MIND
OVER
MATTER

LINDA ZIMMERMANN

Jupiter Books

Also by Linda Zimmermann

Bad Astronomy
Forging A Nation
Civil War Memories
A Funny Thing Happened on the Way to Gettysburg
Ghosts of Rockland County
Haunted Hudson Valley
More Haunted Hudson Valley
Rockland County, NY: Century of History
Home Run

Cover Art: Gordon Bond

Special thanks to David H. Hamilton for his technical support and to Robert A. Strong for his universal support.

MIND OVER MATTER

ISBN:0-9645133-6-6

To my brother Walter,
another man ahead of his time

CHAPTER 1

It was bad enough when they saw Walter hovering. Of course, they immediately removed the d-chip from his brain, but to their surprise things only got worse. Or better, if you looked at it from Walter's point of view.

The Council of Monitors, however, never looked at things from any point of view other than their own, which meant a back alley-narrow, unidimensional, one-for-all mentality; the public being the one and the Council the all. The onset of Walter Danan's extraordinary abilities was naturally a shock to everyone, but more so to the ten Monitors who looked upon themselves as state-of-the-art humanity.

"I want that charlatan found and cast adrift to the blackest depths of the universe!" Monitor Silas Lindquist growled, the veins on his pale temples throbbing an angry purple that matched the color of his new cloak of office.

In the eternity it seemed to take for someone to reply, Silas' mind raced with thoughts of his overnight rise to the Council. Due to his family's numerous connections with people of questionable character, they were quietly able to "persuade" Monitor Ramos to accept early retirement. Everyone smelled a coup, one of the strongest smelling ones in years, but no one dared speak lest the slightest noise unearth their own indiscretions. So Silas now sat among them, the shimmering circle of purple satin that expanded and contracted its will around the fate of many worlds.

"Do you wish your first act as a Monitor to be one of personal vendetta?" a calm, almost velvety, voice asked the newest member who had imprudently risen and slammed his fist on the mirror-finished obsidian table.

"No, sir, I... I wish my first act to be one of eradicating a serious threat to our worlds," a subdued Silas replied, returning to his seat.

Even the bold, brash Lindquist felt humbled beneath the penetrating eyes of Shiro Oku, the man many claimed had the power to overthrow the entire Council and their families. Unlike the other Monitors, Oku had vast popular support and wealth that stretched far beyond the first and second colonial zones. More baffling than the meaning of life, was the mystery of why Oku had not attempted to take over. The mystery and constant suspense made him all the more terrifying beneath that seemingly benign smile.

"To whom is he a threat, Monitor Lindquist, the Union or your ego?" Oku continued as if questioning a child.

"Walter Danan is a threat to every citizen of the Union!" Silas declared with renewed emphasis.

It was a struggle to keep his anger in check, an intense, all-pervading anger and hatred for all Danans. Silas was the great-grandson of the man Walter's great-grandfather had expelled from the Council of Monitors. Even though the incident had occurred years before Silas was born, no self-respecting Lindquist would ever forget, nor rest, until revenge was exacted.

As a child, Silas had tried to make Walter's life miserable by bribing and coercing other upper circle children into ostracizing and taunting the innocent boy. But Walter triumphed over the cruel attempts and won respect and eventually friendship from many of his former persecutors, which only fanned the flames of Silas' hatred.

"Don't you feel you're exaggerating just a bit?" Monitor Idrella Croix laughed, enjoying the obvious discomfort her novice colleague was experiencing. "We would all like to save the universe, but few of us have attempted to do so on our very first day!"

"Idrel...Monitor Croix, you know what this man is capable of doing. I don't think it would be wise to treat this situation so cavalierly. It is no great secret that there is bad blood between our families, but now that I am a Monitor my personal feelings toward Danan are no longer an issue," he declared with practiced sincerity, trying to ignore Idrella's undisguised snickering and the rolling eyes of the other Council members. "I tell you all now, if Walter Danan is not stopped, it will be the end of our world as we know it!"

"Perhaps that would not be such a bad thing?" Oku said with a smile that could have been described as being impish, had he not been a distinguished Monitor.

The simple words and playful grin struck fear into the other nine Monitors. Each heard a threat in those words; each saw an ominous expression of a predator bearing his teeth. Unnerved by the apparently harmless remark, several Council members agreed to adjourn immediately on flimsy pretexts, leaving several issues, including Danan's fate, unresolved. Quickly scattering to their private chambers, the communications networks began buzzing as the latest Oku rumor raced through the upper circle like adrenaline through a trapped animal.

****

Monitor Croix stretched slowly and sensuously in an observation chair. Reflected in her eyes were the unceasing cascades of white-hot, blazing orange and brilliant red bursts that exploded before the long viewing portal of the orbiting Council Hall. It had been her great-grandfather's idea to construct the sumptuous seat of government in the thick of the asteroid belt. A combination of audacity, engineering miracles and questionable sanity made the dream reality and Idrella never tired of watching the beamcutters slice a fiery path through the micro fine debris and occasional massive chunks of rock which yielded to the beams in spectacular bursts of energy.

"Jupiter" Croix, irreverent, radical, self-made trillionaire, still lived out there somewhere beyond the asteroids, circling in synchrony with the mighty planet for which he was nicknamed. Actually, living was probably the wrong choice of words. While quite old, but still vigorous, Jupiter had chosen to place himself in suspended animation and await the day when a new, more enlightened world would replace what he often referred to as "the cesspool of human vanities."

Lost in her thoughts, Monitor Croix hadn't noticed the tall, muscular figure that had slipped into the observation lounge. Moving to within a few feet behind her chair, the man stood breathless as she sighed deeply. Extending her arms above her head, the sleeves of Idrella's cloak slid down, exposing the stark white, sun-neglected flesh that rose like the necks of swans out of the purple folds.

Springing forward, the man grabbed each wrist as if trying to squeeze the life out of the birds and he laughed like a naughty child as Idrella screamed in an uncharacteristic split-second of terror.

"Silas, you bastard!" she yelled in embarrassment and exasperation, struggling helplessly to wrench herself free of his powerful grip.

"What's this?" he asked, laughing even harder. "A member of the mighty house of Croix showing fear?"

Spinning her chair around, Silas yanked the squirming Idrella to her feet, locked both of her arms behind her, and pressed her tightly against him.

"What other emotions have we become capable of expressing?" he whispered in her ear, taunting his immobile captive.

"You haven't changed one damn bit, have you?" Idrella said, giving up the struggle and giving into a smile. "Once a pain in the ass, always a pain in the ass."

"At least I'm consistent," he added, releasing her and taking note of the fact that she didn't seem too eager to be released. "You weren't exactly being sweetness and light yourself in the Council Hall this morning. After all, it was my first day. Didn't your mother ever tell you if you don't have anything nice to say, don't say anything at all?"

"You know that my mother would fly through a supernova if it would hurt someone's feelings," she said as if to remind him of something the entire universe knew, which they probably did. "And you should be thankful that I'm not more like her."

"I can't argue with that. At least you have your father's eyes. Those sparkling little beauties always manage to soften your razor-sharp edges," Silas said as if speaking from experience, as he settled into the observation chair, still warm from Idrella's body.

"I'm sure you didn't come here to talk about my eyes, as much as I enjoy hearing it," Idrella replied in her neutral, official voice, while settling down onto his lap as if it was simply another chair. "You want me to back your plans for Walter Danan."

"Your vote could sway the others," he said, realizing flattery would be wasted on her. "He must be stopped. Permanently."

For a few moments there was silence. Idrella leaned back against his broad chest and gazed out into the bright shower of destruction. While she considered her options, Silas curled some strands of her auburn hair around his fingers and brought them close to his cheek to inhale the arousing scent of the exotic perfume created exclusively for her. He was glad Idrella's parents had not chosen to make her taller and stronger like some of the other upper circle females. Although he had learned long ago that her diminutive size was deceptive, some part of him liked to believe that she was vulnerable, that she felt more secure by his presence.

"Due to the nature of our past relationship, casting my support to you could compromise my integrity with the Council. However, the risk may be worthwhile if I received some kind of appropriate compensation."

So much for vulnerability, Silas thought as he let her hair slide off his fingers and assumed his own strictly business tone.

"Just what type of compensation did you have in mind?"

"I don't know, there doesn't seem to be anything worthwhile you can give me that I haven't already had," she replied coldly, sounding too much like her mother.

"What if I could protect you from Oku when he makes his move?"

"If you could do that I would even sleep with you again," Idrella said eagerly as she turned to face him, green eyes flashing.

"What makes you think I would want to?" he replied, by far surpassing the ice of her previous tone.

Idrella's immediate impulse was to smack him, but she wouldn't allow Silas the satisfaction of knowing he had gotten to her. Instead, she simply got up, straightened her hair and cloak and spoke as one Monitor to another.

"If you can give me assurances that I will be protected from Oku, I will support any action you wish to take against Danan. Until such time, Monitor Lindquist, I will remain neutral on the issue." As the door closed behind her, she cursed at herself for letting him get under her skin one more time.

Silas punched the arm of the chair, cursing his own stubbornness that had helped to alienate Idrella years ago. As children, they had always been so much alike, perhaps too much so, and the two families had hoped their relationship would bring an important alliance. For a time they were happy together, but Idrella's rise to the Council two years earlier created a storm of jealousy and their unchecked ambitions fouled any tender feelings that might have taken root. Their reactions had been childish, on both their parts, and they each harbored secret hopes that things would be resolved once Silas became a Monitor. The ugly scene that just transpired quickly crushed those illusions. There might be a compelling attraction between them, but as long as pride and competition still seasoned every thought, no alliance would be possible.

The scent of Idrella's perfume still lingered on Silas' fingertips as he tried to rub the tension out of the sides of his head. Reality was not what he needed at the moment; he had more than his share in the last twenty-four hours. Sliding his hand behind his right ear, Silas flicked the tiny switch that activated the d-chip deep in his brain. As the beamcutters sliced a precarious swath through the rocky jungle, the lone observer closed his eyes and saw a younger, carefree Idrella waiting beside a riverbank with a picnic basket. There was no Council, no Union and the only purple to be seen was the orchid with which she caressed her golden-tan cheek.

CHAPTER 2

Scholars tracing the evolution of the d-chip often disagree, which all academicians must to some extent in order to perpetuate their professions. Many argue that it had no precursors, some say it began ages ago with television and a few felt obliged to take up the position that the d-chip was the direct descendant of the dramas of Sophocles.

There are some points on which they all agree, which to some extent they must in order to perpetuate their professions. The universally acknowledged breakthrough occurred when the giant pharmaceutical industry was finally superseded by the new science of electroneurophysiology. Rather than subject the body to an ever-increasing list of side effects from even the most sophisticated drugs, electroneurophysiology, or ENP, attained equal, if not superior, results without discernible harm to the rest of the body. After years of painstakingly mapping brain sites, the International Center for Electroneurophysiological Stimulus Research released the *Handbook of ENP* which told the world how to apply electrical "current x" to "site y" to obtain "response z". For a period of seventeen years, the beneficent company that developed the technology strove to alleviate all of mankind's suffering. Aggressive research and development teams continued to find new applications such as surgery without anesthesia, the control of mental disorders, enhancement of the body's own immune responses and their crowning achievement, eliminating the mood swings of PMS.

As years passed, the ENP instrumentation became more compact and the implants less invasive, but overall, the limited vision of the designers kept the devices fairly benign and unimaginative. It wasn't until the original patent expired that the real brains and money got to work in the labs of Oku Interplanetary Technologies. Hideki Oku, realizing that scientists were as sensitive as artists and no less motivated by money than the average man, promised a hefty percentage of profits to his senior researchers Victor Ramos, Ivan Lindquist and Marshall Danan, and gave them carte blanche for budgets and schedules. The founder of the huge conglomerate was determined to use ENP to help capture the field where real money was made, the entertainment industry.

The "Brain Benders", as their boss christened the three, combined the new technology with the exhausted fields of virtual reality and holography. The novelty had long ago worn off of the Three-Dimensional Image Rooms, or D's as they were simply called, but the introduction of authentic sensory stimuli from ENP implants taught an old dog some exciting new tricks.

After only two years of development and testing, Oku Interplanetary Technologies introduced *Space Pirates*, the first truly interactive, action-adventure where participants felt the sting of enemy lasers, the terror of pursuit and the insatiable desire for the seductive, obliging piratess, or pirate, given your sexual preference. It was an instant and overwhelming success and money poured in from every corner of the Union. The Brain Benders were almost embarrassed by their hefty fortunes. Almost.

Not ones to rest on their laurels, or bank accounts, the group continued to refine and expand their repertoire. *Space Pirates* was soon followed by *Alien Encounters* and their number one best seller, *Hot Nights on Venus*. O.I.T. stock split half a dozen times and the company made the rest of the Fortune 100 look like hot dog vendors. But despite their incredible success, the Brain Benders still saw the D's and bulky implants as primitive and grossly limited.

After nine years of unrelenting research, they finally produced the d-chip, a tiny, implantable unit that produced its own, user-determined images. In fact, when the unit was activated, what the user saw and felt was completely indistinguishable from reality and several thousand people starved to death in the first few weeks after its introduction.

While completely absorbed in their fantasy worlds, their brains were unable to respond to the body's frantic cries for help. Blissfully ignorant of hunger, thirst and the need to sleep, the body would waste away, although the victim would always be discovered with a smile on his withered face.

Timers were hastily added to the d-chips to limit its use to four hours per day and a brilliant series of legal maneuvers avoided what would have been catastrophic lawsuits. The government then set up a committee to monitor d-chip distribution, use, abuse and most importantly, the collection of d-chip taxes throughout the Union. The original Brain Benders were included in the first committee of ten members and as the solar system's obsession and dependency for the d-chip grew, the Council of Monitors evolved into the premier governing body. The rest, as they say, is history.

On these points there is no quarrel among scholars. Another point upon which they agree is that the fascination for the d-chip resides in mankind's unceasing and childlike desire to be entertained. One student of d-chipology found this view to be overly simplistic, however, and claimed that there was a much more profound force at work.

In an epic paper, officially banned by the Council of Monitors, Walter Danan, descendant of a Brain Bender, asserted that man's fascination for the d-chip arose from a subconscious yearning for higher states of consciousness, which could be obtained without the use of any devices. It was the human race's destiny, Walter asserted, for mankind to evolve into beings with extraordinary abilities, and the d-chip was inhibiting that evolution.

Universally denounced by scholars as nothing more than absurd speculation, they nonetheless nervously demanded some kind of proof for these outlandish claims. Walter Danan obligingly provided it.

CHAPTER 3

"You were right, Silas is a Monitor!"

The young man who had just run into the room was sweating and panting more from anxiety than the oppressive heat and humidity, although that, too, would quickly become part of the problem. The powerful winds coming off the ocean had no cooling effect, they only added to his agitated state. The man to whom he was reporting the awful news, however, sat peacefully on the terrace, seemingly absorbing strength from the hot, driving mist.

"Walter, didn't you hear what I-" the man instantly fell silent when the calm figure raised a hand slightly, signaling for a few moments of quiet to return his focus from wherever it had gone.

"The eastern section of the island is still cooling. I find the steam that is produced to be most invigorating," Walter Danan finally said, pointing to the rising cloud of vapor in the distance, shimmering silver against the vibrant, turquoise backdrop.

It was a brand new island, thanks to some recent volcanic activity, and the perfect place to get away from it all, the Council being the all. The primordial nature of the area also appealed strongly to Danan; the emergence of a new land from the ocean's depths was the perfect place to continue his research into the evolution of consciousness. Even if his name was cleared from the infamous List, he would probably remain living there.

"I heard what you said, Jess," Walter continued, coming in to greet his friend and place a reassuring hand on his shoulder, "and I wish this was one instance where I was wrong. Here, have something to drink and join me on the terrace."

"If you don't mind, I would prefer someplace a little less like a sauna," Jesse replied, wiping the stinging sweat from his eyes.

"Sorry, I keep forgetting you space babies aren't used to real atmosphere," Walter laughed as he led the other man down into the climate-controlled chambers that had been carved into the fledgling rock.

The two men were very similar in build and appearance. They had dark hair and brown eyes, stood at average height and were slightly thinner than most, definitely not the engineered Adonises of the upper circle. However, whereas Walter's parents had chosen to let nature take its course, Jesse's family financially had no choice in the matter. But both men did possess something upper circle offspring never had, a rich, glowing vitality that somehow appeared both savage in intensity, yet sophisticated in its refinement. Few people possessed the strange qualities. Jesse's sister had been one of them, and that was one reason why Walter had married her.

"Tell me all about it," Walter said somberly, after he had let his friend refresh himself. "How did Lindquist pull it off?"

"Monitor Ramos mysteriously beat a hasty retreat to her Martian hideaway. Word is she received substantial 'encouragement' to resign. They say Lindquist was in so fast that he had one arm in her cloak before she even finished taking it off."

"What a coincidence."

"Yeah, right. And how's this for a coincidence, my sources also tell me you were his first order of business."

"What was the verdict?" Walter asked without a visible change in expression.

"The matter was put on hold. Seems Oku scared the hell out the other Purples with some kind of threat and they took off with their tails between their cloaks," Jesse said, finally able to smile at the last part of his news.

When Jesse broke into that dimpled grin, he looked almost identical to Valery. They had, in fact, been twins, but the similarity was never so obvious as when they smiled. Closing his eyes, Walter brought up the image of Val, listened to her laugh, watched her brush her shiny, black hair that spilled to the ground when she untied it. When they removed his d-chip, Walter's first concern was that he would lose that ability to relive his memories, but he quickly discovered that she could never be removed from his mind.

"Hey, you fading away on me again?" Jesse asked softly, not wishing to disturb anything important.

"No, just thinking of Val," he replied with profound sadness in his voice and face. "Sometimes it's hard to look at you and not think of her."

"If you want me to leave-"

"Don't be silly! It's something I have to come to terms with; I guess it will just take a little more time. Please be patient with me. Anyway, we have the present to deal with now. Any suggestions?"

"Mardo's got a ship that's heading out of the system to establish a colony. It's got one of those no-questions-asked crews," Jesse offered optimistically.

"I don't think that applies to people on the List, Jess. Besides, I can't just run away from all this."

"Yes you can, if it means your life!" Jesse declared emphatically with a power he seldom disclosed. "You're not the only one who misses Valery. When she died I lost a big part of my life and I don't intend to lose you, too!"

After an awkward silence, Walter suggested that they get out of the house and take a tour of the island. It was clear that he took pride in it like a child with a new toy and as much as Jesse hated to go back out into the heat, he couldn't say no in the face of such enthusiasm.

"I had some soil brought in for around the compound," Walter began the moment they stepped outside. "All the vegetation here is stuff I planted. Look at those deep pink blossoms, and those yellow ones! And all these birds started showing up the day I finished planting. Look, look over there, Jess! Look at those bright blue feathers, and that one with the long neck."

"You shouldn't be spending so much time alone," Jesse deadpanned.

"Don't you think it's beautiful?" Walter asked a little hurt and completely deflated.

"Of course it's beautiful, Walter. I'm just pulling your leg. It's just that I'm not used to seeing you so, so..."

"So what?"

"So carefree, I guess."

"You're right, I do feel different here, I feel like I'm part of this island. Sometimes I even forget what's going on in the rest of the system. But wait till you see the other side, the part I haven't done anything to," Walter said with renewed enthusiasm, taking hold of Jesse's arm and hurrying him along.

As they headed east along a high ridge, the scenery reminded Jesse more of a d-chip fantasy than an actual place on Earth. He had spent most of his young life in ships and at colonies and it was strange enough having dirt at his feet, wind in his face and a blazing sun overhead. This landscape seemed to break all the known rules. It was as if he had been transported back in time to witness creation itself.

"What the hell was that!" Jesse screamed, hopping up and down on one foot while violently shaking his pant leg.

"That, my friend, was a member of the lizard family that has recently taken up residence on the island," Walter replied, clearly delighted with the reaction he had undoubtedly been anticipating. "I quickly discovered they like to crawl up legs, but they're harmless.   Imagine, we're at least a hundred nautical miles from the next nearest scrap of land and lizards are already showing up!"

"That's just wonderful. Any other creatures I should know about?" Jesse asked, trying to look annoyed, but failing miserably as he wiggled another shiny purple lizard out of his pants.

Continuing along the ridge, they soon began descending toward the eastern tip of the island. The sight was breathtaking; molten rock was squeezing through cracks where the merciless ocean pounded against it in enraged, self-annihilation. Billows of steam hissed toward the sky as the waves sacrificed themselves against the lava to create solid earth. The air was heavy with the primordial stench of death and life and a mild tremor reminded them of the fine line between the two.

"Are you sure this island is safe? I mean, is it stable?" Jesse asked, cautiously peering down at the battle raging below.

"It's about as safe and stable as the rest of my life," Walter replied with a shrug.

"That bad, huh?" Jesse replied grinning and then continued to step gingerly along the warm, new stones.

Walter's guided tour continued past rainbow-colored pools of algae and swarms of blue-green crabs that rapidly and gracefully danced sideways across the craggy terrain. In the tiniest of cracks, wind-blown seeds sprouted and clung desperately to their tenuous existence. Here and there an exotic bloom stood out against the deep, black rock and fluorescent insects eagerly flocked around the few, precious flowers.

"You can't stop life on this island," Walter declared in awe of his surroundings. "Anywhere there's the slightest chance, it grabs hold, flourishes, reproduces! In all my life I've never witnessed anything so magnificent."

"It is incredible," Jesse agreed in a whisper, far more effected by what he saw than he ever would have imagined. "Is the rest of the planet like this?"

"I think the rest of the universe is like this," Walter replied after a moment of thought. "It's just everywhere else there are so many things to distract you, there's so much diversity. Here, everything begins at ground zero; it's only the basics. By stripping away all the abundance, you're compelled to come face to face with the elemental forces of nature."

Jesse knew from experience that Walter was seeing more than just rocks and plants. An extra brightness filled his eyes when he spoke like that and it seemed as if he was able to look through things, beyond their surface reality to a subtler, yet far more powerful, level. What to Jesse was an indistinct feeling about the true nature of things, was to Walter as plain as the lizard scurrying up his leg.

"Whoa! They get me every time," Walter yelled, roused from his vision as if ice water had been dumped on him while he was sleeping. "I think they came to this island just to keep my head from getting too far into the clouds and to remind me that my feet are on the ground."

"The heat alone is sufficient to remind me where I am," Jesse said as he used the bottom of his shirt to dab his face.

"I'm sorry," Walter apologized sincerely. "Here I am dragging you around in the noonday heat. How about a swim to cool you off?"

"I thought you would never ask!"

Below the compound to the south, the ridge ran smoothly down to the ocean. The island was too new to have any sand, but Walter had brought his own. In the midst of the wild, untamed wilderness, a soft, powdery beach lay nestled in a sheltered cove.

"You thought of everything, didn't you?" Jesse said a second before he stripped down and plunged headlong into the refreshing surf.

"Watch out for those rocks out to the left," Walter shouted after him. "They're like pieces of broken glass."

As Jesse floated on his back in the big, blue ocean under the big, blue sky, he realized that one of the things he regretted about spending so much time in space was the lack of water. Only the biggest ships had pools and their shallow, tepid water could not compare to the vastness of the invigorating oceans. As the strong current began to carry him out from the shore, however, he suddenly regretted not spending more hours in those pools improving his swimming skills.

As Walter was spending most of the time diving beneath the surface, it wasn't until Jesse's third cry for help that he was heard. His brother-in-law had drifted dangerously close to the series of tooth-like rocks that bared themselves as each wave pulled back to sea. Swimming as fast as he could, Walter was no more than fifty feet away when he saw a huge swell pick up Jesse like a piece of cork and throw him between two of the knife-sharp projections. Before Jesse's scream had left his throat, Walter had an arm around him and headed for the beach.

"Oh god, Walter, oh god help me!" Jesse moaned as he gripped his bleeding stomach with both hands.

"You're going to be fine, I'll take care of it. Relax, relax, Jess, and let go," Walter said with perfect calm as he slid Jesse's hand away from the gaping wound.

The deadly rocks had sliced a foot-long gash across his abdomen and he was losing blood at a perilous rate. If Walter ran to the house for a medkit, his brother-in-law, Valery's twin, might bleed to death before he returned. Knowing that something had to be done immediately, Walter took a deep breath and spread his hands over the torn flesh.

"Hang on, buddy. You're going to be fine. Just hang on," Walter whispered over and over.

The agonizing pain slowly began to subside and Jesse was certain he was passing out, or worse. A warm, tingling sensation began shooting through his body and bursts of light were exploding in his head. As all of the pain drained from his body, he began to shake uncontrollably and believed every breath would be his last. Suddenly, the shaking stopped, the lights went dark and Jesse was afraid to open his eyes for fear of glimpsing hell.

"Do you plan to lie around here like a beached whale all day?" said a voice that seemed identical to Walter's. "Hello? Earth to Jesse."

Cautiously opening one eye, Jesse saw Walter's smiling face framed by the burning sun. Opening his other eye, he glanced down to his stomach and saw a reddish discoloration on his skin, but no wound. Without a word, he sat up and repeatedly looked back and forth between his healed stomach and Walter's blood-soaked fingers. Walter stood up, also without a word, and went to the water's edge to rinse his hands. Returning to his friend, he sat in front of him and just smiled. After several minutes of silence, Jesse simply shook his head, grabbed his clothes, and followed Walter back to the house.

CHAPTER 4

"Permission to reveal identity?"

"Permission denied."

"Permission to reveal qualification records?"

"Permission granted."

The burly man with the sour expression finished answering the computer's questions, disconnected the wire from his d-chip and then stepped back from the console so the interviewing officers could see what abilities he possessed. The screen lit up with a single blue square and three yellow circles, indicating he was only a level one pilot, but had level three expertise in maintenance. The officers nodded their approval, gave the man a packet of instructions and release forms and called the next applicant.

A sheepish-looking elderly man entered the room, removed his cap and bowed respectfully to the pair of officers who sat to the left of the records terminal. Deep lines traced paths of anguish across his cheeks and forehead and his spine arched forward as if physically bearing a great weight. Instead of moving forward to connect himself, he stood near the door and nervously twisted the brim of his hat.

"Look, buddy, we don't all have day," the senior officer barked, looking very much like an aggravated bulldog, a 291-pound bulldog. "We need to know your qualifications."

"I have a level three in science, three in medical and two in maintenance," the old man replied, wringing his hat like a dishrag.

"Sorry, we're fresh out of trust today, so would you mind if we verified that?" the officer said rising to his feet to display his foot-taller-than-average height. "It's been a very long day and I don't appreciate someone wasting my time."

"I, I swear I'm telling the truth!" the fully intimidated applicant replied nervously. "I would be a great asset to your vessel."

"We don't require an identity check, sir," the younger officer said kindly, putting a hand on his superior's arm, silently requesting him to ease off the old man. "And we could definitely use someone of your substantial abilities, if you would just let the computer check them out."

The huge senior officer they called Granny (short for granite, which everyone swore he was made of) straightened the somber brown tunic of his uniform, forced a smile to his rigid features and returned to his seat.

"I'm sorry, sir, it's just that we've got a large crew to assemble and you wouldn't believe the no-talent scum that comes in here," Granny said with his unique brand of diplomacy. "If you would please just connect yourself to the terminal, we can verify your qualifications and you can be on your way."

The terminal was flashing a soothing, pale green light, indicating it was in a stand-by mode, waiting patiently to review the next applicant. Once the lead was attached to the switch of the d-chip, the complete file of a person's life could be immediately accessed. Apart from providing entertainment, each d-chip was individually coded with the user's central information number, a handy way of ascertaining anyone's identity from anywhere in the system. However, to assure sufficient numbers to fill the ranks for such a lengthy mission, the usual identity requirements were waived, thereby assembling a kind of interstellar foreign legion.

The trembling applicant looked slightly reassured and cautiously approached the terminal. Lifting the wire slowly to his head, he held his breath as he touched it to the d-chip. Instantly, he cried out in pain and the crackle of high current punctuated his screams. As his body went limp, the terminal howled with a piercing alarm and angry, red lights flashed in everyone's eyes. Guards rushed into the room, squinting, and had secured the stunned man's hands and feet before he even realized what was happening.

"Priority override!" Granny shouted to the terminal and waited several long seconds for the computer to identify him. "Reset to standby and release full record of fugitive."

A blessed silence descended as the incriminating, crimson beacons faded to innocuous green.

"Richard Anderson Salvid, Council Warrant number 9328-B. Wanted for questioning in embezzlement case, DZ8/373," the computer droned. "Detain suspect for questioning."

"I'm innocent! Please, let me go!" the old man pleaded as he suddenly came back to his senses. "My son took the money. I haven't even seen him in years. Please don't turn me in to the Council! I swear, I'm innocent!"

The man's sobs slowly faded from hearing as he was dragged away by security for immediate transportation to Central Detention. Granny and his assistant, Vrovski, were at somewhat of a loss for words until their captain hailed them.

"What the hell's going on down there, Commander? You all okay?"

"We're fine Mardo. Some old guy on the List just tried to apply, but we nailed him," Granny replied, sounding pleased with himself and already planning how he would spend the reward.

"What did he do?" Captain Mardo asked from his ship orbiting high above the recruiting station on the Moon.

"Probably nothing, but since when did that stop the Council," Granny responded uneasily, realizing what would probably happen to the old man, guilty or innocent.

The right to privacy had been extended only to common criminals, which could include anyone from small-time thieves to murderers. What made criminals uncommon was a warrant from the Council itself, placing those individuals on the exclusive List. Only those accused of committing offenses to Monitors, their families and their businesses were put on the Council Warrant List and top priority was then given to those cases. Mardo and Granny both knew that the father of a man who embezzled money from a Monitor's company was in deeper trouble than a mass murderer seen by a dozen witnesses.

"Poor bastard," Mardo sighed. "Well, you had better get on with it, Granny, we've got an awfully big roster to fill and time is running out."

"Yes, sir," the Commander replied and then motioned the other officer to call the next applicant.

A diminutive, oriental woman in a plain, black worker's jumpsuit entered. Without a word or glance to acknowledge the officer's presence, the woman strutted up to the terminal and connected herself.

"Permission denied for identity check, granted for qualification records pertaining only to requirements for this mission," she stated with authority before the computer even had time to ask.

Removing the lead, she stepped back and for the first time looked at the officers. Her eyes flashed with sensual defiance and both men were too distracted to notice that the terminal screen that had lit up like a Christmas tree.

"Aren't you supposed to verify my *qualifications*?" she asked with enticing contempt.

"Uh, yes, of course..." Gran's words faded in his throat when he turned to see the rows of brightly colored circles, squares, triangles, octagons and every other shape that would fit on the screen, indicating level four expertise in almost everything.

"Ah, would you reconnect, for a moment, please, if you don't mind, that is?" Vrovski stammered politely, obviously mesmerized by the arrogant applicant.

With a beguiling sneer, she went through the process again, with the same incredible results. Granny requested a functions check, but the computer indicated that it was in perfect working order.

"I guess good things do come in small packages," Granny said sarcastically, coming around to the front of the desk so he could look down on his feisty applicant. "It looks like we've got a regular Brain Bender among us. How come someone of your abilities is applying for a lousy mission like this, instead of working at the Institute?"

"Am I correct that the requirements for identity checks have been waived?" she asked without flinching, obviously not at all impressed by the Commander's massive size and stern expression.

"Yes, we have dropped those requirements," he admitted, slowly circling and scanning her head to foot, as if hoping to find a chink in her armor.

"Good. I was afraid you were unfamiliar with your own rules," she replied with a smirk playing across her full lips.

Her impudence was maddening and her beauty no less unnerving. Granny wasn't sure if he felt more like slugging her or kissing her, but that's the way he usually felt around women.

"You are, of course, aware that the duration of this mission is projected to be a minimum of eight years? And that during that time every member of the crew is subject to the absolute orders of Captain Mardo and myself?" Granny growled, leaning over to deliver the implied threat directly into her ear.

"Absolute command is necessary to maintain discipline on voyages of this nature," she replied stoically.

"As long as you understand that, then it looks like you're too good to pass up," Granny said with mock enthusiasm, while at the same time realizing he would not win the battle of wills. Not yet. "Lieutenant Vrovski will give you the appropriate documentation. Be ready to report on twenty-four hour's notice."

"But aren't we scheduled to leave in two days?" she asked with the first hint of emotion.

"We leave when Captain Mardo and I decide it's time," he said slowly, emphasizing his importance in the decision making process and playing upon her fleeting show of anxiety.

Without another word, she grabbed the crew packet from the lieutenant, threw an identity card on the desk and stormed out the door.

"Are you sure you want a woman like that cooped up with us for eight years, Commander?" Vrovski asked shaking his head. "She is trouble. Big trouble."

"It will spice things up, don't you think? Besides, I do believe she's genuinely fond of me," Granny laughed half-heartedly, as his extreme fatigue exposed the weariness in his face. "Trust me, Vro, if I could have afforded to turn her down, I would have kicked her scrawny ass out of here. But can you imagine the stink she could have made with the company if I refused someone with her expertise just because I didn't like her attitude?"

The lieutenant agreed and picked up the card she had thrown at him to record the name she wished to be called. The card simply read, "Kiya", although he was tempted to list her as Pandora.

"Shall I call in the next applicant?"

"I don't know about you, but I need a break," Granny said rubbing his bloodshot eyes.

They had been interviewing for three days, barely taking the time to eat or sleep. Oku Interplanetary Technologies had announced the mission only two weeks earlier, giving just a small fraction of the usual preparation time. The purpose of the voyage was to establish District 11, which would become the farthest station out beyond the system. For generations, O.I.T. had been building successive links in a long chain of opulent, high tech city-stations some clever critic had dubbed the Florid Keys. They were touted as being the ultimate in research facilities, but everyone knew they were luxurious strongholds for Oku supporters.

Mardo's vessel, the *Hyperion*, was an unusual choice for the mission. It was neither one of the largest nor the fastest in the huge O.I.T. fleet. Pleased with the honor, yet curious about the selection, Mardo's questions to his superiors went unanswered. Not wishing to jeopardize his good fortune, Mardo did not press the issue. In addition to qualifying for a substantial pension after the completion of the voyage, the secret nature of the crew selection would allow him to smuggle Walter Danan through the system, right out from under the Council's noses on one of the Monitor's own ships. That was worth eight years of boredom.

"We've almost completed the selection," the Commander reported to his captain over a private channel. "Has Danan been located yet?"

"Jesse's working on it," Mardo replied with concern. "If he doesn't find him in the next forty-eight hours, we're going to have to come up with a good excuse to delay departure."

"I could drag my heels a little," he offered.

"Thanks, Granny. Every minute might count."

If Mardo completed the mission, he would have wealth and status second only to the upper circle. Every space sailor dreamed about such a golden opportunity, yet Mardo was willing to jeopardize not only the position, but also his life, for Walter Danan. It was Walter who had faith in the aging, unemployed captain, assumed his debts and arranged command of a ship; a ship that one day pulled off a daring rescue of passengers from a disabled vehicle that was plummeting towards the sun. As luck would have it, relatives of two Monitors had been on board the doomed ship and Mardo became an interplanetary hero with more job offers than he could count, including the *Hyperion*, which Oku himself, had dangled before his eyes. Mardo knew that was an offer he couldn't refuse.

Granny's sense of loyalty to Danan was no less, although he personally never had any dealings with him. It was a second-hand loyalty; he would be willing to die for Danan because Mardo was willing to die for Danan. Granny had been a crewmember on the disabled ship and Mardo was seriously injured rescuing him. That, coupled with the fact that the Council had cheated his parents out of valuable property on Mars, was reason enough to risk everything in trying to smuggle the fugitive out of the system.

Walter had many secret supporters throughout the Union. Many were loyal to him due to his numerous acts of generosity and compassion, some by default due to their hatred of the Council, and some actually even understood and agreed with his beliefs. There was nothing that these groups could do overtly, however, due to the ironclad rule of the Council, but they had an efficient underground network that continually added new members and gathered valuable information.

The general public was aware of the situation, but the vast majority couldn't have cared less. The official word was that Danan was an anarchist who wanted to take away everyone's most precious possession, the d-chip. In fact, he was such a dangerous fanatic that he murdered his own wife when she refused to remove hers. Of the two elements of the story, most people were far less concerned over the alleged murder than the idea that someone wanted to take their d-chips. That was the ultimate crime.

The grapevine had a vastly different version of affairs, which it always did when compared with Council rhetoric. The grapevine's rendering involved an upper circle plot that was responsible for Valery Danan's death, and Danan was being persecuted because he had knowledge that would undermine the Monitor's authority. There were also claims that Danan had remarkable powers that would revolutionize the human race. While such stories provided interesting gossip for the public, until something concrete happened that personally affected them, they remained neutral.

The level of curiosity in the situation did rise, however, when word spread of Lindquist's hostile takeover. His great-grandfather's expulsion from the Council was in every history book and no one doubted that Silas' elevation to the supreme position was greasing the gears of an ancient time bomb. Upper circle feuds had become as popular to follow as sporting events and in the more dramatic ones bets were even placed as to the outcome. Feud bookies were carefully watching the Danan-Lindquist case to see if it would generate enough sparks to make it profitable. One suspicious death was insufficient to draw in the high rollers and all ears were open for new reports to sweeten the pot.

CHAPTER 5

A sleek, personal transport maneuvered skillfully through the deadly obstacle course and prepared to dock alongside Monitor Lindquist's private quarters. A gentle, but persistent beeping roused Silas from a troubled sleep. When the security system detected that he was awake, it informed him that a ship was requesting clearance. Although it had supplied the proper code, verbal clearance from a Monitor was required for any vehicle wishing to approach a Council member's private quarters. Silas rubbed his eyes, checked the code, looked at the time, and authorized the docking.

"This had better be damn good, Tilton," Silas said yawning as he propped himself up in bed with genuine feather pillows worth a years pay to the average citizen. "It's been a hell of a day and I don't appreciate an interruption at this hour."

Draped in a black cape, the bony figure that had entered the room silently glided to the bedside as if on hover jets. His angular features had an oily sheen and his long hair was slicked back and bound with a braided silver cord. Rising from an obsequious bow, he displayed a sharp-toothed grin that threatened to crack the thin layer of skin stretched tightly across his skull. Even the air about him had an acrid, greasy smell and was filled with the tension of a thousand compressed springs anxious to uncoil. Silas was always slightly nauseous when Tilton Maas was in his presence, but he was unquestionably the best at what he did.

"I believe I have located Jesse Dimont," he stated in a voice as soothing as a rupturing hull.

"Where?" Silas asked blandly, thoroughly uninterested.

"He was spotted two days ago in lunar zone three," Tilton replied, noisily popping his finger joints one at a time.

"Stop doing that!" Silas yelled as a shudder of disgust raced up his spine. "I hope you didn't wake me in the middle of the night for this. My sources claim Dimont doesn't know where Danan is any more than we do."

"My sources claim he is with Walter Danan at this very moment," Maas said with a slippery smile, as the stinging odor seemed to grow sharper.

"You've found him! He's on the Moon?" Lindquist shouted, leaping from bed, but stopping short of shaking Tilton's skeletal hands. "Why haven't you taken him?"

"Dimont is with Danan, but their whereabouts is unknown. Dimont left zone three and we were unable to trace him."

"Then you've got nothing, you fool!" Silas shouted angrily, stomping to the other side of the room, primarily to get away from the smell. "They could be anywhere in the system by now."

"I am confident in my information," Maas stated smoothly, undaunted by his superior's temper. "Jesse Dimont is expected back in zone three within forty-eight hours. Walter Danan will be with him."

When Tilton Maas' words slid from his taught lips in that cool, calculated manner, Silas knew that his spy had made someone pay dearly for the information. Maas took no pride in secrets that were disclosed freely or through bribery. Only information extracted with his special skills had any value. Only in those circumstances could he be assured of the informant's sincerity.

Legally, the information on Jesse was no more than hearsay, but it was sufficient for a Monitor to issue a warrant, which Silas did without hesitation. This was the first clue to Danan's whereabouts since the day he simply vanished from the maximum security detention center, a feat no one has ever duplicated, and Lindquist was not about to miss any opportunity to be the one to get him back. If he could capture Danan and interrogate him in front of the Council, he had no doubt the fugitive would provide more than enough rope with which to hang himself.

Dismissing Maas with a small bonus, Silas paced the length of his quarters. The thrill of the hunt had him too charged to think of more sleep and for a time he amused himself by bending and straightening the thick metal legs of a chair. It made him feel good to make the bars yield between his massive hands and then pull them back into their original shape as if he was performing some great act of compassion. When he tired of that, he decided to review some of the Council reports that were strictly for the eyes of Monitors.

Protocol usually dictated that the successful candidate read these reports before donning the purple robe and attending a meeting, but Silas had made a most unusual ascension. Most of the upper circle didn't even hear the news until it was officially announced, which was a serious breach in their normal lines of communication. The fear and turmoil his political blitz created among his peers gave him an almost erotic kind of pleasure, the stuff of which d-chip dreams were made. Perhaps some day he would even be able to provoke the same intense terror in his associates that Oku could with the slightest gesture. Even Monitor's had something for which to strive.

Requesting the most recent financial reports, Lindquist had barely settled back in an overstuffed chair when the first display startled him into a bolt upright position. The innocent-looking series of numbers was divided into three columns; tax revenues, amount allocated to Union projects and the amount distributed to Council members. For things such as import and income taxes, the standard Council cut was half of a percentage point, more than enough to outfit a small planet. But those figures were petty cash compared to the twenty-third item on the list, d-chip revenues.

The same clever Council that fifty years ago had instituted a special tax on every individual that used a d-chip, which effectively was every individual, had also thought to prohibit the disclosure of official government income and expenditures concerning the device. Those two acts of genius kept the rest of the solar system ignorant of the fact that every cent of d-chip revenue went directly into the ten deep, purple pockets of the Monitors.

Even Silas Lindquist, born and raised in upper circle extravagance, was stunned by the obscene amount of money to which he would now be entitled. This was unquestionably the best-kept secret in the Union and if word of this leaked out even to family members, outrage and greed would find an end to the Council and its lucrative practices. Silas continued to pore over financial reports with childlike zeal until his security system began the soft beeping once again.

"What is it now?" he barked angrily, half fearing that Maas had returned.

"Only two point five hours remain in the sleep cycle and your physiology has not obtained the minimum requirement of rest," the artificial female voice stated like a mechanized mother.

"I'm busy."

"You have a full schedule of briefing meetings and you will not be at the peak efficiency expected of a Monitor," the computer replied with a noticeably nagging tone.

"Are you my wife or my computer?" Silas said allowing himself to laugh as he abandoned his reports and went back to bed.

"Silas Lindquist does not have a wife, unless my records-"

"Give it up, you win! Now shut up so I can get this precious sleep you're insisting upon."

There was a long silence, punctuated by a few rare bursts of static. Silas knew the computer was pouting and it would probably have some inexplicable malfunction in the next few days if he didn't apologize.

"I'm sorry. As you yourself observed, I'm overtired," Silas said, shaking his head in disbelief that he was actually apologizing to a computer.

"If you had followed the pre-arranged sleep schedule you would not be in this condition," it said, still being somewhat aloof, but wishing to have the last word.

As Silas began to relax, all the events of the last two days ran through his mind looking for places in his memory to settle in. These had been the most important forty-eight hours of his life, but the prospect of finding Danan remained the issue that demanded the most attention in his consciousness. The heaviness of his fatigue pushed him deeper toward sleep and just as his mind was about to relinquish its grasp, he realized he had completely overlooked the fact that the Council must have a private file on Danan. His mouth tried to move to request the report, but his waking state had given up too much ground. Thoughts swirled around dreams, spinning him downward into a black, unconscious vortex of sleep.

While his boss rested between outrageously expensive silk sheets, Tilton Maas was combing the seediest parts of the Moon looking for fresh information. Some of the characters he encountered even repulsed him, but none were capable of inspiring a moment's fear in the ice-hearted spy. When he felt assured that nothing had changed from his last reports, he ordered, by Lindquist's authority, the tightest security surveillance the Moon had ever seen. Trying to find two men in the flood of interplanetary traffic could be likened to searching for a particular grain of sand at a beach during a windstorm, but Maas thrived on such challenges.

The most difficult part was to make the manhunt look like anything but a manhunt; a forewarned fugitive remains a fugitive. There were ways it could be done, with great inconvenience to the general public, but he felt it was better to detain ten thousand innocent people than let one of the guilty escape. It would have to be a silent, all-encompassing net thrown around the Moon, like slipping a plastic bag over someone's head while he slept, Maas thought proudly.

Silas ignored the slowly brightening lights and the gentle sounds of birdsong that the security system was generating. He even managed to remain sleeping when the soft twitter rose to an Amazon jungle cacophony and the lights began to flash. When the mighty roar of lions surrounded him and blinding strobes beat at his eyelids, however, he knew he must succumb to the inevitable.

"All right, damn it! I give up," he yelled, hurling a pillow in the direction of one of the hidden speakers. "Just get me the biggest, most energizing breakfast you've got."

"Breakfast is served," the computer responded as a heaping tray of food slid out of a panel beside his bed. "I warned you that you would not be at optimum condition this morning. The sleep period is the most extensively documented cycle. A child knows that no one can sidestep nature's cycles."

"Thanks for the sermon. Now would you please review my schedule for today," he said as he jammed half of a banana in his mouth and then changed his mind about the request, although the computer was almost finished by the time his garbled speech could be understood.

"Cancel request. Display Council's file on Walter Danan."

"Your first meeting is in twenty minutes. There's no time to-"

"Display file or I'll tear you out and toss you into a beamcutter!"

"Unable to access Danan file," the computer replied with smug satisfaction.

"Don't lie to me!" he shouted as he manually requested the secret report from his console.

After a considerable pause, the screen displayed a one-line message:

"Access to this file denied to Monitor Lindquist."

"How can this be?" he yelled pounding the helpless terminal. "I am a Monitor! I am entitled to any Council file!"

"May I remind Monitor Lindquist that he is on probation for a period of three months," the computer said with an overtone of spite. "The established Council members have the right to exclude any information they choose during that time."

"This is ridiculous!" he growled, bending the leg of the chair, but not straightening it out again before he hurled it across the room. "They let me see that they're robbing the system blind, but I can't review a fugitive file!"

"Perhaps you can inquire as to the Council's motives during this afternoon's meeting," the computer said as it flashed his schedule on the wall above his desk, highlighting the first meeting that he would have to rush to make on time. "At the very least, it is not expected that a Monitor is late for appointments, especially his second day."

As powerful, wealthy and dishonest as the Council was, its members were punctual. They had their set of rules and Silas knew he would have to adjust to being part of a team, although he would do everything he could to be the star player. For the time being, he would adhere to the irritating rules, until he was in a position to impose his own.

Across the station, another schedule was flashing before the eyes of a Monitor who was running late. Idrella Croix was slipping into her purple cloak, moving toward the door and trying to get a word in edgewise with the woman speaking over her private channel.

"And another thing, your father and I do not expect the Croix name to die with you. What do you want, your poor mother to go through another pregnancy because you're too picky to find someone to give us an heir? And another-"

"Shut up, Mother! For god's sake just shut up!" Idrella screamed, fist raised, at the startled image of usually unflappable Rial Croix. "I am not going to marry Silas so you can have a grandchild to parade around the system. I am a Monitor, not a breeding cow!"

"Aren't we sensitive!" Mrs. Croix said in the singsong voice that drove Idrella up the wall. "I see Silas has already gotten you all hot and bothered. You know, if you would just-"

"End transmission!" Idrella ordered, instantly silencing the voice and dissolving the image of her mother.

Storming out of her private chambers, her massive bodyguard, Boa, had to step quickly to keep up with her. His only garment was a short purple cloth, bearing the Croix family crest in the most conspicuous spot, tied around his waist and he was considerably taller and more muscular than even upper circle men. Idrella requested that he let his thick, brown hair grow long and he looked like a prehistoric giant hovering over his petite mistress. The need for personal bodyguards had long since been eliminated due to the all-pervading security systems, but Monitor's and some of their family members still retained them as status symbols. And even if they had no real role in protection, they were still good for sex, and therefore well worth the exorbitant salaries they commanded.

Boa trotted obediently behind his mistress until he saw an unfamiliar man running toward her from one of the side halls.

With a few swift and mighty strides, he intercepted the man, lifted him off his feet by his neck and pinned him against the wall like a big, blond bug.

"I'm a Monitor, you idiot!" Silas gasped between half-strangled breaths, unable with even his considerable strength to break free of the bodyguard's grip.

"He is a Monitor, Boa" Idrella said laughing, delighted by the sight of the mighty Lindquist's arms and legs flailing, "but he's the idiot for rushing at me like that. Remember, Silas, you're a new face around here. And where's your cloak?"

Boa apologized, but not too humbly, released his hold and let him drop to the floor, but not too gently. He then returned to his place behind his mistress as if nothing had happened.

"I was running late...I forgot...look I have to talk to you about something very important," Silas said, tenderly pressing his throat with his fingertips to make sure there was no permanent damage.

"I'm running late too, thanks to mother," Idrella complained with disgust.

"Rial? And I thought I had problems," Silas shuddered. "But seriously, it's about-"

"I don't have the time now, the Agriculture Committee is meeting in two minutes and I know you've got a full schedule. I'll see you at lunch," Idrella said as she turned and hurried down the hall. "And don't forget your cloak!"

The morning dragged on through a seemingly endless series of facts, figures, rules, regulations and protocols. The Council's huge support staff began with individual introductions and each gave a brief talk on his or her specialty. Silas had no idea of the intricacies of the Union's government; what appeared to outsiders as a ten-pillared core of function and authority was in actuality a vast, branching coral reef teeming with departments, cabinets, committees, sub-councils, sub-committees and delegations. The smallest details of life that he always took for granted were all categorized, monitored, recorded and scrutinized by a specialized commission. It made any of Earth's historic bureaucracies look like a children's tea party, and it would be weeks before each member of the support staff was heard.

When the lunch period mercifully arrived, Silas received a message from Idrella informing him that her meeting was running late due to some potato crisis on Mars and they would have to meet later. It was difficult to curb his impatience, and even more difficult to try to find a time to see her in private in the next twenty-four hours. As soon as the day's meetings were over there would be a gala reception to introduce the new Monitor to all the highest officials of the system's local branches of government. He already knew most of them, in fact many were relatives, but traditions must be followed and his ego was actually looking forward to the event.

Returning to his private quarters, Silas made short work of an enormous meal. He checked with Maas to see if there was any news and then stretched out on the bed just to rest his eyes for a minute. A persistent beeping suddenly snapped into his awareness and he saw that he had slept almost until the time of his next meeting. Leaping out of bed in a groggy daze, he smacked his cheeks, fumbled with his cloak and rushed to the door.

"I warned you that you would not be in optimum condition if you-"

The door slid shut, cutting short the computer's admonition as Monitor Lindquist hurried to hear the report on the forecasted yields and employee-management disputes of the Outer Planet's Department of the Interior Mining Council. Once Danan was dealt with, Silas thought, he might ask ex-Monitor Ramos if she wanted her job back.

CHAPTER 6

As silhouettes began to emerge against the predawn horizon, one figure stood out among the harsh angles of the new landscape. Bending forward and then arching way back, his rhythmic curvatures seemed to inhale and exhale the entire universe with every breath. Raising his arms high above his head, the first rays of light climbed over the edge of the ocean and raced to his fingertips and palms as if pulled by some inexorable force. Standing perfectly still, the rising sun slowly bathed the length of his entire form.

Only when the full disk of energizing fire was safely above the wave's crests, did Walter Danan acknowledge the lizards that had been running up and down his legs. Scooping one up in his hand as it reached his knee, he stroked the shiny purple skin that draped loosely like satin over its knobby joints.

"Don't tell me you're a Monitor lizard," he laughed softly. "Actually, you do remind me of Silas with those suspicious eyes darting around."

"Talking to lizards now, are we?" Jesse asked, only half-joking as he watched Walter gently place the animal back on the ground, where it immediately made a run for his own leg. "Oh no you don't! I saw you coming this time."

Lifting his foot at precisely the right instant, the lizard raced by and went splashing into a puddle of rainwater. Surprised, but unhurt, it remained standing eye-deep in its private pond, obviously deciding it had had enough excitement for one day.

"Jesse, how are you feeling?" Walter asked as he motioned for his friend to sit and enjoy the fresh sunrise.

"Like Lazarus, thanks to you," he replied, patting the skin of his stomach from which even the redness had disappeared. "I had heard that you could do some pretty weird stuff, but I, I had no idea!"

"I had no idea that I could do that either, until yesterday," Walter said in the same tone of amazement. "When I pulled you out of the water and saw that horrible gash, my hands started tingling and there was a warm, calmness that flooded me. It was almost as if I was standing behind myself, watching someone else healing you. When it was finished, I kind of snapped back into my body. What a rush it was!"

"I'm glad you had a good time," Jesse chuckled. "I'll have to see what other part of my body I can rip open for your amusement."

"Don't you dare! I'm never sure when I can duplicate these things."

"How do you do it, Walter? I believe it because I've seen it, but I just don't understand, not one clue," he said shaking his head, eyes scanning the horizon as if searching for answers.

"I don't know, not completely anyway. But I think its as simple as recognizing that matter arises out of consciousness, and when you learn to operate from that higher level, everything that you see, taste and touch can be manipulated," Walter said softly with that distant look of an ancient sage.

"It's that simple, huh?" Jesse replied sarcastically, even more confused than before.

"Yes, it is. But I shouldn't have used the word manipulated, that has too many negative connotations. What happens to me is all very positive, and very natural. You see, Jesse, you become aware of a gap, or need, and you fill that gap by calling upon the creative source of everything, your own consciousness."

Jesse picked up a pebble, examined it thoughtfully and then tossed it down the hill. He didn't speak until it came to rest on a ledge far below.

'That's fine, for you. Maybe you are in touch with whatever your source is and maybe you are lucky enough to be able to create things for yourself. But how were you able to heal my wound? I'm not in touch with anything that I know of."

"There's the trick," Walter said grinning, pointing a knowing finger at his bewildered friend and then aiming it out to sea. "That's what has the Council scared out their wits. Consciousness is like a vast ocean and we all think we're drifting helplessly in its cruel currents, totally isolated from everyone else on our own, tiny rafts."

"That sounds about right."

"I used to think that, too. But the day I jumped overboard, I discovered I was the ocean! Consciousness was not an enemy to be stifled in a d-chip fantasy or superseded by our sophisticated technology. It was our true nature and I realized that focusing on the world presented by our five senses was a hideous mistake."

"So, what you're saying, is that you, and me and everyone else, and even these rocks, are really the same thing?" Jesse said slowly, struggling to catch a glimpse of the light that shone so brightly for his friend.

"Exactly! And I think people used to be aware of it long ago, but we got so wrapped up in our space colonies and d-chips and biotechnology that could make people better than nature could, that we completely lost sight of it. We had conquered hunger and disease, reduced everything to formulas and principles, proudly thought all the mysteries were solved and promptly settled down onto our complacent, self-satisfied, ignorant butts."

"It sounds like it makes sense," Jesse said and then paused to throw a few more pebbles, "but there's nothing in my personal experience that supports it. Maybe you're the only one who can do it."

"There's nothing special about me," Walter stated emphatically, almost annoyed. "Look, you're very hot right now, aren't you?"

"Yeah, I can't get used to this weather," Jesse agreed, wiping the sweat from his burning brow.

"What would happen if you stayed out here, with your d-chip on for the full four hours, and pictured yourself in the arctic, sitting in a tub of ice water?"

"I'd think I was cold, of course, but I would be giving my body a hell of a case of sunstroke, sunburn and heat exhaustion."

"I want you to try it," Walter said as if he was requesting nothing more than the time of day.

"No way! I'm not going to hurt myself just so you can see if you can fix me again!" Jesse replied in a tone he immediately regretted. "Walter, I didn't mean-"

"It's okay, I know it sounds crazy," Walter said, clearly not offended. "I just want to prove everything I've been saying. Trust me."

It seemed to be an act of sheer stupidity, but Jesse had no reason not to trust the man who saved his life. Walter unquestionably knew something he didn't, and if there was a chance he might find out what that was...

"All right, I'll do it," Jesse finally blurted out as if wanting to get it over with before he came to his senses.

"Good. Now just relax, get comfortable and begin to picture yourself in frigid, icy water. I'll switch on the chip and you just keep picturing yourself on the snowbound, overcast landscape, with cold winds howling all around you. Can you see it? Believe that it's possible, feel the burning sun frost over and the stifling humidity crystallize in the sub-zero temperatures. Believe it, create it..."

Walter silently watched his friend, hoping that he would be able to last the four hours. After less than an hour, however, he shook Jesse's arm and called to him loudly. It took a moment, but Jesse's eyelids slowly slid back and remained only partially opened, squinting against the blinding sun. He had expected to come out of it feeling like he was roasting on a bed of coals, but instead he was shivering. Moving his half-numb fingers to his face and then his arms, he rubbed off tiny pellets of ice that had once been beads of sweat. His skin was blue and he could see the vapor of his breath dissipate into the frigid air that surrounded him, air that was in the unprotected sunlight of an island near the equator!

"What the hell is going on? Am I delirious?" he asked, trying to pound warmth back into his limbs. "How long was the d-chip on?"

"I never turned it on," Walter replied with one of those maddening, enigmatic smiles.

"But the snow, the ice, I saw it!"

"You created it in your mind, and you created it in your reality. The power of your consciousness transformed the thought to matter, and as you can see you did such a good job I was afraid you would get frostbite," Walter laughed as he fanned the hot air toward his chilled friend. "In an important way, the d-chip has been a good thing, because it has trained people's nervous systems to disregard the senses and create an alternate reality. The problem is all those damn electric impulses it shoots out which disrupt access to the higher levels of consciousness that would naturally result from these practices. It trained your mind to go to the door and then barred you from opening it."

"This isn't possible! It was, it was too easy!" Jesse cried in protest, but unable to stop the wide grin and feeling of euphoria from spreading. "Do you realize what this means?"

"Dumb question, Jess. And not only do I know what it means, but now the Council does, too. Unfortunately, I was foolish enough to explain it to them and they locked me up. They would have launched me out of the system in an isolation pod if I hadn't 'excused myself' from the detention center."

"How did you escape, anyway?"

"I recognized the fact that 99.9 percent of matter is empty space, and the passage of a few molecules in that vastness is inconsequential."

"You can't mean...You walked through the walls!"

"Just one. Although I did get a few bruises and a bloody nose before I mastered the technique, " Walter confessed, now able to laugh at the danger that had passed. "So, Jess, you still think I should run away and let the Monitors continue to withhold this knowledge from the entire system?"

"No! We have to tell everyone! We have to remove everybody's d-chip and let them see for themselves," Jesse shouted, leaping to his feet as if ready to rush into battle.

"Hold on, Napoleon. The last thing a few billion bored citizens want to hear is that we want to take away their greatest pleasure in life," Walter said rising and placing a cautioning hand on his friend's twitching shoulder. "Besides, I told you that I don't even know the whole story yet. I'm learning a lot, but there are days when I can't seem to do anything. Then there's the small matter of the Council Warrant with my name on it."

"That's where I come in. No one's looking for me, I can move freely around the system teaching people the truth," Jesse said with unrestrainable enthusiasm.

"Just because you almost froze yourself to death doesn't mean you know what you're doing. It's probably going to take years of refinement before-"

"Think of how the entire system will be changed! We will transform the entire universe! Think of it!"

"Think of what they did to Valery," Walter said with quiet pain in his words.

Jesse immediately sobered, stopped pacing and, thankfully, stopped raving. Although no one had been able to prove it, Walter had no doubt that his wife had been murdered by agents of the Council. Soon after Danan's paper on d-chips and higher consciousness was published, and he had giving a few levitation demonstrations, Valery was found dead. The timer on her d-chip had failed and while her husband was lecturing on the other end of the system, she sat in their secluded Martian home and starved to death. Walter knew it was no accident for the simple fact that his wife had stopped using the d-chip a year earlier and had planned to have it removed. The day following the discovery of her body, the Council issued a warrant on Danan for conspiracy, treason and murder.

"Take it slow, Jess. The Council will stop at nothing to silence us," Walter said, tears welling up in the corners of his eyes as he recalled the emaciated figure of his beloved wife. "Come on, let's go in. It's too damn hot out here."

As the pair turned to go back to the house, a series of sirens began screeching across the length of the island. Warning lights flashed and a battery of defense weapons sprang out of the rocks and simultaneously pivoted in the direction of a speck of red light coming in from the west.

"They've found you!" Jesse screamed, as he tried to drag Danan into the house.

"Hang on, don't panic," Walter said calmly. "Computer, identify incoming intruder."

"Type R cargo transport pod. Proper entry code transmitted. Awaiting verbal approval."

"Entry approved. Return to standby."

The impressive weapons systems slid silently back into their recessed chambers, the lights went out and the sirens ended their howling. Despite Walter's assurances, Jesse nervously watched the ten-meter diameter craft approach and land less than five meters from the front door. Walter hurried over like a kid on Christmas morning and rapidly punched a sequence of numbers into the pod's security panel. Jesse couldn't help but jump back when the door suddenly slid open. Fully expecting one of the deadliest of the Council's Enforcer Robots to spring out, Jesse felt like a complete idiot when he cautiously peered over Walter's shoulder and saw a cargo bay jammed with fresh fruit and vegetables.

"Pretty scary, huh Jess!" Walter laughed. "All those Brussels sprouts, and ooh, look out for those terrifying beets!"

"Very funny. Why didn't you tell me you were just having your groceries delivered?" Jesse said, still keeping his distance when he heard there were Brussels sprouts on board.

"Isn't this great? A friend of mine regularly drops off a shipment of fresh food. This is the real stuff," he said, lovingly cradling a huge watermelon as if it was a child. "This is stuff grown on Earth on real trees and vines, not that hydroponics crap that never sees the sun."

"Hey, I grew up on that stuff," Jesse said with mock indignation.

"That explains a lot," Walter deadpanned, tossing a ripe peach to him. "Try this and see what soil, rain and fresh air can taste like."

The sweet juice trickled down the sides of his face as he grunted his approval. Food like this was a rarity in the rest of the system, a very expensive rarity.

"This must cost a fortune," Jesse finally exclaimed once he had sucked every scrap of fruit-flesh off the pit.

"Actually, I get it on the barter system," Walter said slurping on his own fist-sized peach. "I give him lessons in 'life after the d-chip' and he slips me a few tokens of his appreciation. Just look at the size of these mangoes!"

"The immortal fruit of knowledge!" Jesse said bowing with exaggerated reverence.

Jesse was referring to the episode that first showed Danan that there was more in heaven and Earth than was dreamt of in the Council's philosophy. During one of Walter's early experiments with consciousness, his d-chip shut off after four hours, but he continued unknowingly with the fantasy. Feeling a twinge of hunger, which he assumed was part of the program, he thought he was directing his neural delusion to provide some exotic tropical fruit to satisfy the phantom desire. Hours later Valery came to check on her long-absent husband and found him sitting cross-legged on the floor, seemingly lost in a deep, d-chip fantasy, with a half-eaten mango in his lap.

Knowing that the time limit must have long ago expired, and wondering where the fruit came from, Valery felt behind her husband's ear and discovered that the switch was in the off position. Fearing he was ill, she shook him, finally rousing him back to wakefulness. It was days before he finally believed his wife's adamant claims that his chip was off and she did not put the fruit in his lap. It was weeks before he even had a clue as to what had happened. From that point, however, materializing mangoes was to become the least of his accomplishments.

"By the way, how come you didn't suggest that fruit experiment with me, instead of that cryogenic nightmare?" Jesse asked, nosing around the numerous containers in the pod until he found some plump, red grapes.

"Because I didn't want you to spoil your appetite for these lovely turnips," Walter said waving a bunch that drove Jesse back like garlic against a vampire.

Picking up as many cases as they could carry, they went down into the cool, lower chambers and feasted on all the best the Earth had to offer. Since it was no longer fashionable to actually live on the planet, towns and cities had been replaced by farms; highly profitable farms that catered to a wealthy, far-flung Union. And some of the food actually stayed on Earth to be eaten by those generally anti-social few who clung to the outdated lifestyle of a real atmosphere, sunlight and water which fell from the sky.

While they ate, Jesse drained as much knowledge as he could from his brother-in-law. His new desire was insatiable and the instant he grasped one concept, he was questioning another. Long after the sun had set, Walter finally asked for a time out.

"I can't talk anymore, Jesse!" he protested hoarsely. "Let's get some sleep and we can do some more experiments in the morning. Please!"

Jesse reluctantly agreed, but found it impossible to sleep. Remembering Mardo and Granny, he decided that rather than toss and turn all night he would go to the Moon and tell them they would not be needing the ship. After all, Jesse rationalized, wasn't it safer to go in person then risk having their communications intercepted?

Quietly slipping out of the house, he climbed into his transport, gleaming beneath the full, tropical Moon. Before taking off, he left a message for Walter to clean some of those huge strawberries, because he would be back in time for breakfast.

CHAPTER 7

Silas liked the man who looked back at him from the mirror. He was tall, strong, had features that were rugged yet refined, and his sandy blond hair coordinated splendidly with the penetrating sky-blue eyes that never failed to see an opportunity.

"How could I possibly improve upon this?" he asked his reflection and then feigning surprise, reached for his cloak. "What's this! A splash of royal purple to accent my nobility."

Whipping the cape once around like a toreador, he placed it on his shoulders with dramatic ceremony. Satisfied that it hung just right, he slipped the gold dress sash around his waist, making sure the Lindquist family crest was perfectly centered. Sashes were worn only on the most important and most formal occasions and a Monitor's first reception was unquestionably the most prestigious event that ever took place.

Beneath the sash and cloak he wore the standard, plain black pants and tunic, which were supposed to show the humble nature of a Monitor who's purpose was to serve the public. Of course, no one even noticed that part of the outfit with so much rich satin spilling across every limb. And there would be another glittering addition by evening's end, the platinum medallion studded with a gem representing each world in the Union, the Council's ostentatious and most coveted symbol of authority.

"You're going to be late again," the maternal data/security system said as it superimposed the reception information over his image in the mirror.

"A lot you know. Weren't you ever programmed to understand the practice of being fashionably late? Besides, this reception is for me and if I go rushing in there on time it will look like I'm too eager. Maintaining one's dignity is an essential function for a Monitor," Silas declared. "I thought you things were knowledgeable in protocol."

There was a noticeable pause, which meant the computer was checking every record in the main bank to see if there was any truth to his statements. When a full minute passed, Silas knew it must have come upon some reference to 'fashionably late', and was then trying to decide if it was indeed appropriate behavior.

"Well?" Silas asked innocently. "Should I stay or should I go?"

"There may be some validity to your statements, although I am unable to ascertain just how late 'late' should be," the computer replied, obviously uneasy with the fact that there might be an unpredictable variable in its precious time schedule.

"Well, while you chew on that for a while, I have somewhere to go," he said, heading for the door with practiced strides.

"There are no appointments scheduled before the reception. If you-"

The door closed on the agitated voice of his anal-compulsive computer and he hurried toward the private quarters of Monitor Croix. As he turned the corner of the hallway leading to her one-tenth of the luxurious residence section, he was relieved to see Boa still standing outside of her door, which meant she had not yet left. The twinge in his neck reminded him of that morning's rough introduction to her bodyguard and he automatically slowed to a non-threatening pace.

"Good evening, Monitor Lindquist," the massive man said coldly, without even glancing down.

"Good evening, Boa," Silas replied, glad to have been recognized this time. "I would like to see Monitor Croix."

The bodyguard announced Silas and then reluctantly stood aside to let him pass after his mistress gave her permission to let him enter. He found Idrella in her dressing chamber, still in her lounging clothes.

"You're not even ready yet?" Silas asked in surprise.

"Haven't you ever heard of being fashionably late?" she said as she carefully lowered the ultra-fine netting of tiny diamonds over the silken waves of her auburn hair. Once in place, it looked like every strand of hair was a fluid, sparkling gem.

"I always loved when you wore that," Silas almost whispered, completely forgetting why he was there.

"I'm sure you didn't come here to watch me get dressed," she said, standing up and slipping off her robe. "Or did you?"

"No, but it's not a bad idea now that you mention it," he said with a charmingly lecherous grin, scanning the flimsy undergarments that clung to her curves as if under high gravity.

In the old days, the natural next step would have caused them to be very, very late. But the fact that Idrella continued to dress and Silas continued his business showed just how far apart they had drifted.

"Why can't I access the Danan file?" he asked bluntly.

"Because we didn't want you to," she replied just as bluntly, but then softened her tone. "Now before you get all steamed up, let me explain. There is an awful lot to learn when you become a Monitor, as you're beginning to see. Someone voiced the concern that you might become too absorbed in the Danan case at the expense of all your other responsibilities. We all agreed."

"None of you understand how important this is! You have to...Wait, who 'voiced the concern'?" he asked trying to keep his temper in check.

"It doesn't matter, we all agreed."

"Who was it? Was it you, Idrella? It was you wasn't it?"

"No, it wasn't me."

"Then who!" he shouted angrily.

"Oku," she shouted back, tossing the shoe at him, which she had distractedly been trying to put on the wrong foot. "And he was right if you ask me. Look at you! It's the biggest night of your life and all you can think of is Walter Danan. You're obsessed Silas, and an obsession is too costly a thing for a Monitor."

"Oku? What the hell does he care? The bastard must want to get Danan himself and take all the glory. Won't he be surprised!" Silas gloated, shaking his fist in premature victory.

"Surprised? Silas, what are you up to? Listen to me, you've just ascended to the most powerful position in the Union, don't blow it!" she said with genuine concern. "Come on, let's go to the celebration. This is a night for triumph!"

"I hope so," he whispered to himself, wishing he had a chair to bend.

Idrella quickly finished dressing and graciously accepted the arm Silas graciously extended. He escorted her to the door and it slid open to reveal the scourge of the social scene, Mrs. Rial Croix.

"Well, well, well!" she grinned, eyes wide with an I-knew-it look. "No wonder you two are late. A pleasure to see you again, my dear, dear Silas."

Silas respectfully kissed her outstretched hand and almost choked on the dense cloud of perfume that surrounded her flesh. Her dress was an airy weave of gold thread with the tongues of ruby-studded flames leaping up to accent all the right places. A net of rubies also seemed to ignite her hair and the precious stone's finely ground powder gave the illusion of life to her pale cheeks and the swell of her breasts. The combination of looks and sumptuous clothes would have been viewed as startling beauty for any other woman, but for Mrs. Rial Croix the only term that came to mind was formidable.

"You haven't changed a bit, Mrs. Croix," Lindquist said diplomatically, summoning up his well-worn social smile.

"Rial, please, dear Silas. And may I be the first to extend my congratulations; purple is a most becoming color on you. My daughter doesn't look so bad on your arm, either," she said with an exaggerated wink.

"With beauty such as yours, how could I ever look at another woman," he said kissing her overly fragrant hand again.

Such obvious flattery was an insult to most women, but it was the staff of life to Rial Croix. She was like a two-legged black hole, a parasite sucking the life out of everyone within her sphere of influence, which, unfortunately, was vast. Rial needed constant attention like plants needed the sun and it was the wise man who got the complements over with quickly so she would move on to the next victim.

"Silas, if I didn't care so much about my dear daughter's happiness I would grab you for myself," she purred, pressing too close against him and kissing him on the lips much too long.

Breaking off abruptly, she headed down the hall, snapping her fingers sharply. A huge figure suddenly lurched forward and obediently trotted along behind her. Silas was amazed that he hadn't noticed the enormous bodyguard before, but he had assumed that the wall of flesh he saw out of the corner of his eye was Boa.

"Cobra is my big brother," Boa laughed when he saw the look of astonishment on the Monitor's face. "I got the brains in the family and he got the muscle."

"A frightening thought any way you look at it," Silas said smiling, knowing the oaf would take it as a complement.

"Mother always has to outdo me," Idrella snarled. "I have half a mind to put a warrant out on her."

"Please, Drel, there are quite enough people with half a mind as it is. Come on, let's go make a spectacular entrance!"

As the orchestra began the first strains of a heroic, Wagneresque theme, the inner shield doors pulled back to reveal the breathtaking vista of the asteroid fragments exploding in the fiery path of the beamcutters, with mighty Jupiter looming majestically in the background. The lights dimmed and a single, intense spot illuminated the threshold of the grand staircase. Idrella stepped aside right before they entered so that Silas would get the full attention from the crowd, and also to limit the rumors.

Silas did take full advantage of the situation, entering gracefully and regally like a triumphant emperor. Horns sounded, fresh rose petals from Earth cascaded from the ceiling and everyone competed for being the one who applauded and clapped the loudest. He felt he was being hailed as a god, worshipped as an immortal descending from Olympus. And with every step, he imagined that even at that very moment, his almighty hands were growing tighter around the throat of Walter Danan.

At the base of the stairs, waiting to bestow the Council medallion, was the mysterious representative of the esoteric side of life, the supreme Astromancer. Schooled in the science of cycles from the age of five, Astromancers knew how a perturbation in the orbit of an outer planet would eventually effect the pulse of a man on Earth. They precisely calculated death rates based upon solar flare activity and knew without a doubt the ore price fluctuations resulting from the variations in oxygen consumption at the Board of Trade.

Astromancers scared the hell out of most people, especially those in the upper circle. With a handful of facts about one's birth and vital signs, a skilled Astromancer could read you like a book. Often, the individual didn't like the future that was forecast for him and he would spend outrageous sums to discover exactly where in the system he should go for the appropriate gravitational and electromagnetic forces in order to avert the unpleasantness. Naturally, such an important field produced a host of charlatans claiming to have the intensive training, when in fact, they possessed no more than a cursory understanding and an extensive greed.

The Supreme Astromancer was no fraud. Within his brain was contained the memory of every geological, economic, biological, astrophysical and social cycle ever documented. To him all life was a series of pulses, highs and lows on a chart that could be calculated with intricate, yet infallible, mathematics. A thousand variables played with one's future, but they all adhered to a rhythmic, master cycle, the pattern of which was to him clearly visible.

Wearing a long, white silk robe that touched the floor, he had masses of gray hair and a beard that reached almost as far. He had allowed his face to remain wrinkled and also had refused treatment for the eye that was sheathed in a milky, opaque cloud. Among the pampered, seemingly ageless elite he was, at the very least, an unnerving sight.

"Are you prepared, Silas Lindquist, to take on the responsibilities of a Monitor and to bear them with honor?" he asked in a profoundly resonating voice that rang like medieval church bells through the silent hall.

"I am, with honor," Silas replied on cue. "And do you, Supreme Astromancer, in your wisdom, give your consent?"

The question was merely a formality; a hundred Astromancer's objections had no weight against the Council.

"I do. Indeed, I do most heartily consent," he replied as his bad eye rolled aimlessly in its socket.

A wave of whispers, murmuring and gasps rolled through the crowd and even Silas felt his heart begin to race. For as many years as these ceremonies had been taking place, no Astromancer ever said more than simply, yes. Unable to speak, Silas mechanically lowered his head so the medallion could be placed around his neck. When he straightened, he glanced at Idrella who was frantically signaling him to say something.

"Uh... Great Sir," he began, trying to emerge from the shock, "can you elaborate upon your generous words?"

The ancient Astromancer slowly shook his head in the affirmative and turned to face the crowd. Squinting at the cream of the political and economic crop from behind deep folds of skin, he scanned the audience and waited until only the faint hum of the beamcutters could be heard. In a voice that made many tremble, he finally spoke.

"Many are blind to the obvious cycles of life," he thundered. "I can see them! I can feel them! And I say to all of you that this day begins a cycle that will change the course of all humanity. I will not live to see the fruit, but the seed is now planted."

No one dared speak, or was capable of doing so, as the old man withdrew a knife, bunched his hair and beard together just above the shoulder and sliced clean through them. Holding the severed tresses over his head for all to see, he then let them fall to the floor. Without another word, he moved with deliberate strides through the crowd and exited the great hall. He would make no more appearances, no more predictions. When an Astromancer knew his cycle was complete, he cut the hair that had grown since the day his training began, thereby proclaiming his own imminent death.

****

Jesse could get nothing over the radios except chatter about the Council celebration. Realizing that traffic and security would be extra high on an inaugural night, he decided to avoid his usual landing bay and head for the less crowded far side of the Moon. For Walter's sake, it would be best if no one asked any questions, so Jesse slipped through the outer surveillance shield riding piggyback on a large freighter piloted by an old co-worker to keep his vehicle registration from being recorded.

Leaving his ship in a half-deserted garage in an isolated section, he felt like a master spy weaving his way to the recruiting station for the *Hyperion*. It was late, but numerous signs on the trains indicated that last minute applications for the crew were still being accepted. It would be safer to see Granny than docking on one of Oku's ships and requesting to see its captain. Though the secrecy was a complete waste of time, Jesse was having fun pretending to be a wanted man.

There was no line at the recruitment station; in fact only two people remained to work the late shift. Granny was filing some reports at the desk and a bored security guard was nodding off in the corner.

"Jesse!" Granny whispered in surprise. "You've found him?"

"Yes, he got a message to me and I've seen him. Granny, you wouldn't believe what he can do! And then I was even able to-"

"Couldn't you wait until morning to apply?" the aggravated guard growled, disturbed from his nap.

"I... I had to work late, and I just decided I needed to get away from that crummy job of mine," Jesse said laughing nervously.

"Well, go on," the guard said, trying to get comfortable again in the hard chair. "Don't waste the Commander's time."

"You had better hook up or he'll get suspicious," Granny said softly and then raised his voice. "Just step over to the computer so we can verify your qualifications, please."

With a sly wink, Jesse sauntered over to the verifier and raised the wire to his head. As contact was made, a sharp bolt of paralyzing current shot through his limbs and the sirens began to scream. Seeing that the groggy guard was temporarily disoriented by the commotion and knowing that he wouldn't have another chance to find out Danan's location, Granny leapt over the table onto the stunned Jesse and pretended to wrestle him under the desk.

"Where is he? For god's sake, where is he," Granny whispered into his ear, trying to shake some sense back into him.

By now the guard had realized what was happening and had raced to the desk, weapon drawn.

"Do you have him? Do you have him?" the guard shouted as he jumped around trying to get a clear shot between the struggling men.

In the confusion, Granny managed to hook one of his massive feet around the guard's ankle and haul him to the ground, but that maneuver only bought a few seconds as more security personnel came pouring into the room.

"Q, bay twenty-three," Jesse whispered into Granny's ear an instant before a pair of guards yanked the fugitive to his feet and slapped a placater on the back of his neck.

"Good work, Commander," the first guard said as his associates dragged away the limp figure. "You were very quick to respond."

"I was afraid he had a weapon and I guess my self-preservation instinct just kicked in," Granny replied humbly, trying to mask his anguish. "By the way, what did the guy do?"

"I don't know, let me see," he said, removing a small screen from his pocket, tapped a few buttons and began chuckling. "This guy must have the worst luck in the galaxy, the warrant was only issued this morning. Seems he's got something to do with that crazy Danan guy. Looks like we have a little inauguration present for Monitor Lindquist."

"Yes, I guess so. The bookies are going to love this," Granny said forcing a smile.

"Well my money will be on Lindquist. The guy's definitely got the system in the palm of his hand," the guard said and then softened his voice. "Hey, thanks for not mentioning I was, well, not at full readiness before. I owe you one, Commander."

"There's one thing you could do for me right now."

"Name it."

"Get me a replacement, I've had it!"

"No problem. I'll cover until I can get someone else down from the *Hyperion*. Go get some rest. Thanks again."

The moment the door closed behind Granny, he ran with his giant strides to the officer's private lounge and called Mardo.

"God damn it! God damn Lindquist!" Mardo shouted in rage. "Poor Jesse's as good as dead now. God damn. Did he at least have time to tell you where Walter was?"

"No, but I think he told me where he left his ship. Sector Q, bay twenty-three," Granny replied anxiously, quickly becoming overwhelmed with guilt. "It's my fault! I never should have told him to hook up."

"Get a hold of yourself, Gran. How did you know that bastard would put out a warrant the second he stepped into the Council Hall. You had better get back to the ship."

"But Jesse's ship might still have Walter's coordinates in the navigator-"

"Which is why I'm going down there right now. I've got clearance passes so I can't be traced."

"But it's my fault! I should be the one to go," Granny protested, fully prepared to sacrifice himself.

"No, I can't ask you to do this. Besides, I need you to assemble the crew. We're leaving in twenty-four hours," Mardo said and ended the transmission before Granny could try and talk him out of it.

Anyone caught with Danan would share his fate, and Mardo wouldn't let anyone else take that risk. The Union's form of justice was known as the three I's, interrogation, incarceration and finally, isolation. Suspects were interrogated by a professional panel of judges and in the case of a Council warrant, those judges were the Monitors themselves. If they were found guilty, they were sentenced to prison, the period of incarceration being predetermined by the first Council's original list of penalties and punishments; there was no bargaining and no chance of parole. If a convict attempted escape, caused trouble, was a repeat offender, or in any way threatened the security of the Council, his fate was isolation.

Supposedly the humane answer to capital punishment, the prisoner was placed in a modest-sized, converted cargo pod with a survival food generator, but with no engine or communications equipment. The pod was aimed toward uninhabited regions of space, fitted with detachable thrusters and launched. Once the pod was racing toward nowhere at a sufficiently high speed, the thrusters ejected, dooming the prisoner to a life of eternal, solitary confinement. And the cruelest part of the punishment, was the removal of the prisoner's d-chip.

This most likely would have been Danan's fate if he hadn't escaped from prison, and it would definitely be Mardo's if he got caught. Jesse might even be less fortunate, because he had information Lindquist wanted, and many a prisoner in the past had mysteriously dropped from sight after 'private' interrogations. There was nothing Mardo could do for Jesse now, but there was still time to save Danan.

Leaving his s/d system with the instructions that temporary command would be given to Granny while he conducted some personal business, Mardo entered his private vessel and raced full-speed to sector Q on the far side of the Moon. One perk of being a captain in Oku's fleet was the clearance pass that effectively made him invisible to all security systems. Oku had argued that such men had earned privacy, but the real reason, of course, was that he wanted his top officers to be able to conduct business of questionable legality unhampered.

Wearing ordinary worker's clothes and a full sun visor to mask his face, Mardo exited his craft in the temporary parking bay of section Q. Strolling nonchalantly over to bay twenty-three and triple-checking that no one was in sight, he removed a fist-sized device from his vest and placed it over the security panel. Another of Oku's perks, the device could break a thirty-digit code in less than ten seconds. A gratifying series of beeps and green lights preceded the door opening and a few seconds later, Mardo was inside Jesse's ship. As he had feared, the navigator still contained the course of the last flight, a potentially fatal oversight by Jesse. Mardo quickly entered his override codes and programmed the ship to go back from where it came.

****

Wading through a sea of adulation, Lindquist moved steadily toward the very tall, very voluptuous brunette near the center of the room. It was not the woman with whom he wanted to speak, although in private it would be a different story, but the man she supposedly guarded. While it was customary to take a bodyguard of the opposite sex, most female guards were a brutish sort, often recognizable as women only by the extra section of cloth tied around their chests. The employer of this guard not only had taste, but the ability to afford the best. Natalia was unquestionably the best, as all the bug-eyed men in the room would have attested, and Oku could definitely afford her.

"Well Monitor Lindquist, it seems you have a flare for the dramatic," Oku said, graciously extending his hand in congratulations.

It was not the reaction Silas had anticipated and momentarily disarmed, he found himself smiling and thanking his rival.

"I had better be wary, or you might steal Natalia away from me," Oku laughed, as the obliging guard massaged her master's shoulders, but winked sensuously at Silas.

"I never felt the need for a bodyguard," Silas replied smoothly. "But I'm beginning to see that it can have its advantages."

Lindquist continued with some half-hearted small talk with Oku and Monitor Rizzic, while debating whether or not to confront Oku about the Danan file. After the stir created by the Astromancer, Silas was on a high, experiencing a feeling of invincibility that was telling him that nothing could stand in his way. At the moment of his greatest euphoria, a messenger pushed through the crowd and bowed respectfully before the three Monitors.

"I'm most sorry to disturb you, Monitor Lindquist, but there is an urgent message," the frightened boy said, not daring to lift his eyes in the presence of so many powerful people.

"From the Moon?" Silas whispered brimming with anticipation as he pulled the boy aside.

"Yes, Sir. I was told it was something you were expecting."

Excusing himself from the two suspicious Monitors, and promising the messenger a healthy tip, Lindquist took a corner of his cape in each hand and strode out of the hall gloating with satisfaction.

"You have him!" Silas stated triumphantly to the image of Tilton Maas that awaited him in his chambers.

"Not Danan, not yet," Maas replied, uncharacteristically downcast. "But we have Dimont. He was trying to apply for the *Hyperion*."

"Damn you! You told me he would be with Danan!" Silas shouted, his voice trembling in fury. "Where is Danan!"

"Dimont has been resistant to questioning, so far," Maas said, clearly ashamed by his unprecedented failure, but then added with confidence. "However, I have no doubt that Dr. Frye could convince him to cooperate."

"That butcher! I want him interrogated, not lobotomized," Silas replied in disgust, kicking a twisted chair across the room.

"He was quite effective with Valery Danan," the undaunted spy replied coolly and watched as his boss slowly and silently nodded his consent.

****

Walter Danan was startled out of a sound sleep by the overwhelming feeling that something was wrong. Asking the computer to check on Jesse, he was informed that his brother-in-law had left for the Moon. Requesting a trace, Walter tried to settle his troubled mind while waiting for the response. Only a few seconds passed before he had an answer.

"Jesse Randolph Dimont, Council Warrant number 11032-A, has been apprehended at the recruitment station for the *Hyperion*," the computer stated as if reporting the weather. "His place of detention has not been placed on record. No hearing date has been set. No additional information is available at this time. Shall I maintain scan for further news?"

"Yes. Yes, maintain scan," Walter replied, barely able to form words.

This was one of those times when even the power of rational thought eluded him. The turmoil of twisting emotions wreaked havoc upon his balance and clarity. His animal passions told him to charge the Council Hall, guns blazing, and put an end to Silas Lindquist once and for all. With heart pumping and muscles aching for revenge, Walter Danan managed to force himself to sit down, to harness his anger and clear his thoughts. If he was to save Jesse, he would need abilities far beyond what he had already demonstrated. As light finally overcame his dark thoughts, warning alarms began to shriek and the weapons banks emerged fully charged and ready.

"Identify vessel!" Walter shouted over the din.

"Vessel registered to Jesse Dimont. Proper entry codes transmitted."

"Lock weapons on target and prepare to fire on my command. Are there any other vessels approaching?"

"Negative. Weapons locked on target. Awaiting command."

The targeting system was state of the art, the amount of firepower, enormous. Walter had anticipated that when the day came that he was discovered, he would need to fend off at least a dozen battle cruisers. If the police knew his whereabouts, they would not send a single, personal transport, unless it was a trick to take him alive.

"Target in optimum range," the computer announced.

"Still no other vessels approaching?"

"Negative."

"Open channel to approaching vessel," he ordered, probing the approaching craft with his own thoughts, searching for signs of danger.

"Establishing communications could compromise-"

"Open channel!"

An image of a man concealed behind a full face shield appeared in the cockpit. Walter demanded that the pilot to identify himself or he would commence firing.

"Walter, for god's sake it's me!" Mardo said, throwing off the helmet. "Jesse's been taken. I've got to get you to the *Hyperion*, immediately."

"Cancel alert. Allow entry," Walter yelled as he hurried down to the landing area.

A few minutes later he was embracing his old friend and making plans to elude the noose that Lindquist was dangling before his face.

CHAPTER 8

The reception was well into the early morning hours before it began to break up. It was clearly the most exciting social event anyone could remember, which actually wasn't saying much. One participant did put it in the proper perspective, however, when he said it was more thrilling than a d-chip fantasy, the greatest and rarest of all compliments. In a week's time, there would no doubt be at least twice as many people that attended who would claim to have been there, and as the years passed that number would continue to multiply. In the world of the upper circle, lying was often the sincerest form of flattery.

Silas had taken a moment to compose himself after the disappointing conversation with Maas before returning to the party. He had hoped to be able to announce Danan's capture and then decided to keep the news about Jesse Dimont quiet. He was not a big enough fish to waste time on, yet. Depending on what Maas and Dr. Frye could get out of him, Jesse's degree of notoriety could either greatly increase or sink into obscurity.

Lindquist scanned the thinning crowd for Oku, or more accurately, his curvaceous signpost, but neither could be found. Oku generally detested social functions, so it was not unusual that he would be long gone. Unfortunately, one social butterfly, or dragonfly as the case may be, was still buzzing through the crowd.

"Silas! My dear, dear Silas!" Rial cooed as she latched onto his arm with all the charm of a perfumed barnacle. "You simply must let me have you to dinner next week so I can show you off to all my friends! Besides, my husband will be out of the system on business and I'll need someone to keep me company on all those dreary, lonely nights."

Mrs. Croix had let her right hand slide down onto Silas' thigh and had her mouth so close to his ear that he could feel her lips brush against his lobe. Breaking into a sweat, not because of her actions, but because he was afraid he wouldn't be able to gracefully talk his way out, he started squirming and struggled to find the appropriate excuse.

"Sorry, mother," Idrella said, attaching herself to his other arm, "but new Monitors are much to busy to baby-sit overgrown adolescents."

Rial's eyes and nostrils flared and the gentle fingertips on Silas' thigh became biting nails.

"Ow!"

"Forgive me, dear Silas," Rial said breaking away and stepping back, "but I never could tolerate disobedient children."

Idrella also let go of Lindquist and planted herself between him and her mother. For an instant, Silas believed they were actually going to come to blows, a sight many in the room would have paid handsomely to see, but Idrella merely grabbed her mother's arm and half-dragged her to a quiet corner for a good old-fashioned verbal battle. Silas never thought it possible, but he was tired of the party and the fawning guests and while all eyes were on the Croix War, he slipped away.

At first, he headed toward his private rooms, but he couldn't resist seeing if the Astromancer would grant him an audience. They never met with anyone after cutting their hair, but perhaps in lieu of the extraordinary circumstances this one would speak to the Monitor who would revolutionize mankind. Doubling back, he passed a handful of well-wishers to whom he only nodded respectfully and kept going. As he began to round the corner of the hall that contained the Astromancer's room, he heard voices and stopped.

Peering around the wall, he saw an old acquaintance of his, one of the governors from the outer planets. He was a notorious ladies man, but he was failing miserably with some of his best lines. The object of his intended affection looked down on him passively and simply shook her head no. The dejected governor moved on and Natalia kept her place before the Astromancer's door.

"Computer!" Silas barked the instant he stepped through the door of his chambers. "How long has Monitor Oku been with the Astromancer?"

"Monitors' whereabouts are confidential unless present at a scheduled meeting," came the bland reply.

"All right, all right," he said pacing nervously. "Let's try this. How long has Natalia been in residence corridor seven?"

"One hour, twenty-one minutes."

Silas didn't care what anybody said, computers were still stupid.

****

Dr. Frye entered Jesse's cell with slow, determined steps. He was medium height and build, but had a grotesque, uneven, Picassoesque face. His appearance didn't bother him, however, he enjoyed the terrifying reactions they inspired. Some brave souls suggested surgery, but he gleefully replied that it would be a sin to ruin god's work.

What Doctor Nathan Frye did was anything but god's work. With the charm and compassion of a Nazi war criminal, he meticulously tortured people in ways that could not be detected. Considering himself an artist, he demanded, and received, huge sums of money for the performance of his craft. While others claimed that drugs or certain forms of electro-neuro stimulation were excellent, harmless ways to obtain information, Frye held fast to the belief that nothing surpassed the simplicity and efficacy of pure, agonizing pain.

Jesse had volunteered no information; in fact, he had yet to say a word. Maas' interrogation techniques had made him scream, and almost broke him, but his love of Walter and memory of Valery kept him strong. The torment didn't end until he mercifully lost consciousness. When he awoke, Jesse was alone in a dark, windowless detention cell. He desperately tried to use the techniques Walter had taught him to calm his thoughts and ease his pain. Not only did they fail to produce those results, he couldn't even make himself feel cold.

A chill did sweep through him, however, when the cell door opened and he saw Dr. Frye. Though they had never met and he had no idea who he was, Jesse experienced a wave of fear and contempt that he was barely able to control.

"Have you come to take my order for breakfast?" Jesse asked with courageous sarcasm. "Or maybe you've come to fluff my pillow?"

"My name is Dr. Frye and either you tell me everything you know about Walter Danan or I will inflict severe pain upon you," he replied with a country-doctor smile.

"You sure don't waste time, pal," Jesse said trying to laugh, but discovering he couldn't force enough air out of his constricting lungs.

"Where is Walter Danan?"

"No idea."

"When did you last see him?"

"Could you repeat the question?"

"Good. I was hoping you wouldn't cooperate," Frye said with a grin that exposed teeth even more crooked than his features. "I don't mind telling you I'm going to enjoy this."

****

There were numerous reasons why Lindquist would be unable to sleep. The Astromancer, Jesse Dimont and Walter Danan were a few, not to mention whatever it was Oku was up to. But apparently, all of the reasons put together weren't sufficient to keep him from falling into a deep sleep the instant he sprawled across the bed, still fully clothed. As fatigue overwhelmed him, his last thought was of the utmost importance; all morning meetings were canceled in honor of the inauguration.

When the subtle alarm began its increasingly persuasive beckoning at an early hour, he was sure the computer was doing it just to antagonize him.

"Let me sleep you bitch!" he growled, pulling his cloak over his head to block the flashing lights.

"Priority message from Tilton Maas. Shall I inform him you will not-"

"Put him on!" Silas shouted as he suddenly found himself standing, fully alert.

The image of Maas appeared a few feet in front of him, and if he didn't know any better, Silas could have sworn that a rancid smell accompanied the hologram.

"Well?" Silas asked menacingly.

"Dimont has proved unusually...resilient, sir," Maas confessed as he nervously ran his hand across the top of his oily head. "We did manage to get the bay number of his vessel, but not the location of the garage itself. A search of every area is underway."

"And the *Hyperion*?"

The crew has begun boarding and it's scheduled to leave tonight, sir."

"I want the ship emptied and everyone re-verified," Silas said extending a threatening finger. "And I want answers by this afternoon's Council meeting."

Silas had undressed, gotten back into bed and just dozed off when another call roused him.

"Now who?" he asked with exhausted frustration.

"Monitor Oku wishes to speak with you, if it's convenient."

"Why not," he said resigning himself to no more sleep.

"Why not what?" the computer asked.

"That means yes, stupid."

There was a noticeable pause before Oku's image appeared uncomfortably close to the bed where Silas was still reclining.

"I hear you have been busy, my young Monitor," Oku said with his ineffable ambiguity. "I'm surprised to see someone so industrious still in bed at this hour."

"Even Monitors must rest. And how were your extra-curricular activities last night?" Silas parried.

"Quite good and thank you for asking," Oku said without missing a beat. "May I ask why you are interfering with the operation of one of my ships?"

"Jesse Dimont was apprehended applying for work aboard the *Hyperion*. We had good reason to believe Danan would be with him. If you would like to put this to a Council vote..."

"That will not be necessary, I quite agree with your motives," Oku interrupted, still showing no hint of emotion.

"You what?" Silas asked, mildly annoyed that just when he thought he knew how Oku would react, he did the opposite.

"Yes, I agree that it is a wise move. After all, how would I look if a dangerous fugitive escaped on one of my ships?"

"Covering your ass, Oku?" Silas smirked.

"Upholding the law, Monitor Lindquist, as you will no doubt do when you bring Dimont to this afternoon's meeting."

"This afternoon?"

"Need I remind you that the law requires all Council warrant defendants be given a chance to speak at the next scheduled meeting?" Oku said like a teacher scolding a forgetful child.

With that, Oku terminated the call and left Silas to gnaw on his pillow. Due to increasing pressure from the general public, the present Council was unable to be so indulgent with the notorious, private interrogations of their predecessors. Silas knew that if Dimont remembered anything that happened, or even looked like he was anything but well treated, there would be an investigation he couldn't afford to have take place.

"Get me Maas!" Silas ordered and only had to wait a moment for his dutiful spy. "Tell Frye to clean up and get Dimont over here as soon as possible."

"Yes, sir. And Monitor Lindquist, we've located his vessel, but the navigator memory had been erased," Maas said, not at all pleased at the progression of events. "However, soil samples from the landing pads are being analyzed as well as particles from the hull. We believe they are from somewhere on Earth."

"That really narrows it down," Lindquist replied sarcastically, obviously rapidly losing faith in his hired hand.

****

Mardo eased his personal transport up against his private docking area adjacent to his quarters. He was shocked and outraged to find Union Special Security Forces sitting in his living room.

"How dare you!" he said with dignified vehemence. "What is the meaning of this?"

"I'm sorry for the intrusion, Captain Mardo, but we have orders to verify everyone who boards," the apologetic officer explained, jumping to attention.

"Wait until I inform Monitor Oku!" Mardo declared, expecting the men to flee in terror at the mere mention of the mighty Oku.

"It was Monitor Oku who authorized the search. We are going to have to search your transport, also," the officer said, clearly not pleased that he was chosen to barge in on the Captain of the ship, regardless of who issued the order.

"You will not take another step until I verify those orders," Mardo said softly, but in a deep, threatening tone.

"Of course, sir," the man replied, quickly returning to his spot on the couch.

A quick check revealed that the Special Forces officer had indeed been telling the truth. There was nothing Mardo could do but let the men search the vessel. As they entered the craft, a muted beeping sound announced that someone else was requesting entry.

"Come in," Mardo said, while he kept his eyes fixed on the docking portal.

"Captain Mardo?" a low voice asked.

"Look, this isn't a good time-" he began and then glanced over his shoulder to see a woman in a crisp, new *Hyperion* uniform. She was beautiful, with delicate porcelain-doll features and sensuous almond-shaped eyes. "Who are you?"

"My name is Kiya. Here are my qualifications," she replied, handing him a screen lit up like a scoreboard.

"Very impressive, Kiya, but I'm afraid I'm a little busy at the moment," Mardo said returning his gaze to the portal. "Perhaps if you make an appointment with my assistant..."

"I *am* your assistant," she said more forcefully.

"You?" he asked, turning again to look at the cold, but lovely statue-like face.

"I had the best qualifications, as you could see."

"I didn't think this thing had so many lights," he laughed, tossing the screen back to her. "I'm sorry for being abrupt, but I'm being searched at the moment."

"We all suffered that indignity," Kiya said, as Mardo doubted she knew the meaning of the word suffer.

"Yeah, but Captains are supposed to be above such things. And anyway, how the hell did they get in my private quarters?"

"I let them in," she stated plainly.

"You? Who the hell are you to let these weasels invade my privacy?" Mardo bellowed, wondering just how far he could throw the pint-sized menace.

"I am your assistant. I fail to see the problem," she continued, stone-faced. "Do you have something to hide?"

"Do you have another job lined up?" he yelled, moving toward her until they were toe to toe. "Because you're going to need one if you keep up that attitude with me. Either you get the icicles out of your butt or I'm going to kick it across the system. Do I make myself understood?"

"Perfectly, Captain," she replied with cloying sweetness, suddenly producing a smile.

"And don't you ever let anyone in here again without my permission, and that includes you."

"Yes, sir. Is there anything else the Captain requires?" Kiya asked with maddening pseudo-innocence.

"I want a status report on every inch of this ship," Mardo said, knowing it would take the rest of the day.

Kiya nodded and turned to leave, but hesitated when she saw the security forces exiting the portal.

"Well, gentlemen, did I have anything to hide?" Mardo asked them while looking straight at Kiya.

"All clear, sir. Sorry again for the intrusion."

In a few seconds all his unwanted guests were finally gone and Mardo immediately hailed his Commander.

"Is everything going according to schedule?" Granny asked, not daring to mention Danan even on personal inter-ship communications.

"So far so good," Mardo replied with a smile, and then his features abruptly darkened. "But what's the big idea of assigning that succubus as my assistant?"

"Unfortunately, she has enough qualifications to take my job. There wasn't much else to choose from. But I'm confident that if anyone can whip her into shape, you're the man," Granny said with an exaggerated wink.

"No thanks," Mardo groaned. "I prefer my women to have a pulse."

"You may not be that picky a few years into the voyage," Granny said grinning, clearly amused by his Captain's discomfort. "By the way, what the hell did she do to make such a wonderful impression on you?"

Mardo recounted to Granny every detail of his conversation with Kiya and the Commander struggled, and failed, to keep a straight face. After the two friends had a good laugh discussing creative ways of disposing of Kiya, they scheduled a private meeting for later on that afternoon and got back to the business of preparing for an eight-year voyage.

CHAPTER 9

Jesse stood before the Council of Monitors in a daze. Thanks to an illegal drug that obliterates short-term memory, and often wreaks havoc on the long-term as well, Dr. Frye was able to keep his handiwork from finding a place in his victim's mind. The last twelve hours were a blur and even the present couldn't find a foothold in the swirl of confusion. The effects were usually only temporary. Usually.

"All right, Lindquist, what did you do to him?" Monitor M'bai asked the moment she saw the prisoner's glassy eyes.

"I could easily take offense at your accusation, Monitor M'bai, but considering the appearance of Mr. Dimont your supposition is correct, at least partially," the new Monitor lied like a seasoned professional. "Something has been done to the poor man, but not by my hand. He was like this when we apprehended him. I contend that Walter Danan's little mind games did this to him."

There was a moment of murmuring as the Monitors exchanged comments amongst themselves. Idrella looked deeply into her ex-lover's eyes, trying to discover the truth, but as usual got no further than his veneer of charm and innocence.

"Would someone please get the man a chair?" she asked as she watched Jesse swaying unsteadily.

"Of course, how thoughtless of me," Silas said, motioning for a guard to bring over a chair.

"I suppose, Monitor Lindquist, that if we ran a few tests on Mr. Dimont we would not find any clues as to why he is in this condition?" Idrella asked as she began to refit some of the suspicious pieces of Silas' character. The picture that started to emerge wasn't pretty, and with no small pang of guilt, she realized it was a picture to which she had been turning a blind eye for many years.

"How can I say? It is certainly worth a try," Silas said, hoping the other Monitors wouldn't think it was worth a try.

"Mr. Dimont," Oku began as everyone in the room instantly fell silent. "Have you been with Walter Danan recently?"

Jesse tried to focus his eyes on the man asking the question, but couldn't be sure whether or not he was real or part of a dream. At the sound of Walter's name, however, the memory of the accident in the ocean suddenly sprang up before his inner eye and he clutched his stomach as if in agony. Idrella rushed from her seat and knelt before the prisoner.

"Is something wrong? Are you hurt?"

"No, no, I'm okay now," he said looking kindly on the woman before him, thinking of how his sister used to take care of him when he was a child. "Walter fixed me. You remind me of Valery, but she's dead. Some bastard from the upper circle murdered her."

Nine Monitor's attentions turned to the part about the murder; one only heard the name Walter.

"So you have seen him?" Lindquist said starting to rise, but forced himself to remain seated, trying not to look too eager. "Jesse, how did Walter 'fix you'?"

Jesse didn't even look over to Lindquist because he couldn't seem to take his eyes off of Idrella's face. It was an exquisite face, not like the hideous features of the man in his nightmare.

"Do I know you?" he asked her like a lost child, completely ignoring Lindquist's question.

"I don't think we've met," she said, almost blushing under the direct stare. "Were you hurt, Jesse? Did Walter help you?"

Jesse didn't know who all these people were and he wasn't sure if he should trust them. He knew that the gargoyle from his terrifying dream was trying to hurt him and he shouldn't tell him anything. But the woman before him was so beautiful, it must be all right to at least tell her something so wonderful.

"The rocks, those awful jagged rocks," he began, clutching his stomach again. "He warned me, but the current was so strong."

"Did they cut you?" she asked softly.

"It was very bad. I thought I was going to die," he told her, raising the front of his shirt. "But look! It's all gone!"

"Did Walter perform surgery?"

"Oh no, oh no! He just put his hands right here and it went away!" Jesse declared proudly.

"The defendant is obviously not coherent," M'bai protested as the others agreed. "This testimony is not only invalid, it's a waste of our valuable time."

"You all fail to see, my fellow Council members, the important point here," Lindquist said calmly, smelling the sweet fragrance of victory. "Regardless of whether or not Danan possesses these miraculous healing powers, he has made Jesse think he does. And whatever he has actually done to this poor man, we can all see the tragic results."

"Perhaps you will allow us to await the results of some tests before we judge what has really happened to this man? And I also move that the defendant immediately be put under the care of physicians to see if some clarity can be restored to his mind," Oku said as he looked directly at each Monitor with an expression that clearly indicated he expected no opposition to his suggestions.

Lindquist bit hard on the inside of his lip until he tasted warm, salty blood running over his tongue. His anger was like a team of wild horses straining to break free and trample Oku. Just as he had seemed to convince the majority of the Council, that damned meddler had to ruin everything.

"Jesse Dimont!" Silas shouted, barely hanging on the edge of control. "Where is Walter Danan?"

The shouting snapped Jesse out his trance-like obsession with Idrella's face and he looked fearfully at the man who was yelling at him. The man was familiar, he knew he should remember who it was, but there was too much fog and confusion clouding his mind. Somewhere in the swirl of thoughts he came up with the idea that if he told where Walter was, then Walter could heal the whole Union. But as he was about to reveal the location of the island hideaway, he felt Idrella's hand squeezing his arm and saw her eyes open wide in warning.

"I don't know where Walter is," Jesse said with his stupor-like believability and felt very happy when Idrella showed him a fleeting smile of approval.

"You seemed rather smitten with the prisoner, Idrella," Silas said as he pulled her aside before the beginning of her next meeting. "Do dangerous men excite you?"

"Maybe they do," she replied defiantly, wrenching her arm free of his grasp and signaling Boa to stand next to Lindquist.

The massive bodyguard gladly moved within inches of Lindquist, staring down with such intensity that the Monitor swore he could feel the top of his head heating up.

"Then maybe you should reconsider me," he said, giving her a look that made the hair on her neck stand up. "Because I am a very dangerous man. I know what I want and I will turn this Union upside down to get it, whether you're with me or not. Reconsider, Monitor Croix."

"I intend to reconsider a lot of things," Idrella shot back. "This is a risky game you're playing Silas, and don't forget you're not the only Monitor who knows how to play. Boa, wait for me here."

Idrella turned and entered the meeting room and Boa obediently stood in front of the door, not taking his eyes off Lindquist for an instant.

"Your mistress is a fool," Silas spat contemptuously. "She heard the Astromancer's prediction. The day will come when I will rule the Union and she will beg me to take her back."

Silas whipped his cape around for emphasis and strode off feeling invincible. Boa watched placidly, thinking that no matter how powerful some people got, they could still be very stupid.

****

"The status reports you ordered, Captain," Kiya stated coldly as she placed the stack of data screens on Mardo's desk.

"Anything that should be brought to my attention?" he asked without looking up.

"Some minor malfunctions in the auxiliary communications system, some couches missing from the crew's lounge on deck four and a fight in maintenance that prompted the expulsion of both parties involved. Nothing that should delay our departure," she replied with steel-hard efficiency.

"And the security checks?"

"Complete."

"Thank you, that will be all."

Kiya lingered for a moment as if to ask a question, but when Mardo ignored her she kept her silence and left. Before the door closed behind her, Mardo hailed Granny and told him to get the *Hyperion* underway. When Kiya entered her substantially smaller assistant's quarters next to Mardo's, she perched on the end of her bunk and listened to the Captain begin the usual "welcome aboard" pep talk. After a couple of minutes, she silenced the transmission and removed a small cosmetics box from her bedside table. Sliding open the lid, the box revealed a sophisticated communication device; a device far beyond the means of an officer's assistant. Skillfully manipulating the controls, Kiya transmitted a private, multi-coded message to somewhere outside the *Hyperion*, which had just released its docking clamps and began moving out toward the unknown.

****

Silas Lindquist was furious. He didn't like when things didn't go his way, or when people disagreed with him. Surely everyone must realize how important he was? Never before in history had an Astromancer, and the Supreme Astromancer at that, given such a ringing endorsement. The old man had practically said that he was going to be a new messiah.

"Computer, I wish to speak with the Supreme Astromancer," Silas ordered as he paced his usual course around his opulent quarters.

"The Supreme Astromancer is dead."

"Dead! When?" Silas demanded, stopping in his tracks.

"Four hours, forty-nine minutes ago."

"Why wasn't I informed? Did he leave me any messages?" Silas asked, sure that his dying words must have concerned the man who would change history.

"No messages for Monitor Lindquist."

"That can't be right. Check his last statement again."

"No messages for Monitor Lindquist."

"Who did he leave messages for?" he asked with paranoid intensity.

"It is unlawful to disclose confidential statements. You were not mentioned, therefore you have no right to know," the computer said with more than just a hint of satisfaction.

Silas' ego quickly convinced him it was just an oversight by a dying old man, until he seized on the idea that Oku must have somehow coerced the Astromancer on his deathbed.

"Let Oku play his little games!" Lindquist yelled to no one in particular. "The world heard the Astromancer's prediction, nothing can change the immutable cycles of life!"

"Priority message," the computer said coldly.

"Maas?"

"Affirmative."

The instant Maas' image appeared Lindquist began screaming at him for delivering Jesse Dimont in such a wretched condition. He ranted and raved about Frye's incompetence and how his seat on the Council could be in jeopardy if the truth was discovered. Throughout the tirade, Maas stood patiently, like a nanny waiting for her spoiled charge to end his tantrum.

"Well! What do you have to say for yourself?" Silas shouted, crimson-cheeked and about two octaves above his usual tone.

"We believe we have located Danan," Maas stated unemotionally, although the grease in his hair did shimmer just a bit more as he delivered the news.

"Where? Have you sent troops?" Silas almost whispered, breathless.

"There is a recent volcanic island on Earth, in the Pacific, which would fit our test results on the residue samples taken from Dimont's ship. Our scans have indicated a few small buildings, although there are no signs of weapons systems or vessels."

"He would be trying to keep a low profile, fool. Do you think he would park a few cruisers and mount a dozen megacannons? I want a full squadron down there. Now. Oh, and Maas, don't worry about taking him alive," Silas added smiling, as his henchman nodded approvingly and disappeared.

Lindquist made himself cozy in his custom-made lounge chair, contoured specifically for his muscular physique, and ordered a pitcher of a refreshing tropical drink in honor of the occasion. He then requested that the lead ship's viewscreen be tied into his system so he would have a front row seat to the action. Instantly, the wall before him lit up a bright blue that almost hurt his eyes, as the ships were already descending over the targeted area of the ocean. The half-dozen vessels fanned out into a wide v-shape and approached from the south with no sign of resistance.

Lindquist ordered higher magnification so he could see the island. A black dot slowly resolved itself into an irregular, craggy scrap of rock with nothing more than a shack on one of its ridges. He knew Danan would keep a low profile, but this was ridiculous.

"Commander," Silas said to the lead pilot, " are you sure that flyspeck is-"

There was no chance to finish his sentence as a dozen megacannons reared their deadly heads, like mighty dragons emerging from solid rock, and fired before the squadron's warning indicators even had a chance to flicker. Lindquist instinctively threw his arms in front of his face, upsetting the pitcher of cold liquid into his lap. A split-second later the brilliant blue was shattered by a ghastly, scarlet blaze and the screen went blank.

"Commander!" Silas shouted, leaping from his chair and sending ice cubes flying around the room. "Commander, come in! Can anyone from the squadron hear me!"

There was a long, tense moment of complete silence and then Maas appeared to his right.

"All vessels have gone down," he reported in shock. "We're not sure of the casualties-"

"I don't give a damn about casualties! Bring in the cruisers. Now I want him alive!" Lindquist growled, hurling a chunk of pineapple that sailed through the stomach of Maas' image as he faded from sight.

As the *Hyperion* left the moon's orbit, four heavy cruisers raced by headed toward Earth. Those who were off-duty watched the news and discovered that some big battle was taking place in the Pacific and the Union was suffering heavy losses, but reports were neither confirmed nor denied by official sources. There was also no indication as to who was launching this unprovoked attack against a Union that had maintained peace for generations. Word spread quickly through the crew as the final systems' checks were performed and the ship began to accelerate.

Another ship was also on the move. From the southern tip of the island, a wall of rock swung open beneath the sea and a highly modified, Viper-class personal transport shot into the atmosphere like a streak of lightning. The extensive, and expensive, modifications made it blindingly fast, even when compared with the top-of-the-line Laserswift, which already cost more than an average man made in a lifetime.

But that was what upper circle wealth could do for you, especially if you were the descendant of a Brain Bender. Regardless of how many warrants, or even convictions, a member of the upper circle had, his private holdings remained untouched and untraceable. The "Swiss Bank Amendment" was another convenient law passed by an early Council that recognized the fact that they and their families had the most to lose and that political currents could turn upon anyone at any time. If one of their numbers was unlucky enough to suddenly find himself as a wanted man, at least he would be able to quietly sneak away and live in luxury, or provide himself with the fastest vessel and most sophisticated defense system money could buy.

Two of the cruisers and twenty smaller craft turned to pursue the Viper, but it was like sending a herd of hippos after a cheetah. The best they could hope for was to intercept it if it passed within range of any stationary installations or other squadrons ahead of its path. Alerts were issued far beyond the outer planets, but the vessel's course was not toward the black depths of the system's edge. Instead, it was headed straight for the glorious, radiant source of all life, the sun.

Eight more squadrons of lighter craft joined the remaining two cruisers and they began their descent and prepared to assault the tiny piece of earth, which barely held its head above water. A dozen additional megacannons arose from the rock to join the barrage, while scores of defensive weapons sprang up from the ocean waves in a five-mile radius around the island, preventing anything bigger than a pebble from breaking through. It was clear that if Danan was still on the island and was to be taken alive, it would require a massive attack force and a lot of patience.

Patience was one of the qualities Monitor Lindquist was lacking at the moment, and after assessing the strategists reports, calmly ordered the total annihilation of the island. As the mighty cruisers prepared to blow the island, and a sizable chunk of that region of the Pacific, off of the globe, the megacannons suddenly stopped. The defense batteries returned to the sea and for a moment there was silence. Then a thin wisp of smoke rose from the only structure on the island as the underground chambers quietly and unceremoniously self-destructed.

It was a mystery to everyone in the fleet why the guns stopped. They couldn't have known that the sophisticated defense system was programmed to disengage the instant it sensed the weapons of mass destruction charging in the bellies of the cruisers. The man who programmed the state-of-the-art defense computer couldn't bear to have the fragile foliage on his island incinerated, or hurt any of the shiny, purple lizards which were now merrily racing up and down the legs of the landing force.

The charges in the underground chambers had been set deep in a shaft. When they blew, a column of lava swelled upward, filling the rooms and igniting the structure on the surface, obliterating any clues the landing forces might have found. Every inch of the island was searched, but no more surprises were uncovered.

Lindquist and the fleet turned their full attention to the vessel streaking toward the sun. Long-range weapons fired hopelessly at the elusive craft as promises of fair treatment were broadcast, if the pilot turned about and surrendered immediately.

As outer-hull temperatures soared to dangerous heights, the fleet was forced to stop their pursuit and wait to see if their prey would return, or make the ultimate sacrifice.

Silas held his breath in an almost erotic moment of tension as the screen indicated that there was only seconds before the point of no return was reached by the renegade craft. Suddenly, the speeding vessel broke silence with two words of an ancient Earth curse. Then a bright orange-yellow speck appeared, flared into a glowing cinder with a fiery tail and quickly faded to nothingness.

CHAPTER 10

The bookmakers were under heavy fire. Those who had wagered on the Lindquist side of the feud claimed that Danan must have been immolated in the sun's heat, or no less fried by the lava in the underground chambers. Those who had taken Danan and the odds, held fast to the facts; no body had been recovered from the island and, though the voice that uttered the now re-popularized phrase was positively identified as Danan's, it could not be determined whether or not the message had been pre-recorded.

The beleaguered bookies froze all wagering and gave their customers the option of a refund and if they declined, they would have to wait an indefinite period until something definite was officially decided about Danan's fate. Though all regular gambling activity on the feud ceased, one particularly daring bookie accepted an enormous bet on Walter Danan at thousand-to-one odds. It was whispered that someone on the Council placed the wager.

****

The *Hyperion* moved passed highly fashionable, and therefore densely populated, Mars and was traversing the rock-strewn gap between it and Jupiter when Kiya returned to Mardo's quarters.

"Did I call for you?" Mardo asked rhetorically as he looked up from a sea of reports.

"No, sir. But I thought you would be interested in the news from Earth," she said, watching his every move like a hawk scanning for mice.

"I will have years of free time to listen to the news," he said with convincing disinterest. "But right now, it seems like I have years of work to finish before I get a chance to sleep."

"They claim to have killed Walter Danan," she blurted out anyway.

"So?" he replied with pointed frigidity.

"So, he was a friend of yours, was he not? He gave you a job when you were broke," she said as Mardo wondered whether she was the worst spy in the galaxy or simply the rudest woman alive. Or both.

"Oku gave me a better job, with a much higher pay. Now where do you think my allegiance lies?" he asked impassively, leaning back in his chair and putting his feet on the polished mahogany desk, a standard issue for a Captain in Oku's fleet.

"If you are motivated solely by money, than your loyalty is to Oku," she said, still pressing her Captain harder than anyone else ever dared.

"Then there you have it," Mardo said, raising both hands as if the case was closed.

"But I do not believe that you are a man motivated by greed," she replied, leaning on the hand she had boldly placed on the other side of his desk.

"Our five minutes together have revealed my entire character to you? Or have you been checking up on me?" he growled, turning a threatening shade of crimson.

"A good assistant should know the nature of the man she will be assisting for the next eight years," Kiya replied, prudently retreating physically as well as verbally.

"A good assistant knows when to get the hell out of my face!"

When she left, Mardo quickly returned to the latest news from Earth. The media was portraying the disastrous assault as a daring victory against great odds, but then the major networks were owned by the Lindquist family. Walter Danan was described as no less than a fiendish, murdering anarchist and the entire system should be thankful that someone like Silas was now on the Council to protect everyone from such villains.

Unfortunately, the majority of mankind was not yet beyond believing such obvious propaganda.

Though the raid was portrayed as a rousing success, the reporters were cleverly skirting the issue of Danan's fate. Without evidence, no one would even speculate if he was dead or alive. As the reports droned on, with graphic scenes of the conflict blazing in the background, Mardo went to his expansive viewing port and paced anxiously. Before every turn, he paused to scan the heavens. After requesting that the news broadcast be terminated, the captain of the *Hyperion* checked the speed of his vessel for at least the tenth time that hour. They were running fifteen percent slower than the usual trans-system speed and after ordering another two-percent reduction, he told himself that was as low as he dared go.

****

Idrella Croix was not happy, not with Lindquist, her mother, the Council and definitely not with herself. She had done a lot of things in her life of which she was not proud. Just the act of being a Monitor meant she was cheating planets-full of people out of billions that should be used to improve their subsistence existences. She had flexed her political muscle to remove her enemies, helped suppress ideas and technologies which would have lessened the people's dependence on the Council and generally succumbed to everything her great-grandfather abhorred.

Requesting magnification on her viewing portal, she watched the chaotic, angry red spot on Jupiter's surface and thought that her heart must not look too different at that moment. And she pretended, as she always did as a child, that she could see her ancestor's stasis pod orbiting high above that spot. Idrella recalled how she used to have "conversations" with him, asking questions out loud and then imagining what wise answers he would have given. The confused Monitor would gladly have parted with a year's income to have someone like the great Jupiter Croix to talk with for just a few minutes.

An emergency session of the Council was being held later on that night to discuss Lindquist's little raid and her mind was still plagued with uncertainty as to where the truth resided. The pitiable figure of Jesse Dimont had suddenly transformed her apathy to sympathy and for once she saw a case as more than merely a point of business; it was literally a life or death struggle for someone who just might be innocent.

"Computer, access Walter Danan file, manual control," she said, stretching across the bed and reaching for a small keypad.

A list of options appeared on the opposite wall and she chose to begin with Walter's childhood. Quickly scrolling through the birth statistics and official psychological profile, she went on to the actual scenes of his life taped at school and social functions. Official reports were usually worthless, so she muted the commentary and relied on her own memory of those times as she watched.

A small, gangly boy amused himself in the corner of the playground while his taller, stronger, genetically 'clean' peers went about their games ignoring him as if he was invisible. Idrella recalled with shame those early days when she and the other children ostracized Walter because their parents had told them the boy had something terribly wrong with him. It hurt to look at the cruel scenes and the pain suddenly shook loose a memory that had not surfaced for over twenty-five years.

Closing her eyes, Idrella saw herself as a five-year-old girl holding her favorite doll. A group of older children grabbed the doll and they threw it up into a tree. Crying, begging and pleading would not make them retrieve the doll and she was too tiny to get it herself. As the bullies laughed and continued to taunt her, a determined little figure came up behind them. Walter Danan was seven at the time and greatly dwarfed by the ten and eleven-year-old upper circle brats. But there was a look in his eyes, a clear, steady, almost frightening power that silenced the laughter immediately. In an unemotional voice, Walter simply told the group to leave Idrella alone and to go away, which to her amazement, they did without another word. Walter then quickly scaled the tree and gallantly returned her doll.

Thanking him through happy sobs, she ran home and soon forgot the entire incident. At the time, she was too young to appreciate little Walter's special qualities; qualities that most adults still lacked. He was brave, disciplined and above all, deeply compassionate. And there was something else, something about him that couldn't be put into words. She was too young to notice it then, and had been too blind to see it the handful of times she had met Walter in the last ten years.

Requesting the visual file on his marriage, she saw the matured Danan among people who had grown to love him; former antagonists who had been drawn to the strange magnetic force that had strengthened a hundred-fold since childhood. Looking upon it as an obligation, Idrella had attended the wedding, yet had been so wrapped up in her own importance that she barely noticed the happy couple and the warmth they exuded.

And what about Valery Danan, still another irritating puzzle to add to her list? The official report claimed that Walter had murdered her. Idrella had accepted that without a second thought, but the visuals and her memories threw a new, dazzling light on everything, and she realized just how absurd that accusation was. It was clear now that Walter could never be capable of such a horrible deed. However, Jesse's groggy statement about an upper circle plot rang truer than anything she had yet heard about the case. If Walter was incapable of harming his wife and brother-in-law, Idrella concluded, then all ten of her fingers pointed in only one direction, straight at Silas Lindquist.

Tossing the keypad aside, she requested the Council Interrogation Proceedings on Danan. Walter's image appeared, standing before the Monitors to be questioned and receive judgment. He had been captured only a week after his wife's death and the pain and grief of her loss clearly hung on him like a heavy coat of mail. Idrella shook her head at the image, amazed that her impression of the prisoner's attitude at the time had been one of remorseless defiance.

Listening to her own voice ask questions, in an accusatory and patronizing tone, she watched with admiration as Walter answered calmly, point for point. The prisoner was succinct, clear and unwavering in his assertions as one by one, each Monitor grilled the man accused of murder and treason. They all asked the same questions; did he kill Valery because she tried to stop him, did he want to overthrow the government to get revenge for his mistreatment during childhood, and why did he want to punish all of mankind by taking away their d-chips?

The questions were shot at him with such speed that he often only had time to deny the accusation, not explain his real motivations and aspirations, until it was Oku's turn to interrogate the prisoner.

"Mr. Danan, exactly what special powers do you believe you possess, and to what do you attribute them?" Oku had asked with genuine curiosity.

Danan had hesitated for a moment, stared directly at Oku as if trying to gauge his formidable judge, and then began his explanation with eagerness. Idrella almost paused the tape and asked the computer to verify her presence at those proceedings because she had trouble believing all of this went by her.

"Let me first make it clear, Monitor Oku, that the goal of my research is not to pull apples out of the air or to become invisible. Those things are merely 'by-products' of what's really important," Walter stated with unaffected honesty. "Matter is a coarse, surface level of existence. There are numerous other levels, each becoming increasingly refined, and each providing a more expansive awareness of the true reality. The human nervous system is designed to function on these higher levels, but mankind screwed up somewhere along the way and began concentrating solely on the 'concrete' things, like pain and suffering. We completely forgot that in essence *we* create ourselves and everything around us."

"Then it is your assertion that you are not unique?" Oku interrupted, fascination clearly in his voice and eyes.

"Of course I'm not unique!" Walter replied laughing, clearly a different man then the one who was being interrogated only a few minutes earlier. "Oku, if you have a human nervous system, you can do this, too!"

Closing his eyes for a moment, a slight shudder passed through Walter's body and then he slowly rose a meter off the floor. That part Idrella remembered. Seeing ten stunned expressions, Walter decided he had proved his point and gently returned his feet to the plush, purple carpeting. Monitor Ramos called for guards to search him, but no device was found that could have lifted him, or could have created such an illusion. Despite his perilous position, Walter seemed almost delighted by the entire proceedings.

"If that was not a trick, Mr. Danan, how were you able to defy the laws of gravity?" Oku asked, trying to suppress the look of surprise he knew covered all their faces.

Idrella listened intently to the tape, often replaying sections many times, as Walter Danan spoke about his theories of matter, consciousness and the role of the nervous system as a bridge between the two. At the time, she had agreed with the rest of the Council that they were listening to the ravings of a madman, a very dangerous madman who just might have stumbled upon something incredible.

After a brief discussion, it was the unanimous decision of the Council of Monitors that Walter Danan be incarcerated

CHAPTER 11

"Twenty-seven vessels destroyed, eighteen people injured and nothing to show for it!" Monitor M'bai shouted, her tall pretzel-twisted hair shaking with her anger. "Was Walter Danan worth all this!"

Nothing made nine Monitors as frenzied as the scent of the blood of failure oozing from the political wounds of one of their own kind. Lindquist did not expect an easy time of it, but he was far from being defeated.

"If Danan was not dangerous, why did the Council issue a warrant and incarcerate him in the first place?" Silas began calmly. "If he had nothing to hide, why did he outfit his island like a battle cruiser? And if he is the new messiah, why doesn't he materialize right now and show us all the glorious path to salvation?"

M'bai pulled her cloak tightly closed and pursed her lips like a pouting child. The rest of the circle also sat in silence for several moments.

"Was such a massive, and costly, assault necessary against just one man?" Rizzic asked in a more subdued tone.

"Do you mean just one man with just twenty-four megacannons and just the most sophisticated defense network money can buy?" Lindquist replied derisively, sensing the tide turning back in his favor.

To further emphasize his point, he displayed some of the scenes of the fighting and then the substantial list of weaponry confiscated. He became confident the matter would be dropped.

"Monitor Lindquist," Idrella interjected, purposefully ignoring the displays, "what would you do if someone on the Council wanted you dead? Shouldn't a man who believes he is innocent have the right to defend himself? Did you expect Walter Danan to invite you in and surrender himself to that renowned Lindquist mercy?"

Such sharp words coming from someone who had been so close to Lindquist drew everyone's attention. Even Oku slightly raised an eyebrow.

"Innocent, Monitor Croix? Did I hear you use the word innocent?" Silas said as his features darkened. "Were you out sick or on vacation the day the Council voted to imprison Danan, because I could have sworn the vote was unanimous?"

"I said that Danan believes himself innocent. And if you won't be honest, then I will state for the record that if someone raised with generations of revenge and hatred for my family became a Monitor, I would spend my last dollar to ensure my safety."

At that moment, the fine line between love and hatred shattered into a thousand pieces as the former lovers glared at each other across the cool blackness of the stone table. Several Monitors instinctively rolled their chairs back a few inches as if to avoid being scorched by the flames shooting from Lindquist's and Croix's eyes.

"Have I done anything that is not within the bounds of legality?" he appealed to the entire Council with open arms, trying to regain his composure.

"Nothing that can be proven, yet," Idrella said under her breath, just loud enough for Silas to hear, but softly enough for him to pretend that he hadn't.

"You were, of course, within your rights as a Monitor to order an offensive against a fugitive," Oku spoke up, hoping to diffuse the situation, but not by too much. "The losses sustained are, of course, regrettable but often inevitable. However, the sacrifice is worthwhile if some positive results were obtained. Were any positive results obtained, Monitor Lindquist?"

Silas had already grown to hate Oku's ability to sound like he was asking a legitimate question, when it was obvious he was firing a direct hit. It was certainly not a new technique, but Oku had developed it into an art. Taking a deep breath, Silas gathered his thoughts, tried to bury some of his anger and attempted to answer politely.

"There is an eighty-nine percent probability that Danan was killed either in the escaping vessel or the island chambers," he said, displaying a series of strategist's calculations.

"And what course of action do you plan for that unsettling eleven percent?" Oku asked with a smile.

"Our only hope, at this time, is that Jesse Dimont will become lucid enough to provide some answers," he replied, half-hoping he would never become lucid again.

"I'm glad you brought up Mr. Dimont," M'bai said, showing her large white teeth that almost looked sharpened. "Preliminary tests indicate there has obviously been some severe trauma, possibly complicated by some type of drug, but as of yet, clues have eluded all our experts. A mystery indeed, wouldn't you say, Monitor Lindquist? And Mr. Dimont may never recover enough to provide us with answers."

"How unfortunate," Silas said without even bothering to sound convincing.

"Yes, quite unfortunate," M'bai continued, "but not without precedence, however."

"What do you mean?" he asked suspiciously, shielding the fear that had sent a shock wave through his veins.

"Monitor M'bai has reason to believe that there are a handful of unscrupulous individuals trained in a variety of illegal techniques," Idrella said with an air of sweet innocence. "Imagine that, Silas, people who could actually torture others without leaving a trace!"

"This is all very interesting speculation, but it is simply that, speculation," he replied calmly, praying that there was no evidence.

"Perhaps," M'bai added thoughtfully, "but it is worth locating and questioning the few individuals that might be capable of these things, don't you think, Monitor Lindquist?"

"Of course," he answered a little too quickly. "Where are these people? What can I do to help?"

"I don't think our fleet can afford any more of your assistance, but thank you so much for your offer," M'bai said grinning with gritted teeth. "A special team is handling this matter even as we speak."

"I for one see no use in prolonging this meeting at such a late hour," Oku said, as the others looked around nodding in ascent. "You understand, of course, Monitor Lindquist, that this meeting was nothing personal. Any military action of this scale is required to be reviewed immediately. After all, the Council can not afford to have a member functioning independently of the other nine."

"I understand perfectly," Silas said, almost laughing, knowing full well that every purple cloak in the room covered a Monitor that acted as independently as he or she could get away with. "I will prepare an official report tomorrow and I will be happy to answer any questions or listen to any advice anyone has to offer."

With his gracious diplomacy fully restored, Silas Lindquist arose and strode triumphantly out of the Council Hall. After "accidentally" stepping on Boa's foot as he proceeded down the hall, he continued on to his chambers with a renewed sense of satisfaction. There was a much stronger emotion, however, that made his heart beat just a little faster and made him feel not quite so invincible as he would have liked to pretend.

"Get me Maas, immediately!" Lindquist shouted as he yanked off his cape and threw it to the ground.

"Yes, sir?" Maas answered groggily, as his reclining image appeared.

"I'm so glad you're able to get your beauty sleep," Silas said, a short step away from unbridled fury. "I never should have listened to you! Do you realize that inept butcher could cost me my seat on the Council? And god damn it, stand up when I'm yelling at you."

Maas stumbled out of bed, struggling briefly to untangle himself from the sheets that seemed to cling like paper to an oily surface. He was now a far cry from the supremely confident spy who had declared his infallibility and assured Lindquist of Danan's capture only a short time ago. There was an added weight upon him now, a mortal weight that would surely crush him if Lindquist's position on the Council were seriously threatened. The chance was slim, but if Frye was apprehended and made to talk, expulsion would be the least of the Monitor's worries.

"Are they suspicious?" Maas asked sheepishly.

"Suspicious? Are they suspicious? Why should anyone suspect anything when I deliver a fugitive who is supposedly a bright, accomplished engineer, but suddenly has the IQ of a jelly donut?"

"But Frye swore there would be no trace," the humbled spy stated with more of the tone of a question. "And you can trust him to keep his silence, his life is on the line, too."

"I can not afford to trust such a bungling fool," Lindquist said, dropping his voice like a blade of ice-cold steel on warm flesh. "But I want to be able to trust in his silence. Before you get another moment's rest, I sincerely want to have one hundred percent confidence in Dr. Frye's eternal silence."

Tilton Maas suddenly straightened and his spirits lifted at the sound of his master's fatal words. As badly as everything had gone, there was at least one bright spot in the gloom, the spy would soon show the great Dr. Frye what it really meant to perform a task without leaving the slightest trace.

****

"All this work! Doesn't everyone realize that I need my beauty sleep?" Granny joked to Lieutenant Vrovski on the bridge of the *Hyperion*.

It had been somewhere around forty-eight hours since the Commander had been able to get any rest. The first week of a voyage of this nature was always a never-ending nightmare of personnel, purchasing and maintenance problems, both real and imagined. No one wanted to be responsible for an oversight that might not be discovered until they were years away from the supply port, so everything was reported, at least once. Even things that showed absolutely no signs of trouble were often reported, thereby covering the butt of the person in charge in case something happened in the future.

Granny tried to monitor the steady influx of last minute supplies as closely as possible without arousing the suspicion of his lieutenant. Vrovski was a good man, but it was doubtful that the conservative, company man would sympathize with his superior's infamous acquaintances.

"Are you looking for something in particular?" Vrovski asked after he noticed Granny check the general shipping display on the wall and the private screen in his hand for the fourth time.

"Yeah... yeah those new plant specimens. You know how particular Oku is about his vegetation," Granny said rolling his eyes, trying to be convincing.

"Why didn't you say so, those were delivered hours ago. You signed the receiving order yourself," Vrovski said, recalling the order on his own handscreen to prove it.

"Damn, I really must be getting punchy," he laughed, while keeping his eyes fixed on an anonymous entry that just appeared on Mardo's private shipping list. "I know this probably isn't necessary, but would you mind personally examining that shipment? I don't want to get this station built and then discover that all we have is a couple thousand dead posies."

"If it will make you feel any better, I'll go have a look," Vrovski offered, patting his solid commander on his rock-hard shoulder. "If you promise to get off the bridge and get some sleep."

"I'll be out of here by the time you get back," Granny promised, surreptitiously erasing the display from his handscreen.

The instant his lieutenant was gone, Granny reactivated the screen and then carefully compared it to the ship's lists to make sure the transport pod was undetected. Relinquishing his control on the bridge, he hurried to Mardo's quarters. It was only natural that a first officer would be making personal reports to his captain, and friend, even at this late hour, but one tiny pair of eyes watched Granny enter the Captain's quarters with great interest. Examining her handscreen, which was capable of piercing the veil of Oku's clearance passes, she smiled and returned to the modest bedroom that was adjacent to her superior's luxurious quarters.

"This must be the one!" Granny said enthusiastically as he found Mardo already intently watching the approaching vessel.

"The clearance passes?" Mardo asked without turning.

"The *Hyperion* is as blind as a bat to it," Granny answered, having to bend over slightly to watch the transport pod maneuver into position to dock in the captain's bay.

Normally, a second vessel would have to lock onto one of the exterior ports, but this craft was so tiny it fit into the bay alongside Mardo's personal transport. Both men rushed to the bay door and entered the instant the environmental controls flashed green. The battered, circular, ten-meter transport pod had only been designed as a short distance shuttle between cargo ships in orbit to the surface. The high-speed, trans-system jaunt had almost torn the fragile craft to pieces.

Rapidly punching in a series of numbers, Mardo stood back and watched the door of the pod as it groaned reluctantly open. As soon as the seal was breached, a blast of appetizing fragrances shot out. Despite their excitement, both men paused to inhale the sweet scents from a planet they wouldn't see again for almost a decade. Shoving aside some cases of raspberries that had fallen onto the lone passenger during the tumultuous trip, Granny was able to get a good look at the most wanted man in the Union.

Walter Danan did not appear to be such a formidable character, especially with blotches of red raspberry juice dotting his face and clothes. There was a slight smile on his face, but his eyes were still closed as he silently emerged from the deep trance that allowed him to survive the trip. The majority of the energy that normally went to life support systems had to be channeled to the engines in order to intercept the *Hyperion*. By reducing his heart and breathing rate to a hair's margin above death, he escaped that fate at the hands of Lindquist's army.

Lifting him gently, Granny brought him out into the living area where they had already raised the oxygen levels to facilitate his recovery. Mardo lightly touched the palm of Walter's hand with a medical analyzer and smiled to his first officer to assure him that their precious cargo had arrived intact. In a few minutes, Danan's chest began rising and falling in slow, deep breaths. After flexing the fingers of his right hand, he moved them to one of the sticky spots on his cheek. Lightly dabbing his index finger on the spot and then touching the tip of his tongue, the slight smile widened to a bright grin.

"Either my blood has turned to nectar, or I've just ruined a fortune in raspberries," he said softly, finally raising his eyelids as if awakening from a serene sleep.

"You damn fool," Mardo said, much too relieved to sound as stern as he had intended. "If you had dumped the food, the pod might have been light enough so that you wouldn't have had to divert power from life support and be forced to hibernate like a bear!"

"You'll thank me years from now when you crack open a case of oranges that taste like they were just picked," Walter predicted, pulling a few berries out of his collar and popping them merrily into his mouth.

Blood was flowing freely through his limbs again and he stood to accept the outstretched arms of his exasperated friend. Mardo formally introduced his guest to Granny, who immediately tried to apologize for what happened to Jesse.

"It's my fault for not anticipating the warrant," Walter quickly countered. "I should have realized Lindquist would try anything to get to me. How is Jesse? Has anyone heard anything?"

Granny and Mardo glanced at each other as if hoping the other would volunteer to tell him.

"What's the matter? What's happened?" Walter asked fearfully when he saw the men's hesitation. "Jesse, he isn't..."

"No! No, he's alive," Mardo spoke up quickly. "But he's...he's not right. They've done something to his mind."

"My god," Walter whispered, as all the life seemed to drain back out of him in a heartbeat.

"No one's sure what's wrong, but Lindquist is trying to blame it on you," Granny added angrily. "Jesse was fine when I spoke to him, but I'm not allowed to tell the press that. Not that they would do anything about it anyway."

Mardo filled him in on all they had been able to learn. There wasn't any brain damage or trace of a drug, but Jesse did have the classic symptoms of having undergone a severe trauma. He was currently in a hospital on Mars and no sentence would be passed until he was judged mentally competent. Walter took the news hard and Mardo could see in his face that he was having second thoughts about staying on the *Hyperion*.

"The system's too hot for you right now," the captain said anticipating his friend's words.

"But I can't leave him, not like this," Walter protested.

"They aren't going to let you waltz in and take him away," Granny said, feeling uncomfortable as the voice of reason, as his own gut was telling him to storm the hospital with guns blazing. "There's nothing you can do right now. Lindquist is too powerful."

"The fact that they didn't just throw him right in jail is a good sign. I know it's a small consolation, but word has it not all of the Council is thrilled with their latest member. Some even suspect your old pal Silas of some rather unsavory conduct," Mardo said, hoping Danan could be dissuaded from doing something rash. "If anything can be proved, Jesse might be released."

"I can't just run away and abandon him when-"

"His best chance is if everyone thinks you're dead and Lindquist calls off this damn witch hunt," Mardo said like a man used to taking charge.

"You're probably right, Captain," Walter admitted, feeling very helpless despite his unique abilities.

He could try to get to Jesse; walls had already proven to be no obstacle. But there was no guarantee Walter would be able to get him out. There was also the possibility that Walter refused to let enter his mind, that Jesse was already beyond help.

"I've taken advantage of the temporarily chaotic personnel roster," Granny began, to change the subject, "and I was able to enter you as a mid-level scientist in one of the most obscure labs. As of now, you are James Recone, mild mannered botanist."

"Don't you think someone will recognize me?" Walter asked, appreciative for the help, but doubtful that the plan would be successful. "After all, they did empty the ship to look for me and I'm sure my face was plastered on every display."

"Where I put you it could be years before another soul even knows you exist," Granny said proudly, and then realized that wasn't exactly the most appealing prospect.

"And just in case somebody does come along, I managed to procure this handy little device," Mardo said, removing a small, metallic box from a hidden compartment in the wall. "I'll bet you've never seen one of these!"

Mardo was almost giggling as he put the box on the low table in front of Walter. All three men began laughing, even though the captain was the only one who knew the contents of the box. When Walter lifted the lid and looked inside, with Granny peering over his shoulder, the laughter broke into a roar. With his thumb and index finger, Danan gingerly lifted the object as if afraid it might bite, which it certainly looked capable of doing since it was composed of two rows of teeth.

"You're not serious," Walter said, wiping tears from the corners of his eyes.

"Turn it over," Mardo urged. "This is serious stuff."

Flipping the teeth around, Walter was surprised to find what appeared to be some very sophisticated circuitry lining the backs of the fake gums. The teeth were no more than thin facades, designed to fit unobtrusively in the mouth and the device suddenly appeared to be a lot more than a child's toy.

"What the hell?" Granny said to no one in particular as he was as baffled by the choppers as Danan.

"The wonders of modern technology!" Mardo exclaimed, leaning over to activate some switches on the gums and then motioning Walter to put it in his mouth. "You'll feel a slight tingling, but it won't be uncomfortable. Go on, try it, but look in the mirror when you put it in your mouth."

Turning to face the mirror, Walter paused to exchange puzzled looks with Granny and then slipped the fake teeth over his own. There was a fleeting feeling of pins-and-needles type numbness, and then he felt his face begin to change, physically change. Startled, he brought his fingertips to one cheek and felt the muscles contracting, his skin growing tighter in some places and slack in others. The image in the mirror that looked back at him now appeared to have higher cheekbones, narrower eyes, a receding chin and a much rounder face. The new features, coupled with the slightly bucked teeth facade would have made it difficult for his own mother to recognize him.

"Amazing!" Granny said in almost a whisper, and then raised his voice considerably. "Ugly, but damn amazing."

"Do you have anything that's a little more flattering?" Walter asked, examining the considerably less attractive face from all angles.

"Picky, picky, picky," Mardo laughed. "Isn't this thing great? A buddy of mine makes these for a few special clients who would prefer to maintain their anonymity, without the permanence of surgery. A very exclusive item, no more than a dozen of these things exist in the whole Union."

"How does it work?" Granny asked, unable to take his eyes off of the new face of James Recone, mild mannered botanist.

"Little electric pulses are programmed to alter the musculature. And every face reacts differently based on the individual's structure," Mardo replied with admiration. "The only problem is that you can't wear it for more than an hour or so because the muscles will go into spasms-"

"And your face will fall off?" Walter offered.

"Not quite, but you won't be a pretty sight...an even less pretty sight than you are now."

The refreshing spirit of frivolity temporarily prevailed and they each took turns with the fake teeth. Mardo's stately, dignified countenance contorted into buffoon-like features, much to everyone's amusement. The device seemed to be straining to rearrange Granny's chiseled features, but it was worth the wait as his face suddenly snapped into a very effeminate pout.

"Lovely, simply lovely!" his friends complimented, a split second before they began laughing so hard it hurt.

"You're all just jealous," Granny scoffed in his sweetest, highest-pitched voice, puckering up proudly and prancing about the room.

The hilarity was interrupted by the buzz of someone requesting entry.

"Who the hell wants me at this hour?" Mardo growled to the security system.

"Assistant Kiya," the voice replied blankly.

"Tell her to go away."

"She says it's important and requests an immediate audience."

"Damn her," Mardo whispered, motioning for Danan to go into his bedroom, as Granny popped the device out of his mouth and tried to massage his face back to its accustomed rigidity.

With Danan and the device hidden, he authorized Kiya's entry.

"What's so damn important at this hour?" the clearly irritated first officer asked, purposely moving close to the tiny woman to have another try at the intimidation factor.

"The *Hyperion* is running eighteen percent below plotted speed," she shot back without missing a beat, as she tried to surreptitiously scan the room. "Standard procedure dictates-"

"There is nothing standard about a half-assed mission like this," Mardo interrupted, rising to stand next to his Commander as they both attempted to stare her down, with no obvious effect. "We're lucky to be underway at all with the ridiculously short amount of preparation time we were given. Now be a good, little girl and go back to bed and let the officers do their jobs."

Both men were delighted to watch her eyes and nostrils flare in anger as they finally penetrated her defense shields. Mardo would never dream of speaking to anyone else in such a condescending manner, especially someone with her stack of credentials, but with Kiya it was like having to scratch an irresistible itch.

"I am a highly qualified professional trying to do my job," she finally managed to reply through gritted teeth.

"Your *job*," Mardo began slowly, with great emphasis, "is to do *whatever I tell you to do*."

Granny tensed, as he was sure he would have to grab Kiya when she lunged for his captain, but miraculously she held her ground. Forcing her fists to unclench, she turned to leave without another word. She stopped, however, when she stepped on something squishy. Lifting her foot with a look of great curiosity, she seemed pleased to find a bright, red stain on the captain's carpet.

"I'm so sorry, Captain," she said sweetly. "Whatever could have made such a mess? Why, it looks like some kind of fruit."

"Don't worry about the stain," Mardo tried to say nonchalantly. "I'll have it cleaned in the morning."

"Fresh fruit is quite a luxury," she continued, smiling. "But then being a captain does have certain, advantages."

"As well as disadvantages," Granny added, sorry that he was ever crazy enough to assign her to his poor captain. "Kiya, are you sure you want to be Captain Mardo's assistant? There's still time to change your mind."

"Who else could you find with my credentials on such a half-assed mission as this?" she declared, wiping the sole of her shoe across the carpet and continuing out the door.

CHAPTER 12

Dead calm followed the whirlwind of events that began with Lindquist's coup and ended with the alleged death of Walter Danan. After a couple of weeks, things even settled down into a routine. While his extensive spy network remained silently vigilant, Silas went about his numerous administrative responsibilities with something resembling dedication. The infamous Dr. Nathan Frye had disappeared as completely as if he had been pushed into the path of a beamcutter, but otherwise the new Monitor didn't want to do anything that might further antagonize his new colleagues.

Needless to say, Monitor M'bai's special committee was unable to gather sufficient evidence to prove anything. There were many clues, but their star suspect was nowhere to be found. Jesse Dimont's condition improved slightly, but his memory remained too scrambled for any reliable information. The media did its part in molding public opinion by dropping the Danan raid like a piece of radioactive waste and continued showing the Astromancer's inaugural predictions several times a day.

Monitor Croix was a changed woman. The bottom had dropped out of her entire life. Things she had never thought to question became open sores on her conscience. Though tempted in her anguish to abandon everything, she was practical enough to realize that the best place to be to bring about change was right where she was now. The purple cloak also allowed her access to the restricted security section of the hospital where Jesse was being held.

Visiting as often as she could, Idrella tried to tell herself it was professional curiosity that kept drawing her back, but she couldn't help admitting that she enjoyed watching Jesse's face light up when she entered the room. The first two visits, he called her Valery and rambled on about childhood memories as if she was his sister. By the third meeting, his mind had cleared sufficiently for him to realize she was a Monitor and refused to speak at all. After jogging his memory about her actions during the interrogation, Idrella was finally able to convince Jesse that she wanted to help. How much she was willing to help, however, was unclear, even in her own mind.

The last three times they met, Idrella asked a myriad of questions, none of which were for the record. Trying to grasp the bizarre concepts for her personal edification, she listened intently to the scraps of recollections that surfaced in Jesse's abused brain. Even when the details were hazy, the underlying fact remained constant; Walter Danan, if he was still alive, was the most remarkable human being in the known galaxy.

James Recone had managed to spend two solid weeks without encountering another member of the crew. Except for a handful of brief conversations over Mardo's private channel and the submission of one status report, his time was free to be spent as he chose. Sometimes absorbed for days in silent experimentation with consciousness, the boundaries of reality began to dissipate like wisps of smoke. He discovered he did not need to physically be with Jesse to help him. In fact, it began to appear as if eventually he wouldn't physically need anything.

Kiya had proved to be a brilliant and highly efficient assistant to the captain. Her extensive knowledge of the design and function of the *Hyperion* quickly convinced Mardo that she must have had some hand in its conception and construction. Something rather drastic must have happened for someone of her capabilities to be forced to take on the position of assistant on such a mission. Mardo fell short of feeling sorry for her, however, when he thought of Walter's even less enviable position. And then, of course, there was the fact that she still managed to piss him off at least once a day.

Despite her increasing responsibilities, Kiya found the time to begin personally meeting every member of the ship. While she made it appear as if it was a random, unofficial, good will tour to build a rapport between officers and crew, her approach was anything but random. If anyone had cared to notice, it would have become obvious that she was concentrating on the male members of the crew in their thirties of medium height and build. Mardo and Granny were not aware of Kiya's welcome-wagon moonlighting, and neither was a mid-level botanist buried in the bowels of the *Hyperion*.

The security system buzzed three times before Walter Danan realized where, and who, he was. Fumbling for the false teeth he kept in the drawer beside his bed, he asked who was requesting entry. When he heard it was Kiya, he activated the device, popped it in his mouth and waited a few seconds for his face to rearrange itself into the visage of James Recone.

"She may enter," he said, standing up and pushing his lengthening hair into some kind of order.

Kiya entered as if marching to a silent band. Neither her demeanor nor her personality had softened since the mission began and Walter/James found it amusing when she stiffly announced that she had taken it upon herself to greet everybody and give them a warm welcome.

"So tell me Mr. Recone, what is your specialty?" she asked in the same breath as her welcoming speech, scrutinizing every square inch of his face and body.

"Flowering plants, mostly, although I really wouldn't call myself a specialist," he replied in an open, friendly manner, while also examining her features. He had definitely seen Kiya somewhere, many years ago. "Would you like to sit down?"

Taking a seat without taking her eyes off of him, she concluded that the height, weight and build were almost exactly what she was looking for, but the face was all wrong. Of course, simple surgery could have altered the features, but everything she knew about Walter Danan suggested he would never undergo such a procedure. Still, there was something about this man...

"Mr. Recone-"

"Call me Jim."

"Yes, that is less formal. Jim, I also have an interest in certain forms of blossoming vegetation. Have you created any of your own hybrids with which I might be familiar?" she asked, awkwardly groping for a way to engage him in conversation.

"No, not me. I'm more interested in the preservation and cultivation of naturally occurring species."

"Oh, you're one of those," she said with her first genuine smile.

"One of whats?" he asked, thinking that she was almost charming when she stopped gritting her teeth.

"One of those back to nature, live-and-let-live types," Kiya laughed, surprising herself at how comfortable she felt with the stranger. "I know your kind."

"You have my full confession!" the fugitive deadpanned, raising both hands. "But I'm not sorry for anything I've done."

The two continued talking about plants, Earth and the staleness of ship life. Kiya felt an irresistible warmth and magnetism from this man, and he also possessed an insight and wit that aroused her usually unchallenged mind. The bright, if terribly unattractive, botanist was like a breath of fresh air to Kiya and she felt as if she wanted to spend every hour of the day in his presence.

"Uh... I've enjoyed our conversation, but I have things to attend to," Jim said as a sharp twitch in his cheek reminded him his Cinderella hour was up and he was about to revert to Walter, or something far worse. "Maybe we can speak some other time?"

"Of course, I'm sorry to have taken up so much of your time," Kiya replied, genuinely disappointed that she had to leave the company of someone she actually enjoyed.

As he was hurriedly escorting her to the door, she tripped over a box of gardening tools in the cramped quarters and started to fall forward. His arm encircled her waist to prevent her from hitting the floor and her hand grabbed the back of his neck for support. Kiya's fingers were only there for a second until she steadied herself, but it was long enough for her to feel the smooth patch of skin where the d-chip switch should have been.

****

"You rang?" Mardo asked when he returned to his quarters late one evening and found a message from Walter.

"What do you know about your assistant?"

"Besides being a clever pain in the ass, nothing. Why?"

"She just happened to drop by for a little chat this afternoon."

"Did she recognize you?" Mardo asked as he felt his pulse quicken.

"I don't think so, but I can't be sure. I suppose if she did recognize me, though, half the fleet would be after us by now. I know I've seen her somewhere before, maybe one of my lectures," Walter said thoughtfully. "In any event, she was certainly friendly enough."

"Friendly? Are we talking about the same woman?" Mardo asked, incredulous.

"She was a bit cool at first, but we had a great conversation. The only reason I asked her to leave was because my face was getting well done."

"I don't like it," Mardo said with unabated concern. "There are thousands of people on this ship and she happens to find you. Maybe you should just stay in my private quarters."

"And how would we explain the disappearance of Recone? No Mardo, if we have any hope of making this work for any length of time, I'm just going to have to play my part."

"All right, for now. But I'm going to look into the possibility of finding you a safe haven on one of Oku's city-stations."

While the two friends discussed various options for Walter's safety, the captain's assistant paced uneasily up and down the length of her cabin. The absence of the d-chip had confirmed it, but she did not experience the sense of triumph she had expected. There was no doubt in Kiya's mind that this was Walter Danan, but she had every doubt as to what to do the knowledge.

If only she hadn't felt that odd pull, the tugging on some deep level that transfixed her like a nocturnal animal in a bright beam of light. The feeling was beyond her normal boundaries and she was simultaneously enthralled and resentful of the disruption to her peace of mind. When Kiya discovered she was unable to bar the image of his face or the sound of his voice from her consciousness, she decided her only recourse was to settle into a chair, reach behind her ear and activate the switch that would make the world go away.

CHAPTER 13

Rial Croix was furious, a feeling that was well within the spectrum of her emotions, emotions that were strongly shifted toward the negative frequencies. She believed it was her god-given right to at least know everybody's business, if not control or direct it. So when Idrella made a rare appearance at their home in order to have a private meeting with Mr. Croix, Rial deemed it the ultimate affront.

Tersely explaining that it was Croix family business, Idrella went to her father's study and remained there for several hours. Legally, of course, a wife was part of a family, but in the upper circle, blood was the only binding contract. A child was privy to the dealings of both families from which she descended, but a spouse could be, and often was, excluded from important matters of ancestral honor, which generally translated into financial concerns.

Mrs. Croix made a point to keep abreast of the state of the family fortune. Even if they didn't make another cent, they could all frolic in the lap of luxury for at least the next hundred years, give or take a decade. And it was no secret that being a Monitor was an obscenely lucrative position. So Rial felt she could eliminate money from the list of possible topics her daughter and husband were discussing.

As to Idrella's personal life, it appeared as if there was nothing to discuss. The rift between Silas and Idrella now seemed too wide to harbor any further hope. Even if there was a problem in the romantic area, she knew her daughter well enough to know that Idrella wouldn't waste time seeking advice on such a low priority item as love.

What that left was anybody's guess, so Rial consoled herself by calling everybody who might care to venture a guess. If she was also offered sympathy regarding the terrible insult, that was even better. After contacting about a dozen of her acquaintances that possessed the least integrity, Mrs. Croix was able to come to the completely unfounded conclusion that Idrella was planning to resign from the Council. Based solely upon the third-hand information that someone heard that Monitor Croix was not satisfied about certain recent Council proceedings, they deduced that it could be the only possible reason for such an otherwise inexplicable visit.

"You know mother is probably tearing her hair out right now," Idrella said to her father as their meeting drew to a close.

"Oh no, dear, your mother would never do that. Rial would pay people to let her tear their hair out," Mr. Croix laughed like a very weary man.

Justinian Croix was as different from his wife as a palm frond from a bullwhip. He was a man of quiet integrity, intelligent, resourceful and compassionate. Idrella felt good when she was with him and realized that if she ever was to become the person she wanted to be, she would have to nurture the Croix family characteristics.

"I've been dying to ask this question for years," Idrella began and then hesitated.

"How did your mother and I get together?" Justinian finished for her.

"Exactly."

"In the beginning, opposites attract. Unfortunately, just in the beginning. As time passes and the novelty wears off, however, you realize that opposites are like matter and anti-matter just aching to annihilate one another. It certainly wasn't the brightest thing I've ever done," he said shrugging his shoulders in resignation.

"I hope you don't have any doubts about *this*," she said quickly, regretting having brought up a subject that put such pain in his eyes.

The object she held in her hand was clearly an antique, primitive by current standards. It appeared to be some type of transmitter with a formidable series of buttons that afforded the only means of data entry. The designer had the foresight to realize that computer technology was about as static and reproducible as a trendy hairstyle and the best away to ensure the proper operation of a device for generations beyond you was to step back to basics.

"I know I'm not supposed to hand this over until I'm dead, but I have no doubt that my bright, talented and successful daughter knows what she is doing," Justinian replied boldly, instilling great confidence in his daughter, who clearly wasn't sure she was doing the right thing.

"Thanks, I needed that. This whole crazy idea is a long shot, but if I'm right, I want this with me," she said cradling the device almost lovingly in her arms.

"Jupiter Croix would be proud of you!"

"I hope so, Dad. I hope so."

As Idrella left by a back exit, her enraged mother decided she had one more call to make. Putting on one of her more revealing outfits, she primped and preened for an hour before she felt her appearance was just right. Reclining on a couch and practicing a look that conveyed both distress and sensuality, she ordered the call.

"Get me Monitor Lindquist and tell him it's urgent," she said, hoping she wouldn't have to hold the pose for long.

After several long minutes, the puzzled image of Silas appeared appetizingly close to her couch. His expression grew even more disagreeable when he saw what she was wearing, or not wearing as the case may be.

"Mrs. Croix, what an...unexpected pleasure," he said bowing diplomatically.

"Oh Silas, dear, whatever am I to do?" she sighed deeply enough to make her chest heave impressively.

"What seems to be the trouble?" he asked half-heartedly, fully expecting another unwanted invitation to brighten her dark, lonely nights.

"It's Idrella, of course. Isn't it terrible?" she replied cryptically.

"Look, it's over between us-"

"No, no, no! Not that. You mean you haven't heard?"

"Maybe we had better start from the beginning, Mrs. Croix. Just what is going on?" he asked, uncertain if this was some plot of Idrella's against him, or simply mother against daughter, again.

"Rial, please, dear Silas. You mean you don't know that Idrella is planning to resign from the Council?" she declared with great dramatics, making sure her head was thrown back at just the right angle to catch her best features.

Silas had no doubt that he looked stunned, because he was, completely. His mind raced to evaluate every possible motive for Mrs. Croix's announcement, from the truth to just another in a long line of malicious gossip. Before jumping to any conclusion, he required a lot more facts.

"Did she tell you this herself?" he asked with measured restraint.

"Well, no, not in so many words," she replied, slightly offended that he didn't take her every word for gospel. "But you know how strange she's been acting lately, and she just had a long meeting with my husband and they wouldn't tell me anything about it. And you know that rumor has had it she's been thinking of quitting."

"I'm afraid I didn't know rumor had that," he replied with some disgust, believing the entire conversation was a waste of his time. "I really don't think there's any solid evidence here, and anyway, what did you expect me to do?"

Rial saw that her fun was about to be spoiled and knew she had to throw out some tantalizing bait to keep him on the hook.

"Have you lost interest in the Danan case?"

"What has that got to do with it?" he asked with suspicious interest.

"My daughter has become very close to Danan's brother-in-law. Seems she visits him every chance she gets, and that I can prove!" Rial smiled, seeing the spark leap into his eyes.

"I admit I was unaware of this, Rial," Silas replied with newfound respect. "But I still fail to see the connection between that and her possible resignation."

"I really hate to discuss such a sensitive issue this way. Perhaps we could meet in person, to talk?" she said, lowering her voice to a sensuous whisper. "I really do believe I have something you want."

Silas thought carefully for a minute, scanning the numerous peaks and valleys of flesh stretched out before him. If Rial really did have information about Danan, there would be a lot to be gained from a personal meeting. If she was lying, perhaps he could find some way to compensate for his wasted time. After all, Mrs. Croix's notoriety extended far beyond her proclivity for gossip.

"I'll be there as soon as possible. You had better not be lying," he replied with a dangerous look that sent chills up her spine.

"I'll be right here," she cooed, as her mind was already fabricating the elaborate details of her story.

Silas decided to confront Idrella before making the trip to Mars so he had some idea of the truth in the matter. He took great pleasure in seeing the look of hatred Boa shot at him as he approached her quarters. The giant was clearly not content with just the memory of holding the Monitor up by his neck.

"Is your Mistress in?" he asked with a sickenly courteous smile.

Boa made no reply, but turned and entered the chambers. After several minutes, he returned and motioned for Lindquist to enter.

"I must admit, this is most unexpected," Idrella said stiffly as Silas entered her study, restraining herself from saying more until she found out the nature of his visit.

"I know I'm not welcome, but I have some important questions that I would prefer not to ask in front of the entire Council," he replied, annoyed at how uncomfortable he felt.

"Yes, I have been visiting Jesse Dimont," she offered, deciding to beat him to the punch. "But I'm sure your spies have told you that already."

"May I ask why?" he said, trying to hide the surprise at her candor.

"He interests me. Walter Danan's work interests me. Are you going to put me on report?" she asked with defiance.

"You're playing with fire, Idrella. Make sure this doesn't become an obsession. A wise woman once told me that Monitors couldn't afford to have obsessions."

Bowing slightly, he turned and left. He could have pressed her for more information, but he had learned what he came to find out. Mrs. Rial Croix might make a valuable ally after all, Silas thought as his ship left the Council Hall. If Idrella was determined to oppose him, what better weapon to add to his arsenal than her mother's potent venom.

****

For a man of vast wealth, Oku had few pleasures in life. One thing in which he did take great interest and pride was his string of city-stations. Stretching like a sparkling jeweled necklace into the black depths beyond the system, Oku spared no expense in making them garden paradises. Those who disparagingly called them the Florid Keys were generally jealous because they couldn't afford to live there. Personally, Oku preferred the real thing on Earth, but for those who felt the call of space, he was proud to offer the best in off-world living.

Though the first station was officially opened over one hundred years earlier, construction never ceased. To accommodate ever-increasing demand, level after level was added until it resembled glittering clusters of crystals reaching in all directions. They became more than just cities, each station was a self-contained world supplying all the needs of tens of millions of people. The cost of living was very high, more than twice what similar accommodations would run on an outer planet station. The most obvious reason for that was the constant upgrading to state-of-the-art systems as well as the single-minded pursuit of the finest natural materials available.

Oku believed that "composites have no class" and he used natural wood and stone wherever possible in the interior sections. Since such materials needed to be shipped rather than manufactured on sight, the initial construction costs were already far beyond even some upper circle companies' means. While construction costs were generally recouped after only a few years, due to constant maximum occupancy, one cost was absorbed by the governing body of each station.

Oku did not much care for the scores of different "rubber-faced robots" that were produced by his own companies. Designed to be everything from barbers to teachers to doctors, Oku insisted that they made an already artificial habitat unbearable. As part of the non-refundable operating costs, stations housed a large staff of humans to provide truly human services. Those who preferred their cybernetic counterparts were welcome to them, but Oku made it once again fashionable for people to employ people.

Each of the existing ten stations was an official territory in the Union, even though they were under private ownership. And while the stations claimed to be primarily scientific research facilities, the majority of the populations were employed in O.I.T. businesses that had nothing to do with research. These seemingly minor technicalities allowed for enormous tax breaks that many in the system grumbled about, but no one dared openly oppose.

The combination of all these factors produced a long waiting list of potential tenants and companies, making an eleventh station necessary, and it was the *Hyperion*'s job to complete the first phase. One of her two enormous cargo bays held the prefabricated forms that would frame the outer shell. The other bay was loaded with teak, marble, silk carpeting and all the finest the hand of the craftsman could create. Many of the smaller storage areas were filled with seeds and cuttings that would line every street with trees and shrubs and make every communal area a garden. Captain Mardo was to oversee the construction of the core unit of this newest city-station that would house the first tenants as well as a permanent crew to continue additional phases.

Security was considerably less stringent on these stations as Oku had desired to alleviate some of the paranoia common in system worlds. There was also a blatant disregard for many other Union laws that didn't suit the inhabitants, most of which were tax laws. This gradual, bloodless rebellion eventually separated the ten city-stations from the Union as effectively as if there had been a colonial revolution. They only hesitated to declare complete autonomy because they didn't want the Union to crack down. The Union overlooked the stations' "indiscretions" because of the trade and they also reasoned that a small tax revenue was better than nothing.

The more relaxed atmosphere coupled with the sheer size of the off-world complexes made them an excellent place to hide from Union authorities. This is not to say that they were teeming with fugitives, but many a resident had a skeleton or two he preferred to keep in his closet. The local governments kept strict law and order in their communities, but whatever a person might have done elsewhere was of little concern.

People on the List were a different matter. Even Oku conceded to allowing an initial security check to determine if the potential resident had a Council Warrant on his head. With a device similar to the one used for qualifying applicants for the *Hyperion*, everyone entering a city-station was screened. Regular criminals were given the same clearance as the innocent, but those on the List were literally in for a shock.

Mardo knew that Walter would never pass the initial security check, not because he was on the List, but because he had no d-chip with which to connect in the first place. That made him more conspicuous than if he showed up stark naked with a grenade in his teeth. Not even the Captain's special clearance passes could be employed at such a checkpoint, so as ideal as the stations would be for Danan, a way would first have to be found to get him inside.

The advantage of the yet-to-be-built station eleven was that the security checks were already supposed to have taken place before the mission began. The only problem was maintaining Walter's alias for the many years before construction was complete. Mardo and Granny had hoped no one would even notice him, but with the onset of Kiya's inquisitiveness that hope vanished. There was still a chance that she, or anyone else, wouldn't discover James Recone's true identity. If Kiya did, however, Granny was prepared to take a drastic step. In fact, he would be more than happy to keep her locked in his closet for the next few years.

CHAPTER 14

Jesse sat quietly in his windowless room listening to Walter Danan. The words weren't physically spoken, but he heard them as clearly as if Walter was there. At first, he believed it was all part of his scrambled thoughts or a hallucination. As time passed, however, the voice became stronger, more persistent and he again experienced the strange tingling sensation he felt when Walter had healed his terrible wound.

The troubled confusion began to ease as his distant friend helped Jesse's mind undo the damage inflicted by the drugs and Dr. Frye's special skills. Several times a day, Walter's presence flowed over him like warm water and after each encounter his mind became more focused and his memory more organized. Walter recognized that as Jesse regained his mental health, it was important for him to maintain the appearance of illness and confusion. It was that mental message he was transmitting to his brother-in-law when Kiya requested entry.

She had become an almost daily visitor in the last week and Walter enjoyed their stimulating conversations and the depth and sharpness of her mind. As he pulled himself back from his chat with Jesse, he slid the fake teeth in his mouth and authorized Kiya to enter. One look at her shocked expression told him he had forgotten to activate the device.

"I guess I won't need these anymore," he said, casually removing the teeth and tossing them onto the desk.

Except for the look of surprise, Kiya didn't appear to react. One foot did seem to want to go forward and the other back, but the conflict remained unresolved and she continued to stand where she was. Walter watched very carefully for signs of fear, or more importantly, recognition, but what he sensed from her was not either. What he did feel was a great sense of relief, which was finally confirmed by a deep sigh before she spoke.

"I must confess this is a big improvement over your other face, Mr. Danan," Kiya said smiling and taking a seat as if nothing had actually happened.

"Now that you know who I am, what are you going to do about it?" Walter asked with equal calm, taking a seat next to her.

"I've known who you were since the day I discovered you had no d-chip," she said, placing her hand on his neck as she did the day she almost fell. "And as to what I'm going to do about it, I'm not sure. What do you suggest?"

"Well, if I knew who you really were, that might influence my answer."

"I'm sorry, that's one thing I can't tell you. It might influence you too much."

"Since you insist on keeping me at a disadvantage, I will tell you what I would tell anyone who was in a position to have me hanged; give me a chance to prove my innocence," he replied, staring into her eyes with a power that made her blink as if looking into the sun.

"And just how will you accomplish that?" Kiya asked, getting up and walking around the room to dispel the odd feeling vibrating in her spine.

"With patience, an open mind and your cooperation," Walter said, rising to halt her pacing and to place soothing hands on her trembling shoulders.

"I...I guess there wouldn't be any harm in giving you a chance," she almost whispered, an instant before a jolt of energy surged up her spine.

****

Monitor Lindquist lounged in his favorite chair, the only thing he brought with him when he took over the occupancy of Ramos' quarters. Everything else was hers, including the obnoxious security/data system which he planned to have scrapped and replaced with something more agreeable, in other words, more deferential. Everything else in the luxurious and spacious suite could remain as it was; the ex-Monitor had good taste, in addition to the wisdom to know when it was time to retreat.

Silas actually enjoyed the constant reminders of the previous occupant; they provided a constant boost to his conquering spirit and ego. He also enjoyed Ramos' little housewarming gift. Obviously intended as a bitter threat, the new tenant placed the object in the middle of the central hall with which all his other rooms connected so he would see it many times a day. The finely rendered marble bust was of one of the Caesars and it bore the inscription, "Remember Thou Art Mortal."

The ambitious new Monitor's mind chose to disregard the warning and instead, chose to totally identify with the image of imperial Caesar. He felt further justified in that course of thought by the Astromancer's predictions. With his family and some well-placed allies behind him, there was no telling just how far a man of his abilities could go. A man was limited only by his vision, he thought as he watched a tiny speck of rock incinerated as it confronted the awesome power of the beam cutter, and Silas felt as if he could see the entire Union on its knees before him.

As he continued to muse over his possible futures, Silas' thoughts also turned to his most recent past. He had not been completely satisfied with Rial's story about her daughter. However, he had been more than satisfied, and surprisingly so, with the rest she had to offer. In many ways, he still found Mrs. Croix repulsive, a feeling shared by everyone else who knew her. But Silas discovered an inexplicable and perverse pleasure in embracing the object of such universal contempt. And wild excitement overwhelmed his senses as Rial whispered into his ear that she would do anything to anybody to get what she wanted. That was his kind of woman.

Several times during their encounter, his thoughts turned to Idrella and it caused him even greater pleasure to imagine how enraged and disgusted she would be by it all. Many times in the last few days he had been sorely tempted to drop in on his rebellious colleague and tell her about his newest ally, but the revenge would be far sweeter if it came from the lips of her own mother.

Despite all the amusement, the new information about Jesse and Idrella was the most thrilling result. Regardless of what transpired between Silas and Idrella, he always had respected and admired her practicality and ability to see through any scam. However, it now appeared as if she had fallen prey to Danan's mumbo jumbo, seduced by the empty promises of a foolish prophet. That was always a danger; Danan himself might be dead, but as long as Jesse and other's like him still lived, they could uphold his ideals, more cherished now in lieu of the potential martyrdom of their originator.

Patience was important. The disastrous raid on the island had not won him many friends and the obvious tampering with Dimont's mind had made the ice even thinner. It wouldn't be easy, but Silas would have to bide his time until the remainder of the three month probationary period expired. Once that was over nothing could remove him from the Council short of committing atrocities on a public broadcast. Even then it would be difficult.

The following eight weeks would not be a total loss, however, for he would use them to redouble his efforts and reinforce the surveillance network. He would not overlook the poor, confused Jesse, either; the man who still held the keys to both victory and defeat in his addled brain. It was Lindquist's duty to make sure the right people were always near Dimont to ensure his proper treatment. In fact, he might have to see firsthand how the patient was progressing. And if Walter Danan managed to be alive, a couple of months of quiet could be just the thing to lull him into a false sense of security. No, the time would definitely not be wasted.

CHAPTER 15

Remarkably, the public did not lose interest in the Danan-Lindquist feud. The Monitor's fears were being realized as the anonymous Danan supporters injected regular doses of martyrdom into every branch of the grapevine. The possibility that he had escaped death was not overlooked, either. Claims stretched from the plausible to the absurd. Some said he had simply escaped the raid, but others whispered about Danan's disembodied brain being enslaved by the Council for evil purposes.

To combat the growing tide of gossip, the major Lindquist networks and their affiliated stations continued their part in the anti-Danan war. Selected sections of his banned treatise on the d-chip were highlighted, specifically the sections that called for their removal. The idea of life without d-chips was so unthinkable that after a few weeks of the media harping on it, some actually began to start thinking. Inquisitive minds wanted to know why a descendant of a Brain Bender, who could have everything the Union had to offer, suddenly went off on such a dangerous and inexplicable tangent. Perhaps, they reasoned, there was some method in Danan's apparent madness.

Unfortunately, those who began to see the light were forced to remain in the shadows. But there were many shadows in the system and growing numbers of people were gathering in them in secret. It wasn't that they were dissatisfied with their d-chips, far from it. D-chips were the raison d'être for the lower classes. While the Union provided the poor with enough to eat and a place to live, life was suffocatingly static with no hope of improvement. In an era where planet-hopping for a day's shopping spree was common among the upper circle, the economically less fortunate often spent their entire lives in one confined sector of a station or colony, engaged in a token work program to compensate for the government's "generosity".

A daily, four-hour d-chip fantasy was everyone's free ticket to an exciting life of adventure, romance or just plain fresh air, green grass and sunshine. The d-chip justified their existence, gave them a reason to trudge through the other twenty hours a day. Those other twenty hours became a mere formality as no one bothered to pursue hobbies, education or even any form of social interaction. No one complained, however, and it was even looked upon as a desirable situation by those who pointed out that the birth rate continued to plummet in that most burdensome sector of the population.

A few of these people dared to hope that there was more to life than a flick of a switch. Often not knowing where to begin, or even what to look for, they relied heavily on hearsay and the overactive imaginations of pseudo-intellectuals. But something odd began to happen a few weeks after the well-publicized melee on Earth. Information on the nature of consciousness and the possibility of higher states began cropping up in the unlikeliest places across the system.

In the pocket of a new shirt, one man found a data wafer that discussed the basic concepts of how the human nervous system supported consciousness. Many people received anonymous packages containing data wafers that raised doubts about our perception of matter and reality. Some children even found actual printed pages of Danan's banned work scattered around a park. The incidents were often reported and the items quickly confiscated, but not always. Enough of the material was quietly preserved and studied to get the right people going in the right direction. Across the Union, an almost imperceptible tremor of vitality shuddered through long-dormant places.

Though incensed by the counter-propaganda campaign, Silas did not take it as a serious threat. He told Tilton Maas that the masses couldn't possibly grasp any concepts higher than counting on their fingers and toes. What did concern him was who was behind the far-reaching campaign. The manner in which it was being conducted strongly suggested that someone of substantial wealth and influence was spreading the dangerous information. Most agreed it had to be an act of a member of the upper circle. Maas reported that there were even whispers of it being an actual Council member.

Curiosity in Danan's claims was not limited to the lower or even middle classes. Genuine interest was being generated among the highly educated, as well as the simply bored and disillusioned members of the upper circle. The same people who had paid no attention to Danan's work before Valery's death, now eagerly sought every scrap of information in the wake of his apparent, dramatic demise. It had even recently become fashionable to mention that one had personally known the late fugitive.

The wealthy had access to numerous sources of information and a far greater degree of freedom to pursue this risky line of thought. The potential danger of serious repercussions, such as prosecution, was what enticed some of the thrill-seeking elite to embrace this odd notion of a world beyond the physical. Among such people the prospect of uncharted levels of existence swept through their veins like a potent aphrodisiac.

The numbers of those opening their minds to Danan's ideas statistically was minute. But statistics didn't take into account the power of an idea or the tremendous influence one talented and driven person could exert, as opposed to dozens, or thousands, of ineffectual people. The fact that ten individuals held sway over billions stretched the length of the system was sufficient to show that life wasn't strictly a numbers game.

Silas Lindquist, however, felt comforted by the vast number of people under his control. By far, Oku's camp was the largest, but among the runner's up the Lindquist family was the most visible. The Croix empire, built by Jupiter and sustained by capable descendants like Justinian, was arguably larger and wealthier, but the Croix's generally preferred a subtler exercise of power. To be a Lindquist was to be in the headlines, the self-promoting forefront of any undertaking with which the family was connected. And a second cousin, twice removed, living on the ninth city-station, had no less need for publicity than the shining, purple satin star of the family who was not content with deciding only one-tenth of the Union's fate.

Tilton Maas was directed to have Idrella Croix's every move watched. He was to try to decode every transmission, observe every person with whom she came into contact and examine the records of all public meetings and appearances for hints of treasonous behavior. Oku was not to escape the intricate web of intrigue either. Rumors had begun to resurface about an imminent coup, but this time, Oku did not step forward to quell the rising tide of gossip, which made the tide rise even higher. While spying was commonplace throughout the Union, doing it successfully against Monitors who held a full deck of clearance passes was the toughest game in town. It required an enormous amount of manpower and no less staggering sums of money. Lindquist would have no difficulty deciding what to do with his cut of the d-chip tax revenue.

****

On Idrella's next visit to Jesse, her heart skipped a beat when she found his room deserted. There was no sign that anyone had ever occupied the place and she feared the worst. Dressed in ordinary clothes and leaving Boa behind in an attempt to maintain somewhat of a low profile, the Monitor discovered that it was so low that none of the staff would stop what they were doing to give her any information. Frustrated, and worried, Idrella finally cornered an assistant supervisor at the end of a hall and flashed her Council medallion. The previously rude man turned stark white and beads of sweat quickly sprang out of every pore.

"I, I, I had no idea, Monitor," the quaking man stammered. "Please, please forgive me!"

Idrella used to enjoy the reactions she evoked with her medallion or cloak, but the smell of terror oozing out of the frightened man only made her stomach turn now. Nauseated and ashamed at the image she helped create, she felt like running away, but her concern for Jesse kept the facade intact.

"I want to know where Jesse Dimont is, the man who was being held in the maximum security area," she said with seasoned authority.

"Yes, Monitor, right away," he gasped, fumbling with his handscreen. "I believe he has been moved. Yes, here it is, Monitor. Mr. Dimont has been moved to Ward G. That's the minimum security section on the third level."

"By whose authority was this move made?" Idrella asked, not lightening the pressure one bit.

"The order was signed by my supervis-"

"A mere supervisor would not dare move a Council prisoner on his own authority. Where did the order originate?" the Monitor demanded as her voice squeezed him tighter.

"I, I don't know. I'm only-"

"Where!?"

"Mo...Monitor Lindquist suggested we place Mr. Dimont in more hospitable surroundings," the man blurted out, swaying as if about to faint.

Monitor Croix stood staring at the man for what he perceived to be an excruciatingly long time, a time in which his fate was being decided. Though looking right at the shaking assistant supervisor, her mind was on Silas and Jesse and the motive for the move. It didn't take long to figure out that the relentless new Monitor had ordered the move to keep a closer watch on the prisoner. Out of isolation and among other prisoners, Jesse might let vital information slip. As her mind explored the various courses of action, a low whimpering sound distracted her.

"What's the matter with you?" she snapped at the terrified man.

"You won't tell Monitor Lindquist that I talked to you, will you?" he begged between short, shallow breaths.

"I won't if you won't," Idrella replied grinning, patting him on the cheek. "Now, which way to Ward G?"

Following the direction of the trembling finger, she found the elevator up to the third level. The maximum-security section of the hospital was seven levels beneath the surface, with restrictions and surveillance decreasing with every successive level up. Over level three were various administrative offices, and the towering aboveground structure was for regular patients, giving them a view of the city sprawled across the Martian landscape and the diminished glory of the pale sun.

Minimum security was not an accurate description for the hospital wards. There were still the same rigorous checkpoints for everyone entering or exiting, there were just far fewer of them. There were not two guards for every prisoner, but one stood at the door to each ward. And no one could overlook the ominous Peacemaker robots, flanking either side of every entry point like enormous, armored rats. Their appearance was intentionally intimidating; a fearful appearance that was matched only by their reputation for ruthless efficiency.

The Monitor with her set of passes breezed through the checkpoints as if they weren't there, and she also left enough of her medallion showing to avoid any questions. The guard who had just snapped to attention in front of Ward G even opened the door for her.

Small bedrooms radiated out from a large central lounge filled with real plants and a waterfall hologram that was gently hissing in the left back corner. The lighting was more subdued than in the lower levels and chairs and sofas even had cushions. This area was usually populated by corporate executives and government officials who had been convicted of some minor transgressions. They were there temporarily until their tennis elbows and swimmer's ears were cured and then they would be shipped back to the park-like minimum-security detention center on the surface.

It was unheard of to find a Council prisoner, especially one accused of treason, in anything less than level five security. The other detainees were uneasy about the presence of such a hot property. They were even less thrilled when Monitor Croix strutted into the room. Scurrying back to their private chambers or hiding behind potted palms, those who hoped to soon be accepted back into the upper circles desperately tried to look nonchalant about obscuring their identities. The last thing a corrupt official needed was to be seen in prison by a Council member.

A handful of men appeared unconcerned about the possibility of being recognized. In fact, a few even seemed to be studying her with a practiced casualness. As Idrella glared at one of them until his resolve melted and he, too, ran to his room, she thought that Silas could have hired some more professional spies. Slowly circling the ward, the Monitor silently convinced a few more that it had gotten too warm in the lounge. A devilish thought popped into her head as she watched them retreat. Next time she would bring Boa.

Jesse was sitting in the corner of his darkened room at the far right end of the ward. His eyes were fixed on the waterfall out in the lounge, but his mind seemed a light-year away. Not wishing to frighten him, she whispered his name softly until his eyes blinked a few times and then moved to focus on her.

"Idrella! It's good to see you again," he said, as they both were unable to suppress wide smiles.

Before she spoke, Monitor Croix placed a small disk on Jesse's shoulder and one on her own after she sat on the edge of the bed facing him. A dull, blue light emanated from the disks and formed an envelope that surrounded them completely.

"We can speak freely now," she said in a voice that was difficult not to trust. "This blocks all visual and audio surveillance devices, even the ones they've probably sewn into your clothes. When did they move you, Jesse?"

"Two days ago. They said the nicer environment might help me recover," he replied, trying to appear as if he still suffered from something from which he needed to recover.

"Have they treated you well?"

"Yes, they've been nice. But I stay in my room by myself most of the time."

"Good. Don't trust anyone. I'm positive Lindquist has spies in here," Idrella said and then went on to describe the most likely candidates.

"I'll be careful, but I really don't have anything to tell them, Valery," Jesse replied, hoping that he sounded convincingly confused.

"I'm not Valery Danan. I'm Idrella Croix, can't you remember?" she asked sadly, with something resembling tears at the corner of each eye.

"Of course, of course, how stupid of me," he apologized quickly, feeling guilty for making her upset after all the kindness she had shown him.

"It's all right, I know you've been through a lot," she said pulling herself together. "Can you remember anything more about what happened?"

"I remember being taken at the recruiting station and put in some kind of cell. After that I only recall pain, an excruciating fog of pain that clouded my mind. And there was a very ugly man, but he must have been in a nightmare because no one could look like that. Since then it's felt like someone dropped my brains in a blender."

Idrella laughed with him, but only for a moment while she entered a few numbers on her handscreen. Hoping the image that appeared on the screen would do more good than harm, she turned it toward Jesse. His eyes grew wide with horror and his jaw dropped to accommodate the onset of rapid breathing. Afraid that the sight was too much, she quickly erased the image and grabbed hold of his cold, clammy hands.

"Was that the man from your nightmare, Jesse?" she whispered.

"That's him! But that's impossible, how do you know what's in my dreams?" Jesse asked with a shudder.

"Unfortunately, Dr. Frye was a living nightmare. Monitor M'bai was able to track down this picture, but the man himself has completely disappeared."

"Who is he?"

"No one is sure, but we have reason to believe he was more than capable of doing this to you. If he did, Lindquist was surely behind it. But since Frye's fallen into a black hole and you're not a competent witness, there's nothing we can do. Are you sure you don't remember anything else about that night?"

Jesse winced as it pained him to try to pull shreds of recollections out of their drug-induced shells. Walter had helped to remove the debris of the episode from his brain, but the initial impact of the drug permanently deformed the features of its memory. Hanging his head and shaking it from side to side in answer to her question, his spirits suddenly soared when he finally realized Idrella was clasping his hands.

****

Silas was not pleased at the reports he received. Idrella had been to see Dimont, but other than the fact that she went into his room and activated a privacy field, no information was obtained. His well-paid spies were clearly uncomfortable about confronting Monitor Croix's formidable presence and even though he could understand their fear, he was paying for results. It wasn't that he expected Idrella to talk to Jesse in the open, but he was hoping that those in his employ could exhibit some resourcefulness.

There was even less information to be had on Oku. When not residing at the Council Hall during an extended session of meetings, he was hidden away on his vast and secluded estate on Earth. Comprising most of the area of what used to be the state of Arizona, he was the only Monitor to still live on that planet and he was also by far the least accessible. No one was able to infiltrate his household as a servant or administrative assistant because he did not maintain any staff whatsoever. Apart from visits by his immediate family, an occasional close friend and, of course, Natalia, Oku was the sole human inhabitant of the deserts, mountains and canyons.

The other members of the Council all had their primary residences on Mars, each supported by a huge staff, and entertained a steady stream of people. It was easy to get someone on the inside of such a household. In fact, it was assumed that a substantial percentage of one's staff consisted of spies from the other nine Monitor's camps. In recent weeks, however, Idrella drastically reduced both her staff and her entertaining, and she was showing signs of Oku's brand of reclusiveness. But the other eight were more than willing to compensate for their two anti-social colleagues, and Silas actually obtained more information on them than he cared to know.

The unnerving talk about Oku finally making a move had Silas more concerned than he would admit. Reports from his sources in the city-stations claimed that the citizenry was openly discussing future policy under Oku's regime. O.I.T. fleets were conducting extensive "exercises" around the outer planets. The number of vessels located in the inner sectors of the system had quietly doubled and huge sums of money were zigzagging across the Union in a myriad of untraceable deals. And the most distressing fact was that Oku was still not saying a word.

Chapter 16

Granny was baffled. The first time he saw that expression on her face he was sure it was just a new type of grimace. It persisted, however, and now he was forced to come to the nearly impossible conclusion that Kiya could smile. That in itself would have been hard enough to swallow, but Kiya was full of more surprises. A full week went by without her starting any arguments, hurling barbed insults or freely handing out looks-that-could-kill as if they were candy. Granny was tempted to have her report to sick bay or check to see if any toxic fumes were seeping into her quarters. This was not the same woman who was just aching to spit in his face at the recruiting station.

"Good morning, gentlemen!" Kiya said in a perky, singsong voice as she glided by Granny and Vrovski on their way to early morning duty on the bridge.

"Do we know that woman?" Vrovski asked rhetorically as the two confused men shook their heads in amazement.

"Maybe there are two of them and now this one keeps her evil twin locked up."

"That's more plausible than any excuse I've been able to come up with so far," Vrovski laughed as he scanned the reports from the last shift. "Wait a minute, I don't believe this one. It looks like the Captain's assistant isn't the only one who's left orbit."

"What is it now?" Granny asked, pausing his own stream of reports.

"It seems that some of the construction crew was having a friendly game of *Hazard and Pain* with some of the boys in maintenance late last night. As the computer was tallying the final scores, there was some kind of glitch that erased a full round of points. There was a ton of money on the game and witnesses called security because they were sure there was going to be a riot," Vrovski said and then paused to reread the final section of the report several times.

"Well? How many people got hurt this time?"

"No one. By the time security arrived, the rival groups were congratulating each other on a good game and dividing the money evenly! What the hell are we feeding this crew?"

The two groups involved had acted more like street gangs when the mission began and fights had often erupted over far less significant things than money. Violent incidents always increased over the course of time as different individuals or departments tried to establish their dominance for the long flight ahead. Granny had been on missions that were considered a success because the murder rate was kept below average. An eight-year voyage with a crew of second-rate criminals had all the earmarks of a lawless wagon train rumbling through the wild west.

The *Hyperion*'s incident reports had steadily declined since departure. The most serious occurrence in the last three days had been the alleged theft of one of the navigator's desserts, although it was suspected that the corpulent woman had simply forgotten that she had already eaten it. The atmosphere on board was the strangest Granny had ever encountered. An inexplicable feeling of calm and quiet seemed to blanket the ship and the Commander soon realized he was not immune to its effects. Like the rest of the crew, the edge had been taken off his temper, his unruly nervous energy was more subdued and manageable, and petty annoyances that used to gall him now seemed to roll off his back like water off a duck. Granny wasn't sure he liked his altered personality.

Mardo was no less amazed at the transformations sweeping his ship and it was amusing to hear both Kiya and Granny comment on the other's improved demeanor and behavior. But the Captain was not so baffled as his Commander as to the source of the mysterious goodwill generator.

Some feelings are like scents, both good and bad. They evoke a myriad of responses and are generally unforgettable.

Like the fragrances of early morning on Earth, there was a profound sense of awakening to the vibrations permeating the *Hyperion*, a vital creativity wrapped in stillness. When one encounters the slightest breath of such rarefied air, its memory is deeply ingrained. The day Mardo met Walter on the island it was like a thousand dawns were springing aloft, and it had nothing to do with the island itself.

"What are you cooking down there, Walter? I can smell it all the way up here," Mardo chuckled as he contacted his friend on his private channel.

"Sorry about that. It seems like the whole crew has caught a whiff," Walter said in mock apology. "I guess whatever waves I'm generating have a ripple effect all around me. Neat stuff, huh?"

"Very neat, Walter, and please don't turn it off. I think I'm even beginning to like my ornery assistant."

"She has been an excellent pupil," Walter said and then watched to see just how far the Captain's jaw would drop.

"Could you clarify that statement?" Mardo asked, hoping he had misunderstood.

"Kiya's known who I am for a while. I'm sorry I didn't tell you sooner, but I didn't want to worry you needlessly."

"Needlessly? Your life is in danger! It isn't tough to figure out that I got you on board, either. And she's smart enough to know Granny must have had a hand in it," Mardo tried to say as calmly as the shocking news allowed.

"I don't think there's any imminent danger, at least not to you and Granny," Walter said thoughtfully. "Someone undoubtedly sent her here to try to locate me, which, I admit, is not a comforting feeling. But she's agreed to give me time to prove that the Council has made false accusations."

"Why would she do that?"

"Kiya is a bright woman, she knows that my work has some validity. Just how much, well, she's finding that out for herself. And you've said so yourself, she's really changed," Walter added, hoping he sounded upbeat enough to allay his friends fears.

"I don't care how changed she is, Kiya is still a damn clever headhunter sent to bring back your skull on a silver platter. I think you should examine the alternatives to keeping her as a pupil."

"I am not prepared to harm her, no matter what."

The tone of Walter's voice held a compassion and finality that Mardo knew was useless to contest. And as he paused to examine his own thoughts and feelings about his assistant, he discovered that he did not want Kiya's blood on his hands either. Once again, he would have to put his trust in Danan's abilities.

"Well, I guess I'm already so far out on a limb another five and a half feet of trouble won't make much difference," Mardo finally sighed with cheerful resignation. "But the second she tries to harm you, I will personally throw her in a stasis tube."

"Fair enough," Walter agreed. "And you might as well let Gran know what's going on, but I suggest that neither of you let on that you're suspicious. If she feels threatened it might undo all our work."

"You mean we should just keep treating her as badly as we've been doing?" Mardo offered tensely, his humor permeated with a lingering hint of fear.

***

Kiya never asked how Walter got aboard the *Hyperion* or how many accomplices aided him. She didn't care to know the details of his escape from prison or how he spent the last year in hiding. Her sole line of inquiry revolved around consciousness and neurophysiology, the latter being a subject in which she possessed a technical knowledge superior to Danan's, but one completely lacking in an appreciation for the wonder of it.

Walter quickly discovered that Kiya's mind was like a horse with too many jockeys. After gently coaxing her to relinquish some of the overbearing control, she found that dropping the reins altogether brought a marvelous sense of freedom and satisfaction. Once she experienced these deep, relaxing states, he showed her how to maintain them and guide her mind beyond the veil of limits and boundaries. When she returned from these exhilarating mental jaunts, some part of her experience remained and the effects would increase in intensity with every session.

"Can I dare to assume you've gotten more out of the mission than you bargained for?" Walter whispered as they both emerged from a prolonged, meditative state.

Unable to speak right away, Kiya simply smiled. Whatever level she was able to attain in her own quarters was deepened tenfold by Walter's presence. Her ever-widening field of inner vision was systematically exposing the rest of her life as a meaningless charade. And the d-chip, the device that blocked the paths to these realizations, she now viewed as the most insidious invention of mankind.

"You are a master of understatement, among other things," she finally whispered back, gingerly touching the switch to her d-chip as if it was an infected wound.

****

Much to Rial's chagrin, Idrella didn't even flinch when she dropped the obvious hint about her evening with Silas. It wasn't any fun if her daughter didn't scream, cry or hurl threatening remarks and glassware, and it was downright infuriating when her daughter's expression failed to show the slightest hint of emotion.

"Perhaps you didn't understand my meaning," Rial pressed on. "Silas was not here on business. I know how uncomfortable the truth must be to hear, but I simply couldn't live with myself any longer if I didn't confess to spending the night with him."

"So?" Idrella asked, seemingly as bored with this conversation as all the others.

"My dear, you must be in a state of shock. I see that I'll have to leave you alone to think about this. I'm here if you need to talk."

Rial shouted an angry command to end the transmission and her image mercifully faded from sight. Idrella was almost as surprised as her mother by her reaction, or lack of one. A month ago such an announcement would have been devastating and shaken her with a murderous rage. Now she simply couldn't be bothered. There were a lot more important things taking precedence in her mind, and heart. In fact, it seemed quite natural for her mother and Silas to form a liaison; both had sunken so low they were perfect for one another.

As Idrella left her private quarters, with Boa close behind, she knew that Rial would have instantly contacted Silas to complain about her spoiled fun. Her hunch was confirmed when she saw Lindquist speaking to an assistant outside the Council meeting room. Looking up, he saw Idrella's sarcastic smirk and quickly turned away in obvious embarrassment. This was better than she could have hoped.

Heading straight for Silas, the assistant saw Monitor Croix's approach and obediently backed away. Silas took a deep breath and decided to face the inevitable like a man.

"You wish to speak with me, Monitor Croix?" he asked, feeling none of the triumph he had expected.

"You're not looking well, Silas. I hope you haven't eaten anything that's disagreeing with you," she said with overly sweet concern. "Or perhaps it's some kind of parasite?"

Lindquist's desire to gain an ally, and humiliate Idrella at the same time, only half succeeded. The anger and disgust with which he hoped she would be consumed had completely bypassed her and boomeranged back to himself. He tried to believe that the information he received would ultimately be worth the price.

"How kind of you to notice. I'm sure whatever it is will pass soon."

"Don't bank on it, Monitor Lindquist. I dare say it might be chronic," Idrella said with an even wider smile as she tossed one side of her cloak over her shoulder, `a la Lindquist, and entered the meeting room. Boa took his place by the door and couldn't repress a bout of snickering. Silas hastily completed his business with the assistant and followed two other Monitors into the chamber, knowing that if he remained for another second he would surely take an imprudent swing at the significantly bigger bodyguard.

Oku did not take his seat until the last chime of the appointed hour was struck on the ancient grandfather clock. Old analog clocks had been one of Jupiter Croix's passions and not a room or hallway in the entire complex was without at least one. Most people found the incessant ticking and chiming a nuisance and conveniently neglected to wind those pieces in their private offices and chambers. But those in the meeting rooms and hallways were lovingly and meticulously tended to by an official timekeeper.

Idrella's favorite was that grandfather clock which stood against the wall that she now faced. It had been constructed hundreds of years ago in a town once known as Newport, expertly crafted in gleaming cherry wood. Even as a child, Idrella would sneak into the Council Hall to watch the scenes of sailing ships move across the elaborate dial, rotating endlessly around the ornately lettered phrase, "Tempus Fugit".

At the moment, no one was paying any attention to the clock, except for its announcement of the time, because all eyes were on Oku. Even the oldest Monitor's could not recall a single instance when Oku was anything less than ten minutes early for any meeting. Even more startling, was the deeply knitted brow that dominated a usually smooth, placid face. Realizing that all eyes were upon him, he carefully and deliberately straightened his cloak, poured a glass of water and glanced over the agenda.

"Is there any reason we should not begin?" Oku asked innocently, scanning the circle for someone brave enough to question his brief, but glaringly obvious, absence.

No one felt up to the challenge and the business of the day commenced. A dozen different matters were discussed and voted upon in a session that ran long over its scheduled time. During every break, Oku remained in his seat and placed a tiny decoding unit in his ear to which he fed messages from his handscreen. Croix, Lindquist and one or two others took their breaks in the lounge, relaxing and appearing unconcerned, while the rest of the Monitors raced back to their chambers to examine the latest positions of Oku's fleets and check their own intelligence groups for information. There were no outward signs that he was making any big move, so they all strolled back to the meeting hall with rehearsed nonchalance.

After the scheduled business was finally concluded, Silas requested an immediate vote on a non-agenda matter. There was a general grumbling and a few remarks about their already overworked rear ends, but the rules allowed each member to introduce one unscheduled piece of business after every joint session.

"I wonder if I can guess what this will be about?" M'bai asked rhetorically, with her own special brand of venom-spitting sarcasm.

"If you have cleverly deduced that this concerns Jesse Dimont, Monitor M'bai, then your wisdom surpasses even your beauty," Silas replied graciously as he looked into the face that only a mother could love. "I request that we arrange another interrogation at the earliest time convenient to everyone."

"He has sufficiently recovered?" Rizzic asked with suspicion. "What is the latest doctor's report?"

"What's the point, is more like it," Idrella interjected.

"Why must I continue to remind everyone that you unanimously agreed over a year ago that the Danan case was of the utmost importance?" Lindquist said, recalling the Council verdict on the main viewer. "In lieu of this recent epidemic of Danan propaganda, I suggest we question Dimont further, before this gets out of hand."

"I wouldn't call eight incidents an epidemic, and Mr. Dimont is clearly not ready for another interrogation," Idrella stated with a little too much confidence.

"For someone who fails to see the point of all this, you seem to be quite familiar with the case. Perhaps your expertise derives from your frequent visits to Jesse Dimont?"

Silas paused to let his words hang in the air for a moment and then he watched as the circle constricted with surprise. Even Oku seemed interested in the list of dates and the duration of Idrella's visits to Jesse that Lindquist had produced.

"Overlooking the fact that Monitor Lindquist obviously obtained this information through questionable means, may I ask the nature of your business with the prisoner, Monitor Croix?" Oku asked with polite curiosity and no hint of the accusatory tone of his young colleague.

"I find the case interesting... no, fascinating. And I intend to gather as much information as possible, under Monitor Lindquist's watchful eye, no doubt," she replied, sounding refreshingly like a woman who had nothing to hide.

"I trust you would naturally have reported on anything which would have aided in further prosecuting the Council's case?" Oku added.

"Naturally."

"Nonetheless, despite Monitor Croix's single-handed efforts, I still request another interrogation," Lindquist insisted, clearly annoyed by the polite exchange.

There was some further discussion around the table and it was decided that an official vote would not be taken until another thorough medical examination was conducted. Lindquist immediately contacted the chief of staff of the hospital who agreed to begin right away. Idrella shifted uneasily in her seat, knowing that she wouldn't have time to warn Jesse.

****

The artificial waterfall hissed pleasantly, drowning out the chatter of the other men in the ward. Jesse paced the length of his room, repeatedly flicking the switch of his d-chip, which had been deactivated immediately after his capture. Conviction wasn't always necessary for that punishment, suspicion was often sufficient. Jesse didn't plan on ever using it again anyway, but he objected strongly to what he believed was its unlawful deactivation. There was not much more time to ponder the legal aspects, however, as a pair of hulking orderlies appeared to escort him to an examination room.

Trying his best to wear his blankest expression, Jesse answered the doctor's questions with practiced incoherence. While he may have been successful in fooling them, the medical scanners could not be so easily duped. While there was still evidence of trauma in some regions of the brain, the staff was stunned to find an over ninety percent improvement from previous tests. All procedures were repeated in triplicate, but the results were identical.

Jesse Dimont's brain had somehow undergone radical and rapid healing. Still cautious about the results, the official report ambiguously stated that while the trauma appeared no less severe than one might find in a patient who had experienced a slight concussion, no two physiologies reacted exactly alike. Therefore, the symptoms of Dimont's disorder might still be genuine. This middle of the road attitude was an ancient, ass-covering technique frequently employed by the medical profession, conveniently placing the onus on the Council itself.

The report was compiled and sent to each Monitor. By the time it was completed, it was late at night, but three members of the Council had been unable to sleep awaiting the results. Despite their widely differing motives, each read both what he or she wanted, and didn't want, to see. Once the reports were carefully scrutinized, the real work began. Three strategies were planned, three networks of operators contacted and three powerful forces embarked on a collision course.

CHAPTER 17

Tilton Maas personally instructed everyone who would be involved. The mission was necessitated by the Council's defeat of Lindquist's proposal for a second interrogation. By a seven to three margin, it was decided not to waste precious time until the state of Jesse Dimont's mind could be determined with certainty. But Lindquist had planned for that contingency and a week later Maas reported that all was ready.

It couldn't happen soon enough in Silas' opinion, as the number of pro-Danan incidences took a steep rise. Anti-d-chip slogans were being painted in public places across the system. Wildly exaggerated horror stories about the dangers of the device were already circulating through every level of society. Arrests had been made at some college campuses where radical students were having their d-chips removed. Slurs against Lindquist and his family were also daring to leave the lips of a few brave, but anonymous, souls. But the most intolerable, infuriating smear tactic of all was the mysterious reemergence of the story the descendants of Harod Lindquist had hoped was permanently buried with their ancestor.

Harod was the Monitor who was expelled from the Council by Walter Danan's great-grandfather. While even schoolchildren were familiar with the event, time and careful manipulation by generations of Lindquists had muddied the truth and succeeded in portraying Harod as the victim of a great injustice. No one but a handful of historians knew the entire story, and even they had long ago ceased to care.

Now, mysteriously, fragments of the original public records of the events surrounding the dismissal and disgrace were surfacing on densely populated stations, as well as remote, surface colonies. Tantalizingly brief, each piece offered enough information to stimulate both curiosity and anger. Suddenly, library banks across the system were being accessed by millions wishing to learn the details of the past, and their implications for the future.

Harod Lindquist was a man of substantial ambition who made his way to the Council by his political skill, and vast wealth. Possessing none of the scientific expertise of the Brain Benders or frenetic genius of Jupiter Croix, he nonetheless managed to become a towering figure of his time. With center stage promises and back room deals, he won the ultimate honor of wearing the purple cloak. In an age where dizzying technological advances were constantly redefining man's place in the universe, Harod claimed to speak to the immutable heart and soul of humanity, defending them from the cruel onslaught of relentless change. And while he was making those noble claims, his organization was preparing to alter the d-chips so that he could have direct control over the minds of the populace.

The plot was uncovered by Jacob Danan and he exposed Lindquist before the Council, and then the public. The Monitor's immunity saved him from prosecution, but by unanimous decision, the other nine Monitor's stripped him of his cloak and banished him from ever again participating in any form of government. Retiring to his vast estate on Mars, Harod concentrated on multiplying his real estate holdings, as well as personally multiplying until he had enough offspring to practically qualify as a colony. His purpose in this procreative marathon was to produce so many blood relations that chance would favor that at least one descendant might someday avenge him. Hatred for Danans and contempt for mankind was fostered in each child and generations became obsessed with the lust for revenge against a world that for some reason didn't want to be controlled by a little keypad in the hand of a madman.

Needless to say, this revelation began to color the light in which Silas Lindquist was viewed. Instead of the triumphant hero redeeming his family honor, a shadow of suspicion was descending and many began to see him as merely an extension of the sinister Harod. Even some supporters couldn't suppress the fleeting thought that Silas might try to continue his great-grandfather's mind-domination plan. Things were definitely heating up in the system and the bookie who had accepted the enormous pro-Danan bet at thousand-to-one odds was really beginning to sweat.

The Lindquist networks continued to do their share in promoting Silas' image. The programmers decided to pull any reference to Danan, Dimont and the Astromancer, hoping that the public would quickly lose interest in Harod's indiscretions. The only problem was that Oku's in-house networks, serving billions of his employees on the city-stations and colonies, had suddenly decided to go public. That would have been tolerable, except for the fact that Oku had recently given the okay for "alternative programming", which simply translated into flooding the airwaves with whatever issues the Lindquist networks were ignoring.

It was not Oku's style, however, to make open denunciations. So rather than focus on the crimes of Harod Lindquist, the O.I.T. networks ran an entire dramatic series charting the history of the Council of Monitors, dealing with the Harod Lindquist episode so tantalizingly briefly as to give the impression that it was too shameful an event to go into at any length. Interest in the scandal was thus raised to a fever pitch. The Lindquist clan was ready to drink hot blood, but upon Silas' recommendation they kept silent. They also bit their tongues when startlingly objective programs explored some of Danan's theories. Silas didn't believe for an instant that Oku had anything but contempt for Danan and his insane beliefs, but the clever old man knew just where to strike to weaken his new colleague's popularity.

While all these events were disturbing, Silas tried to look at them as nothing more than a few troublesome ants trying to invade his picnic; ants that happened to have names like Croix and Oku. All he needed to do was raise his foot and crush all his problems with a few short steps, when the time was right. Caressing the smooth, marble features of the Caesar bust in his chambers, he envisioned his own nose, his strong jaw and powerful eyes cut into the cool stone. These were just tests, minor obstacles every great man encounters on his path to immortality. With that thought in mind, he ordered Tilton Maas to proceed.

****

Jesse was sleeping soundly. Idrella had personally informed him that Lindquist's request for another interrogation had been voted down. The spies in the ward had practically given up trying to obtain any information, simply because Jesse refused to speak to anyone. And he knew without a doubt that Walter was safely aboard the *Hyperion*, refining and intensifying his abilities. While his own future was still bleak, he didn't lose hope that somehow it would all work out.

Lost in a deep dream, it took a minute for him to realize that a hand was over his mouth and someone was shaking him. Startled to wakefulness, the hand pressed even harder while a second held down one shoulder.

"Jesse, it's all right," a female voice whispered, "Idrella sent me."

Jesse shook his head in agreement that he wouldn't shout and sat up once the hands were removed. A thin, late middle-aged woman dressed in a nurse's uniform with her hair slicked back into a tight bun, knelt by the bedside, and Jesse could see in the dim light that she was trying to overcome a look of anxiety with a sweet smile. The uniform had the proper hospital insignias, but he didn't remember seeing her before, which was not unusual because there were probably a thousand nurses working in the huge complex above the detention levels.

"Why are you here?" he whispered suspiciously.

"I'm here to get you out!"

Jesse's weary mind wanted very much to believe the woman, but he had to be cautious.

"Why would Monitor Croix want to get me out?" he said in a dismissive manner.

"She's in trouble," the nurse stated gravely.

"What kind of trouble?" Jesse asked, trying to appear unconcerned.

"Lindquist is plotting to murder her! He was furious when they broke up and now he thinks she left him because of you."

"But that's ridicu-"

"And he thinks she's responsible for all this pro-Danan stuff that's been surfacing. He wants her dead!"

One of the benefits of minimum security was the privilege of access to outside news. Jesse had been following the string of incidents with great interest, and the hint that someone very high up was responsible had not escaped his attention. He knew Lindquist was capable of just about anything, but actually killing another Monitor seemed beyond even him.

"Lindquist wouldn't dare!" Jesse insisted.

"Do you honestly think that this would be the first time he's had someone killed? Is your mind that far gone or are you just terribly naive?" she said, literally shaking him in exasperation.

"All right, all right, let's say you're telling the truth. What does this have to do with me?"

"If Lindquist would eliminate a Monitor, would he hesitate to arrange an 'accident' for you? Idrella is sick of the intrigue and politics. She's leaving the Council and wants you to go with her where it will be safe. Jesse, she *loves* you."

The last three words pushed aside every fear, suspicion and doubt. Tears sat tenuously on his lower lids before a few escaped down his cheeks. He had longed to hear that phrase, preferably from Idrella's sensuous, peach-blushed lips rather this pair of drawn, gray ones, but his heart embraced the words all the same. The nurse gave Jesse a minute to revel in his dreams of the future and then brought him swiftly back to reality by dangling something shiny in front of his face.

"In case you still didn't believe me, she gave me this," she said as the Monitor's medallion sparkled brightly even in the subdued light. "And this."

A small disk was dropped into his open palm and he could see the identical Monitor insignia embossed in gold on its surface. Jesse had never actually seen one, but there was no doubt that this was a Level One clearance pass, of which only ten were in existence. There could be absolutely no doubt that a Monitor had sent this woman.

"Where are we going? What connection do you have with Idrella?" Jesse asked distractedly as he rushed to get into the civilian clothing the nurse had brought.

"Just in case something goes wrong, it's best for Idrella's sake if you don't know too much," she cautioned. "And if you don't mind, I would rather not hand out my name and address."

"Fair enough. Now what's the plan?" he asked, peering out into the vacant lounge.

"I have staff clearance and the two of us are just going to walk out of here as if we do it every night. And we've also arranged to have a new set of guards on duty to eliminate the chance of someone recognizing you. A ship will be meeting us at a rendezvous point in an hour. That's all I can say. Are you ready?"

"My damn hands are shaking, I hope no one notices," he replied with a nervous smile.

"That's what pockets are for, my boy. Let's go."

Jesse's heart raced, half because of the obvious danger and half because he and Idrella would soon be together. As he and the nurse stepped out of the ward and passed the first guard, Jesse decided that holding his breath would be easier than trying to control the rapid heaving motions in his chest. Once beyond the first hurdle, he followed the nurse as she calmly proceeded toward the nearest exit; an exit where two ominous peacemaker robots stood poised for attack. Jesse forced his eyes to remain on the floor as he approached the security checkpoint by the door.

The woman held her disk into the beam of red light projected between the two robots, it turned a bright green and she walked through. Jesse took a quick gulp of air, pulled the disk from his pocket and shoved it forward. Bracing himself for sirens and stun bolts, he stared dumbly at the innocuous emerald glow that signaled his freedom. No one seemed to take notice of the two figures winding their way through the hospital complex and into the deserted streets of the city. Only essential services personnel were out at that late hour, because it was common knowledge that it was crucial to adhere to an Earth-like circadian cycle, with the most beneficial sleep being obtained at night. This was especially important on other planets and stations.

Since the Mars' day was only an hour longer than Earth's, sticking to the cycle was more comfortable on the red planet due to the familiar visual cues provided by the sunrises and sunsets. But even those born and raised on distant city-stations, where the sun was just another star in the backdrop, found that their physiological rhythms were inexorably linked to the home planet.

While this hemisphere of Mars slept, Jesse anxiously followed the nurse to one of the less desirable parts of town. An occasional dog barked and twice they passed women who obviously weren't concerned about healthy sleep cycles. Jesse graciously declined their generous offers and hurried to keep up with the older woman. It didn't seem possible, but the atmosphere shields in this sector appeared to be the original, low-ceilinged, pointed-arch tubes that he had only seen in museums. The shield thickness was undoubtedly no less than the soaring, modern equivalents, but seeing them only a few meters above his head, they looked like paper-thin membranes. There was a suffocating, claustrophobic feeling in this sector, which only added to Jesse's agitated state of mind.

Stopping in front of a pawnshop that faced a parking bay, she motioned for him to descend a flight of stairs that seemed to go beneath the shop. Although feeling severely boxed-in and vulnerable, he gladly went down the dimly lit staircase and into a dark, musty storage room. At least under the street he wouldn't be able to see the archaic, fragile shell that was the only thing standing between him and a very unpleasant death.

"Hang in there, Jesse," the woman said kindly as she saw the fearful expression and trembling limbs. "We're almost home free."

"This is embarrassing," he apologized, sticking his shaking hands beneath him as he sat on a packing crate. "I don't think I've ever been this nervous, even when I was first captured."

"I bet you never broke out of jail before, either," she smiled sweetly.

"Good point. Still, I don't know why I'm so on edge."

"Relax, my boy. The hard part is over. We just have to wait here until the ship arrives across the street."

The woman made small talk to keep Jesse's mind off of the numerous dangers that could still lie ahead. She was able to make him feel at ease and within minutes his guard was down and he didn't even hesitate to answer her simple questions about Walter Danan. Naturally, she must be curious and if she was willing to risk her life to help him, he could at least satisfy her curiosity. She was probably even one of Walter's silent supporters.

The nurse confirmed his belief when she admitted to having attended some of Walter's early lectures. This confession came in eye-darting whispers, as if fearing that every crate contained a Council spy.

"Now look at me!" she laughed when she realized her paranoia was also showing. "I'm one to talk about relaxing. I guess I'm just getting too old for this kind of thing."

"You've done things like this before?" Jesse asked eagerly. He had always loved spy stories when he was a kid.

"More than you can imagine, my boy. But don't let it fool you. It may sound exciting, but it only gives you ulcers and gray hair," she said, smoothing an errant strand back into place. "Your sister always told me I should just retire and take up knitting."

"You knew Valery?" he asked as a powerful wave of emotion swept over him.

"Not as well as I would have liked," she replied sadly. "To lose her, and then Walter, it's just been too much. I don't know how you can stand it."

"It...it hasn't been easy," Jesse admitted, the tears in his eyes springing up at the thought of his murdered sister.

"If only Walter was still alive! There's a new feeling in the system, people are ready for change, Jesse. If Walter was alive, it would give people courage and a cause for which to fight. Maybe *you* could lead the people, Jesse," she said, placing a surprisingly strong hand on his forearm.

"Me? What could I do?"

"Pick up where Walter left off!" she declared enthusiastically.

"I couldn't lead anyone," he replied dejectedly, thinking of how badly he had bungled everything. "Walter is the leader. Walter is the teacher. I'm just a follower and student."

"Jesse, why did you just speak as if he was alive?" the nurse asked, brightening with hope. "Is he Jesse, did Walter escape the raid?"

He hesitated to answer, but there was such a look of anticipated joy in the old woman's face, and a revolutionary zeal that was contagious. This woman knew Valery, Walter and Idrella, and had probably helped countless other victims of the Council to freedom. She had probably spent her life risking it for others and now longed to hear that her sacrifices had not been in vain. And she was probably in a position to be able to tell all of Danan's supporters that there was still hope, that they should band together and fight the injustices of the Union. Just a few words could renew that hope and give her the strength to carry on.

"Walter Danan is alive!" Jesse suddenly blurted out joyfully. "For his sake I can't tell you where he is, but he is alive!"

"That's all I needed to know," the old woman said as her sweet smile suddenly hardened into a twisted sneer.

CHAPTER 18

"Your generosity is too great," the impostor nurse said, as she glanced at the figure being deposited into her account. "This one was far too easy."

"I'm not accustomed to modesty from your family, Mrs. Maas," Silas laughed. "Believe me, you were well worth the price."

Tilton Maas stood proudly behind his mother, whose greased hair had been freed from the constrictive bun to flow like an oil slick down her bony spine. Pulling a Council medallion and Level One clearance pass from her pocket, she placed them on the desk in front of the jubilant Monitor.

"I suppose you want these back?" she asked rhetorically. "I really wish you two could have seen how he fell for all this like a lead weight. And the puppy dog look in his eyes when I told him Idrella loved him, well I had to keep my mouth shut or else I would have burst out laughing!"

Silas and Tilton made the old spy tell every detail of the mission at least three times. They especially liked her colorful descriptions and reenactments of Jesse's pitiful expressions and nervous twitches. They roared over her hilarious retelling of his capture, when the look of horror and anguish contorted his features as the guards and peacemaker robots burst through the wall of the storage room. And they could barely catch their breaths as she recounted how Jesse had fought gallantly to protect her from harm, until he finally realized he had been setup higher than a comm tower.

****

A humiliated, enraged and terrified Jesse Dimont was back in his maximum-security cell. Desperately trying to calm his whirlwind mind, he sought the deep level of clarity necessary to send a warning message to Walter. Too agitated to realize that Walter had sensed his anxiety before he had even left the hospital in the bogus escape, Jesse was also unable to perceive the return message that Walter already knew the gist of what had transpired. Sheer exhaustion finally pulled Jesse into sleep, and finally ended the distant, frenzied cries ringing in Walter's ears.

****

"They've tricked Jesse. Lindquist knows I'm alive," he said to Kiya as she came for her daily session.

The smile slid from her face like a foot unexpectedly finding a patch of ice. The stiffness was trying to return to her features and posture but she had loosened so much in the past few weeks that it hurt to attempt to impose the old, rigid control mechanisms. Finding the edge of the bed with her hand, she lowered herself slowly, her mind too active to pay attention to her body. Walter sat next to her and waited silently while she recalculated her position.

"There is a high probability that Lindquist will once again suspect you are on the *Hyperion*," Kiya finally said, emotion clearly placing a strain on her ability to speak.

"I'm well aware of my position," he replied, eyes piercing her as no other pair of eyes could do. "What I am interested in knowing is how this changes your position."

"I don't know, Walter. I honestly don't know," she whispered, brushing away what actually looked like a tear. "Obviously, we can not proceed as before. You are once again a most wanted man and our focus must shift from the years ahead to every minute of the day."

"Have I at least convinced you of my innocence?"

"You've convinced me of far more than that," Kiya said, trying to clamp down hard on the softness that was creeping back. "You have forever changed my life and I can not possibly repay you for what you've given me. No matter what happens, please believe I have your best interest at heart."

Rising suddenly, she rushed from the room. Walter felt the turmoil within her, but as always in her case, he was unable to penetrate to the deepest levels of her thoughts. He still didn't know who Kiya was, or more importantly, what she was going to do, which lent a disquieting uncertainty to his future.

As buck-toothed, face-stretched James Recone, he ventured from his quarters for the first time. No sense of danger or anticipation was stirring in the crew, which meant nothing out of the dull ordinary had happened, yet. Making his way to Mardo's quarters, he paused before Kiya's door, but continued on.

"James Recone requesting entry," the Captain's security system informed him.

The ensuing surge of adrenaline brought Mardo from his seat. They had agreed not to meet in person unless it was an emergency. Mardo ordered Granny to be located and sent to him as he rushed across the room and practically punched the door access panel trying to get it open.

"What's wrong?" Mardo asked as he pulled Walter in and shut the door. "Are you all right?"

"I'm fine, for now," Walter replied clumsily as he popped the fake teeth from his mouth. "You had better get Granny up here, I have some bad news."

The Commander was at the door in a matter of seconds, his curiosity at the sudden summons turning to concern at the sight of Walter.

"Of course, I don't know all the details, but Lindquist managed to trick Jesse into telling him I'm alive. I don't think he told them I'm on the *Hyperion*, but it's only a matter of time before they either pry the information out of him or figure it out for themselves," Walter stated gravely.

"Is Jesse okay?" Granny asked almost shyly, still haunted by his first capture.

"He's scared, upset, but I don't think they've hurt him, not this time at least. Is there anything, Mardo?" Walter asked his friend who had immediately begun scanning the most recent classified information to which he was privy.

"If Lindquist or the Council has done anything yet, it's taken place on levels higher than my access. There's been no significant movement of Union fleets and I read no increases in security at any port."

"Are you sure Kiya had nothing to do with this?" Granny asked, refreshing his memory of her early behavior.

"No, it clearly came as a shock," Walter replied with certainty. "But I don't know what she is going to do now."

"We could arrange to keep her quiet for a while," Mardo offered.

"I thought about that, but if she fails to communicate with whoever sent her it will be like sending up a flare."

"Then we just sit and wait?" Granny puffed impatiently.

"There's nothing we can do about Kiya, except trust that she will make the right decision. I know that isn't a desirable option, but we have no choice. As for me, I have to get off this ship. Any suggestions, gentlemen?"

Calling up a schematic on the *Hyperion*'s position, the massive ship appeared to be a speck on the room-sized grid.

"Downsize, include positions of nearest city-stations," Mardo ordered as he walked through the hologram and raised his index finger to the dot which represented them. "We are here, about two day's distance between the first and second stations. In addition to them, there are three small supply outposts, a few private residences and a whole lot of empty space."

Mardo's finger traced the line of tiny spots and then his hand made a sweeping arc through the blues lines of the grid to emphasize the vastness of their surroundings. On this scale, Earth and the Council Hall would be somewhere at the other end of the corridor leading to his quarters. Stretching his arms to encompass the area between the two stations, Mardo requested that section to be enlarged, giving diagrams and information about every possible sanctuary.

The three men examined the data on the supply stations and the scant information on the secluded residences. One of the private homes was owned by an old friend of Danan's, which would be one of the first places the Union would search. The supply depots had minimal staffs under maximum security, not the ideal hideout for a Council warrant fugitive. That left the city-stations, and empty space.

"Well, it seems that I either have to get lost on one of those," Walter said pointing to the two stations and then laughed as his hand made an arc similar to Mardo's, "or get lost out there."

"We don't have the proper equipment, or vehicle for that matter, to let you loose in deep space," Granny protested. "We have to find a way to get you into the city."

Mardo agreed and wouldn't listen to any wild plan involving Walter leaving in the battered, fruit transport and taking his chances. There were some things about which the Captain had to put down his foot.

"I'll get you in that city if I have to blast a hole in the dome and park the damn ship on the front lawn of the Union offices!" Mardo declared emphatically.

"I do believe you would," Walter grinned, glad to have such friends as these.

****

Idrella had planned to visit Jesse after the day's meetings, but there were so many delays, interruptions and complications it was like every committee she was on wanted to deliberately keep her as long as possible. By the time the last session finally ended, not only was she exhausted, but it was so late she would not have time to sleep if she made the trip to the hospital.

As it was, she couldn't sleep anyway, her mind refusing to let her stop thinking of Jesse. She had felt an odd, uneasy feeling all day, but she attributed it to her impatience to be with him, not to mention the constant frustration of the day's business. Now that Idrella was alone in the quiet of her chambers, the feeling grew to one of clear distress, as if Jesse was crying out for help. It was useless to ignore it or explain it away as her imagination.

"Get me the supervisor of Jesse Dimont's ward at the hospital," Idrella ordered as she tossed her cloak over her nightgown and assumed a demeanor of authority.

"Ready," the computer informed her and then began the transmission at her signal.

A quaking image appeared and at first, Idrella thought there was some kind of interference. Then she recognized the terrified assistant supervisor she had previously intimidated so thoroughly.

"Mon...Monitor Croix, how can I b...be of assistance?" he stuttered nervously.

After his first encounter with the Monitor, he had requested to be assigned to the less desirable graveyard shift, thinking he would never have to meet with any Council members again. Much to his obvious dismay, he had been wrong.

"Is Jesse Dimont all right?" she asked after a long pause to give him time to really build up a good sweat.

"As far as I know, Monitor Croix," he replied, dropping his handscreen twice before he was able to verify it. "Yes, Monitor, his condition is listed as good."

Idrella could be fairly certain that this man wouldn't dare give her false information, but still she wasn't convinced. After looking him up and down slowly, she spoke again, slowly and deliberately.

"I want you to check on him personally, right away. If anything is wrong, call me immediately. Is that understood?" she added with threatening emphasis.

"Perfectly! Perfectly understood, Monitor Croix. I'll look in on him right away. Right away!"

"But don't disturb him if he's sleeping."

"Of course not! I'll look right away and let you know if anything is wrong and I won't disturb him if he's sleeping."

Getting back into bed, Idrella went over some reports to kill time while she waited. After half an hour, she assumed that all must be well and tried again to fall asleep. Something was still not right, but fatigue was finally overcoming her agitated senses. It was the assistant supervisor, something about him that was not right. Unfortunately, the fact that he worked on the maximum security level, not the minimum where Jesse was being kept the past several weeks, failed to reach her conscious mind before it succumbed to the inexorable pull of sleep.

Silas had not slept since receiving the news. It had taken fast thinking and considerable influence to get the committee members to drag their feet during their meetings with Idrella. He wanted as much time as possible before the rest of the Council discovered his little maneuver. His most vicious bloodhound squads had been deployed only minutes after Jesse's recapture, and Silas preferred to let them work unhampered by Union interference, or any bothersome laws. He knew the truth would come out in a matter of days, if not hours, but that might be all it would take for his special forces to catch Danan's scent.

This time there would be no question about taking him alive. The fugitive's ability to elude the Union forces, as well as disappear from prison, had proven that he must be eliminated. Lindquist had already prepared the "official" report of Danan's death; how the coward ruthlessly murdered innocent people to try to save himself and then begged pitifully to be spared. There were affidavits awaiting signatures and a death certificate needing only a time and place to be complete. The Monitor wanted to be certain the martyr myth died with the man.

Less than a day away from city-station two, the captain and commander of the *Hyperion* had fabricated a plausible excuse to dock. Erasing the memory of a shipment of vital life-support components for the new station to be built, they would at least be able to enter the port without undo suspicion. Getting Danan off the ship would be another problem. Mardo's clearance passes would give Walter free access throughout the station, but the initial security check involved a verifier hook-up to an individual's d-chip. That would be a little difficult for a person who didn't have one.

Versions of the stowaway plan were examined, but they needed to have someone in the city they could trust to receive the bogus shipment. Everything was scanned before entering, but there were ways of fooling the detectors, if Walter could stop breathing and keep his heart from beating for the few minutes it took to pass through the entry system. That part would be easy, far easier than sifting through the population records of the vast city.

Walter was in his quarters, trying to compile a list of residents willing to take the risk of receiving a fugitive when his computer informed him that Captain Mardo requested his immediate presence. Walter had been so focused on the details of the escape plan that he failed to detect the tremors of fear and alarm resonating through the ship. As he approached Mardo's quarters, however, his intuition told him there was danger behind the door, as clearly as if warning beacons were flashing in the hall. There was still time to back away, run and hope for a lucky break, but he knew that would only be prolonging the inevitable.

Stepping up to the door and requesting entry, the panel immediately slid back to reveal Mardo, Granny, Kiya and at least two dozen, heavily armed, O.I.T. guards, all of whom had their weapons aimed in his direction. Initially, Walter thought that Kiya had been taken prisoner with the others, until he saw that she also had a weapon, held half-heartedly in Granny and Mardo's direction, but held nonetheless.

As six guards rushed forward to put restraining devices on Walter, Granny saw Kiya's attention had turned to the newest prisoner. Thoroughly infuriated by her treachery, and exasperated by his inability to act since Jesse's capture, Granny seized the opportunity and lunged at the traitor. Before the stun bolts reached the massive man, he had grabbed Kiya's shoulders and flung her the length of the room as if tossing a rag doll. As her tiny figure crashed into the opposite wall and hit the floor with a thud, Granny watched with an ecstatic thrill of victory. A spilt-second later, his towering form fell like a giant redwood as three bolts brought his numbed body to the floor.

"Are you all right, Miss Oku?" the squad leader asked nervously as he lifted the dazed woman to her feet.

Walter and Mardo looked at each other in amazement, feeling somewhat stupid that they hadn't realized the obvious. All along they assumed she worked for Lindquist's organization, but now everything made a lot more sense.

"I, I think I'm in one piece," Kiya Oku replied, testing her joints and flexibility and then hobbling over to where Granny was just rising to his knees, restraining devices safely in place. "I suppose you think I deserved that."

"I was just getting started," he growled, aching for one more throw, preferably toward an open airlock.

Walter, who had yet to speak, casually stepped out of the orange glow of the supposedly impenetrable rings of restraining energy and approached Kiya. She motioned for the shocked guards to hold their fire and looked into his eyes with more remorse than defiance.

"This is your heart's idea of acting in my best interest?" Walter said calmly, but with a look that seemed to burn right through her.

Kiya could say nothing. Words got stuck on the big lump lodged in her throat. Turning away, she listened as the panicked guards reattached the restraining rings and led the three prisoners through the door. It was the most difficult moment of her life, but she had a job to do.

CHAPTER 19

The Council Hall moved majestically through the wide path cleared by the beamcutters. Most of the fireworks flashed directly before the orbiting seat of power, but an occasional beam slashed out at debris approaching from the rear or sides. A few small vehicles made their way, slowly and very carefully, to the general docking area. Those cautious crafts were piloted by minor officials or wealthy citizens trying to be first on line to ask favors from the Council. Most residents of the Hall were still sleeping, but the prospect of preferential treatment from a Monitor was well worth the wait.

Half a dozen transports zipped to and from the docking area with remarkable skill and speed. They were the Council runners, paid minimal salaries to deliver messages by hand and conduct a hundred different odd jobs. Those pilots had the reputation for being capable of navigating blindfolded, which anyone who watched their death-defying maneuvers would think they did on a regular basis. They took big risks for small pay, because corporations and members of the upper circle were always looking for good pilots capable of doing things just a little faster than everyone else. So the runner's pool was a kind of showcase, a minor league where the hotshots could prove themselves and move up to where the real money was to be made. If they lived long enough, that is.

Idrella watched one sleek, shiny, red Laserswift dart past a cloud of ultra fine particles, barrel roll left over a jagged hunk of rock and loop end over end before docking as lightly as a butterfly landing on a flower. That had to be the pilot who brought her back from Mars on her last visit to Jesse, she thought as she put a hand to her stomach, recalling both the nausea and exhilaration. He was known simply as Red, not for the unusual color of his ship, but for the flaming locks of hair that ignited his already intense eyes and searing smile. Red claimed he could fly through a sandstorm and not touch a single grain. His daring and audacity brought him numerous job offers, but he continued to hold out. Some said he was greedy, but his friends knew that Red was merely having too much fun.

In the considerably more carefree days before she joined the Council, Idrella always piloted her own ships. That was a simple pleasure her position and schedule would no longer allow, as there was always an endless stream of reports and correspondences demanding her attention. Of course, with Red at the helm she seldom had much time to concentrate on anything anyway.

"Contact Red for me," Idrella directed and then realized she was sitting by the window in her nightgown and quickly added, "Audio only."

"What can I do for you, Monitor Croix?" asked a cheerful voice, high from the thrill of the flight.

"Are you available after session today?" she asked, wondering if she was in her right mind wishing to fly with Red again.

"It will be my pleasure, Monitor. Taking another spin down to Mars?"

"Yes," she replied, afraid that his choice of words would be accurate. "Can you stand by and be prepared to leave as soon as I'm through?"

"I'll have the 'Red' carpet rolled out and waiting!" he said enthusiastically, remembering that she was one of the most generous tippers, not to mention by far having the prettiest face among the other Council sourpusses.

Since she had gotten up so early, Idrella decided she might as well use the time to catch up on business. Not wanting to leave her comfortable chair to get her handscreen, she requested the day's business to be projected in front of her. A schedule materialized, a mercifully light one after yesterday's nightmare marathon. An innocuous purple asterisk flashing in the upper, right-hand corner caught her eye before she dismissed the schedule. The symbol was usually used to indicate that a Monitor was requesting an addition to the agenda or had special information to be reviewed before the session. Believing it to be another annoying request from Silas, she reluctantly asked for the special point of business to be displayed.

The surprise at seeing that the report was submitted by Oku was nothing compared to the stunning shock of its contents. As terse and hard-hitting as the man himself, the few lines stated that with the aid of his daughter, Kiya, his forces were able to capture Walter Danan and two accomplices on the *Hyperion* and they were on their way back to stand trial.

Red swore that it would be no problem getting Idrella to the Martian Hospital and back in time for the first session. When the initial impact of Danan's capture struck her mind, it also jogged loose the recollection that the assistant supervisor with whom she spoke the night before worked in the maximum security wards. She had no doubt that somewhere there was a connection, and at the very least she wanted to tell Jesse the terrible news before he heard it from a stranger.

Red's ship was at her personal docking port in a matter of seconds after her summons and he was surprised, but not displeased, to welcome aboard the nightgown-clad Monitor carrying a bundle of clothes wrapped in a purple, satin cloak. However, he was more than slightly uneasy when the massive Boa squeezed through the hatch behind his mistress.

Silas had finally managed to get a few hours of sleep. His nagging data/security system had been gutted and replaced by one that didn't care how poorly he ate or slept. It had never interrupted his rest before, so when it began its persistent, but refreshingly soothing, tones at such an early hour, he knew it must be important.

"Sorry to wake you, Monitor, but you did request that you be alerted when any special business was posted," the wonderfully subservient voice apologized.

"Who the hell is posting business at this damn hour?"

"Monitor Oku."

"Display!"

It was a moment he had anticipated since the day Danan disappeared from prison, but now he could taste nothing but bitterness. Shiro Oku, the man who had fought and criticized

Silas every step of the way had now captured his most coveted prize. Like a wild animal that only eats a fresh kill, Lindquist turned up his nose at the news and instead of joy, he felt only fury. He almost wished that Danan was still a free man. Killing him now would not be easy.

Not a piece of furniture that wasn't bolted down escaped his wrath. The obedient computer watched patiently, making note of what items to order as replacements. The leg of a small table caught the back of Caesar's head in its flight across the room. The bust wobbled, looked as if it would settle into place and then took a sudden nosedive. Silas was unable to reach it in time and the marble figure of the great leader shattered at his feet. A few discernible features remained intact, an eye here, a lower lip there, as well as the motto intended to instill humbleness in the observer. The words quickly crumbled to dust beneath his heel, however, and the computer scanned furiously through its data banks in search of a sculptor who specialized in ancient Roman busts.

When he had satisfied some of his wrath on the furnishings, Silas decided to turn to more animate prey. Tilton Maas was the obvious choice, the highly paid master of espionage whose infallibility was becoming more and more of a joke.

"Read this," Silas growled softly when Maas' image appeared.

"That's wonderful...isn't it?" he asked nervously, seeing both the dark scowl on Lindquist's face and the twisted furniture littering the floor.

"Why it's simply divine! Makes me want to run right out and pick posies and sing songs!" he shouted with a force Tilton imagined made the walls tremble.

"But, but Danan, he's been captured. It's what you've wanted."

"What I wanted was a corpse, not a prisoner! And I certainly didn't want a symbol of hope against great odds. I spent a fortune outfitting squads of the most ruthless men and women in the Union and Oku's little girl plucks him right out from under your noses!"

Maas could have argued that Oku's organization was much larger than theirs, or that Kiya lucked out because Danan just happened to be fleeing on one of her father's ships, but he saved his breath. He knew from vast experience that such efforts were about as effective as trying to deflect an oncoming asteroid with a popgun. Silas would not be placated. He would be avenged.

"Perhaps if an unexpected tragedy befell some of the squad leaders, the others would be more diligent next time," Lindquist suggested with a pleasant smile.

Maas hated to lose good operatives, but he knew there was no sense arguing that either. The best he could hope for was that things would settle down now that Danan was captured. He would follow orders, lay low, and watch his back.

Normally, the days began quietly in the Council Hall. Gradually, the rooms filled with lobbyists and supplicants, the Monitors and their staffs appeared promptly at the designated times and the same old routine rolled into motion. This morning, however, began as calmly as a pack of greyhounds out of the starting gate. The few lines of Oku's news exploded across the Union like a supernova and everyone clambered to get more details.

The Hall itself was a hotbed of activity with staff members frantically trying to sort fact from fiction. The only reliable information was Oku's brief statement; the rest was speculation and hearsay. Natalia stood her ground before Oku's door, ignoring equally both the pleas and threats of those wishing to see her master. One low-seniority member of Monitor Rizzic's staff lost his balance in the crowd of people and stumbled forward into the naked midsection of the seductive and terrifying bodyguard. Protesting vehemently that staff members should be treated with respect, he was nonetheless hoisted up by the seat of his pants and tossed to the back of the crowd. The sense of urgency suddenly waned among the bystanders and they either left or retreated to a safer distance down the hall.

When there was only a few minutes before the scheduled beginning of the morning session and Oku still hadn't appeared, the disappointed crowd realized that the Monitor must have taken the private corridor that led directly to the inside of the

Council meeting room. The system of entryways connecting the Monitors' quarters was seldom used to go to meetings. Although they were designed for that official purpose, their actual use historically had been for generally more amorous purposes. The staff members and reporters dispersed, but would gather outside the meeting room later in the day to try again.

****

Between Idrella's authority and Red's talent, they were able to cut through the morning rush hour traffic and reach the hospital in record time. The pilot informed the now properly clad Monitor of the minimum time required to get her back to the Council Hall before she rushed off, boldly striding through the main entrance with her cloak waving behind her like the banner of an invincible army, and Boa looking very much like that army.

It was amazing how quickly elevators emptied of dozens of people to allow the two an unhampered route. Employees and patients alike, darted down other corridors or pressed themselves close to the walls and looked the other way as the clearly enraged Monitor and her even more frightening bodyguard cut a path with their eyes as effectively as if they were beamcutters. Descending straight to the maximum-security level, the door opened to the hapless assistant supervisor, on his way out now that the morning shift had finally arrived.

"Here, please, just take it," he begged Idrella, pressing his handscreen into the palm of her hand. "It has all the information you need. Just leave it with security when you're through, please."

The thoroughly frazzled man ran to the stairwell and disappeared through the door before she could speak. Accessing Jesse's file as they breezed through the security checkpoint, she had a pretty good idea of what had transpired in the last twenty-four hours before she reached his cell.

"Monitor Croix wishes to see the prisoner," Boa said, towering over the guard who was only too happy to unlock the door, and then find an excuse to go to the other end of the level.

Boa opened the door for his mistress and then planted himself before it like a giant oak. It was very doubtful that the regulations regarding only one visitor at a time on the maximum-security level would be enforced in this case. In fact, Boa probably could have thrown a party without anyone saying a word.

Crouched in the corner next to his bed, Jesse's head rested on his knees and he appeared to be asleep. Alternating waves of compassion and anger swept through her, and the Monitor finally had to acknowledge the rising tide of an even stronger emotion as she looked at the pitiable figure. Kneeling on the floor beside him, she placed a tender hand on his forehead and whispered his name. Through sobs and curses, the exhausted and completely demoralized man told her the entire story. Holding him tightly in her arms, she fought back her own tears as she listened to the continuing saga of Jesse's torment and anguish.

"At least Silas told the truth about one thing," she said, raising his face close to hers and wiping the tears from his cheeks. "I do love you."

It would be foolish to think that all the terrible things that had happened were worth this one, precious moment, but Jesse's heart couldn't be convinced of that at that moment. All he knew was that her lips were against his and a surge of warmth, passion and vitality swept through him like wildfire. His receding faculties were thrust back into the present and all the grandiose schemes of a man in love seemed as close to his grasp as the woman in his arms. But in the midst of his ecstasy, Idrella pulled away, unable to completely share Jesse's joy in the light of Oku's announcement.

"Idrella, what's wrong? I thought you-"

"Walter's been captured," she stated slowly, as if each word was painful to pronounce. "And the captain and first officer of the *Hyperion* were also arrested."

There was no easy way to break the news; no amount of preparation would have softened the blow. Idrella felt as if she had just plunged a knife into Jesse's heart, but delaying the truth would have made it worse.

"It's my fault. It's all my fault!" he cried, leaping to his feet and slamming his fists against the unyielding walls. "I don't deserve someone like you. I don't even deserve to live after what I've done!"

"Jesse, stop it!" she commanded with the powerful combination of the voices of a Monitor and a woman in love.

"Lindquist has won already if you believe that. Besides, it was Oku's people who captured him. He had his own daughter on the *Hyperion*, so it was only a matter of time. I'm sure that the information you gave that woman had nothing to do with Walter being taken. It was probably just a coincidence that it happened so soon afterward. Jesse, are you listening to me?"

He had stopped pounding the wall, but was still pressing his palms and forehead against it. While it looked as if Jesse was attempting to push his way to freedom, the real struggle was taking place inside, trying to hold off the crushing weight of despair and remorse. The knowledge that Oku, and not Lindquist, had taken Walter was of little consolation, for he knew the result would ultimately be the same. Not even his love for Idrella could ease the pain of that realization.

"Can anything be done?" Jesse asked in a whisper, turning to face her with rigid features.

"I don't know, but you can be assured I will do everything in my power," she said with strength and conviction.

"But how can you fight Lindquist and Oku?"

"I just might have an ace up my sleeve," Idrella replied as a curious grin spread across her face. "Don't count the Croixs out so soon."

Boa knocked loudly before entering to inform the Monitor that it was almost time to leave. He knew he wasn't the smartest man in the Union, but it was obvious even to him that Jesse wasn't too thrilled to see that a mountain of muscle in a loincloth was escorting Idrella.

"I'll wait outside, Monitor Croix. Sorry for the interruption," Boa said, clearing his throat several times and backing away before Idrella could introduce him.

"Who was that?" Jesse asked, his head still tilted at the angle necessary to look up into the face of the half-naked man.

"Uh, that was just Boa," Idrella replied awkwardly. "He's just my bodyguard, that's all. You know, they're just for show, really."

"Oh, now I *am* disappointed. I thought you were a much better liar than that," Jesse said, managing a thin smile.

Promising to return in the evening, it was the only way Idrella could convince Jesse to let her go. Boa led the way as the two rushed back to the parking bay where Red was revved up and waiting. No sooner had the hatch closed then they were accelerating to a dizzying speed.

"I thought we had conquered the problem of motion sickness," Idrella said with a grimace, placing a hand on either side of her head to make sure it remained on her neck.

"There are always new frontiers to conquer, Monitor Croix," Red laughed, an instant before he did a triple spin to avoid a super-heavy transport, emblazoned with warnings concerning its highly explosive cargo. "That's what makes each day a challenge!"

Idrella wished that Red's enthusiasm was contagious. She would need that boldness, that laughter in the face of danger. What she would do in the following days and weeks might determine the fate of the Union; assuming, of course, that her wild pilot got her back in one piece.

CHAPTER 20

The ship was unlike any in the Union fleet. It could keep pace with the swiftest scout vessels, yet hold its own against the largest gunships. The hull was made of a new material developed by an O.I.T. lab on the fifth city-station, and to put it simply, it redefined the current state of technology.

Rather than cast the material into large plates, it was extruded under enormous pressure through tiny orifices to form filaments. The filaments were spun into threads possessing astounding tensile strength, and they in turn were woven into long sheets half a meter thick. The featherweight, airtight sheets were then "sewn" onto the framework with cables of the material; creating a vessel with half the weight of a conventional craft its size and a heat resistance and flexibility that effectively negated the numerous stress-related problems to which a ship's outer skin was subject. The engineers even claimed that if an asteroid collided with the hull it would just bounce off. That experiment had yet to be tried, however.

The obvious advantage to this lightweight "fabric", was that it allowed the addition of greater payloads, or in the case of this premiere Zeppelin-class ship, christened the *Götterdammerung*, more weapons and bigger engines. It bristled with fourth-generation megacannons and had two, state-of-the-art drives capable of powering a heavy cruiser. Its design was so unique and its construction such a well-guarded secret that even the crew members needed to be convinced that it was not some captured alien vessel.

There was another advantage to the material that had not been anticipated during its conception. Even to scanners specifically calibrated to the new substance, the *Götterdammerung* was almost impossible to identify and track. When any results could be obtained, the scanners best guess was that the massive ship resembled a small piece of wood. Needless to say, the first Union outpost observers to see such a signal on their screens were reluctant to report a wooden vessel speeding through their sector.

"This is going to make the fleet commanders wet their pants!" Mardo shouted with glee as he scanned the specs of the ship on which he was nonetheless a prisoner. "And look, it says here that O.I.T built this years ago. I wonder why they haven't used it until now?"

"I guess Oku was just waiting for a special occasion," Walter replied grimly, unable to share his friend's enthusiasm for a ship which would only hasten their trials, and no doubt, their capital punishment.

Isolation was technically not the death penalty, but it might as well be. As Walter sat with Mardo and Granny in the comfortable quarters which were generously granted to them for the trip back to the Council Hall, he realized it would not be impossible for him to escape again, perhaps even before returning to the Hall. But while he might gain his freedom, he would realistically be unable to liberate his friends at the same time. Jesse was already imprisoned on his account, and Walter would not allow two more people for whom he cared to suffer the same fate while he walked away. Kiya must have been aware of that, because no special precautions were being taken for the fugitive who possessed such unique abilities.

"Seriously, Walter, Oku's not one to sit on anything innovative, especially something like the *Götterdammerung*!" Granny said with a sense of awe as he peered over Mardo's shoulder at the screen. "And why are they allowing us to see all this stuff, anyway?"

"Is there anything to that, Mardo? Is Oku up to something beyond the obvious?" Walter asked with eternally springing hope.

"Oku is always up to *something*," he meant as a joke and then realized the truth of his words. "And now that I think of it, the city-stations have been buzzing about Oku finally making a move to take over, and he hasn't denied it. Nothing Oku does is by coincidence; he knew damn well that all eyes would be on the ship that was carrying you back. I bet this is that clever bastard's way of telling the Union and the other Council members that he can do anything. What a statement, parading the number one fugitive through the system on a ship that makes the Union forces obsolete!"

"And our heads will be the first trophies of Oku's new empire," Granny added with considerably diminished enthusiasm.

What his friends said made a lot of sense, but Walter felt there were pieces missing, some very big pieces. He still could not accept Kiya's treachery, perhaps because he simply didn't want to, or perhaps because the situation was more complex than it appeared. Nothing seemed to add up no matter how he calculated it, which always meant the equation was incomplete.

"I don't know, there's got to be more to it," Walter thought out loud.

Walter closed his eyes and began examining the situation from other angles while Mardo and Granny continued their study of the impressive ship. The two officers were probably each facing a life sentence, but at the moment their only regret was that they would never have command of a ship like the *Götterdammerung*.

****

Red was true to his word and returned Monitor Croix in time for the Council meeting. He received a hefty tip, but didn't realize it was actually Idrella's way of expressing how glad she was to still be alive after the hair-raising trip. Boa simply gave him a dirty look, which was far less threatening than intended because of the green cast to the giant's skin and the obvious facial contortions of queasiness. Red could never understand his passengers; he felt nothing but exhilaration and the desire to go right back out and do it again.

Monitor Croix straightened her rumpled clothes and hair and hurried to the meeting room. She had never seen such a large crowd in the Hall before and Boa had to "assert" himself to clear a path for his mistress. Eight Monitors were already seated and as she took her place, Oku emerged from the private entrance. There was nothing in his expression or posture that signaled that this was anything more than just another day to him. Taking his seat, he glanced at the agenda and then looked up to speak. They all braced themselves.

"Monitor Rizzic, I must apologize for the rough treatment of your staff member this morning. Natalia doesn't always know her own strength," he said with a polite smile. "Now, shall we begin?"

The other nine members of the circle didn't move, or speak, expecting that Oku would next present a more detailed report of Danan's capture. Only the muted rhythms of the ancient clock beat softly in their ears, and when he failed to speak for two full minutes, M'bai and Lindquist couldn't stand it anymore.

"Well?" they both blurted out simultaneously.

"Aren't you going to say something about Walter Danan?" M'bai continued.

"There's not much more to say," Oku replied as if surprised. "I was spared the embarrassment of a convicted criminal escaping on one of my vessels. And now the *Götterdammerung* is bringing him back as quickly as possible, which should be about two weeks."

No one had yet heard about the new ship so Oku's reference to it meant nothing. The return time seemed short, but there were small craft capable of the required speed.

"Has he been hurt?" Idrella tried to ask casually.

"I can assure you, Monitor Croix, that all three prisoners are being well treated. I will allow nothing to happen to them while they are in *my* custody," Oku stated with emphasis, clearly taking a stab at Lindquist's handling of Jesse.

"Why haven't you turned them over to Union authorities?" Lindquist asked, aching to tear his grinning adversary limb from limb.

"He is quite safe on my ship. Quite safe," Oku replied, widening his smile.

There were a few more general questions, with equally general answers and it was obvious Oku was not going to show any more cards in his hand. He was probably the only man in the

Union who would prefer to make everyone think he had successfully bluffed, rather than show that he was holding a royal flush.

"Since Monitor Oku has no further tales to tell," Idrella said shifting her attention, and consequently everyone else's, to Silas, "perhaps Monitor Lindquist would like to fill us in on the bedtime story of Jesse Dimont?"

"In lieu of the fact that Danan is already in custody, thanks to Monitor Oku's brilliant work, I don't think that insignificant event is even worth mentioning," Silas replied, knowing full well that Idrella was not going to let him off the hook.

"Don't be so humble, Monitor. It's not every day that a Council prisoner is released in a fake escape attempt in order to obtain information from him," she announced to her peers, who instantly exploded into a volley of questions.

Idrella sat back and let the others grill Lindquist. During his lengthy interrogation, Idrella felt as if she was being watched and glanced over to Oku who was studying her intensely. Even when she returned the direct gaze, he persisted unabashedly. A smile spread across his face, not the usual sarcastic or condescending smile, but one of honesty, approval, in essence, a look of genuine friendship.

Idrella and Oku had never shared anything but professional respect for one another's abilities, and on her side, fear of her mightier colleague.

"I said, Monitor Croix, are you satisfied with my report?" Lindquist was apparently asking for at least the second time.

"Excuse me?" she replied, breaking the momentary spell and returning her focus to the proceedings. "Oh yes, of course, I would like to study your official report later."

"Naturally," he said, wondering what had just transpired between his greatest enemies.

While Lindquist's methods were unconventional, to say the least, they were unexpectedly within the bounds of legality. In fact, his boldness was actually applauded by several Council members. Idrella had hoped for a crucifixion, but was so preoccupied and puzzled by Oku's silent communication that she wasn't upset when her plan backfired. Lindquist was also surprised by the responses and so encouraged that he decided to have his network do a special. If Oku had nothing to say about his work, he would certainly make up for it by showcasing his own.

"Now that we have spent an hour discussing a few individuals, could we please spend at least a few minutes on the other billions of citizens for which we are responsible?" Oku asked, sounding utterly bored and fatigued by the affair. "I don't know about the rest of you, but I'm looking forward to a vacation."

The current Council session was scheduled to adjourn in three weeks. There would be four glorious months of peace and quiet, or raucous, non-stop entertainment for those who preferred, for the Monitors to discover new ways of relieving the pressure of their ponderous bank accounts. No Council in history had ever worked past adjournment date, and Oku's subtle announcement reminded the other members that they did not wish to set precedence, either.

While the Council agreed to put the Danan case on a shelf until the fugitives arrived, the rest of the Union couldn't get enough. Lindquist supporters were shouting ultimate victory, while Danan supporters were whispering that they could not be defeated. The aura of mystery grew around the man who challenged the worlds and regardless of the outcome many already were bestowing Danan with the status of a legend. Of course, few had more than the most elementary understanding of his work, but Walter was actually living a life that others only experienced in a d-chip fantasy. Even if there was a lack of understanding, Danan and his story meant excitement, a rare commodity in their predictable lives.

Wagering rebounded to a frenzied pace with all those who had nullified their bets returning with double and triple the original amounts. Despite Lindquist's exalted position and Danan's precarious predicament, odds were running low in the feud wagering, sparking even wilder speculation. One computerized bookmaking house had calculated that Danan should actually be favored, but they prudently chose to ignore the results for fear that the numerous Lindquists on the Union Fair Gambling Commission would revoke their license.

But if the "Mind Over Matter Melee", as the Danan-Lindquist feud was dubbed, had electrified the populace, the startling revelation of the *Götterdammerung* would elevate that excitement level to a frenzied pitch. When a full forty-eight hours had elapsed without anyone noticing the ship cruising right through the heart of the shipping lanes, the captain was ordered to stop at a supply depot on a flimsy pretext. Several crewmembers were instructed to mingle with the residents in the station lounge and let a few facts about the vessel "slip out". Two hours later as the ship pulled out of port, the name *Götterdammerung* was resounding through the length and breadth of a trembling Union.

Chapter 21

Dinner sat on the table, the rising steam from the once piping-hot food long ago cooled to an unpalatable clamminess. Nothing on the tray had been touched, except for a few grapes torn from the bunch and chewed slowly and deliberately. The discovery of the *Götterdammerung*, which had so alarmed her colleagues, brought an inexplicable thrill of anticipation and hope to Idrella. That single look from Oku seemed to transform him from a dreaded enemy to, potentially, a powerful ally. And who wouldn't want an ally to possess such a vessel, or a fleet of them for that matter?

Reading and rereading every file on Danan, Jesse, the *Hyperion* and the recent trouble throughout the Union, Idrella's mind sorted and evaluated every scrap of information. There wasn't anything to be gained from Oku's file; it contained nothing more than the standard dates and achievements that accompanied every press release. But his daughter's file was another story. Kiya's Intelligence Potential was in the first percentile and she held enough education certificates to outfit a university. Not all her interests were technical, however, as her list of publications showed a distinct tendency toward the esoteric. What a coincidence, Idrella thought with a smirk, that Kiya Oku just happened to be the one to find Walter Danan.

Tackling the series of codes required to open her personal safe, she knew her plan would be the biggest gamble of her life. Removing a platinum attaché sealed with magnetic locks, she placed her thumbs over the print verifiers in each corner and opened the case to check the contents for the tenth time since her father gave it to her. Sliding a square, green button on the left side of the device within the case, Idrella felt reassured by the soft glow that appeared on the screen which a moment later displayed the word, "READY".

"I certainly hope so!" she said on the exhale of a deep breath. Switching off the device, she resealed the case and took one more deep breath before speaking again. "Inform Monitor Oku that I wish to meet with him in private."

"Monitor Oku is not commenting on the *Götterdammerung* at this time," the computer-generated voice reported after a minute.

"Tell Monitor Oku I don't give a damn about the ship, in fact, I'm glad he has it. Tell him I have something that just might put the icing on his cake!" she declared boldly.

There was a few minutes of silence as the odd message was being transmitted and, no doubt, puzzled over.

"Monitor Oku is curious to see your recipe, but he requests you come by way of the private corridor and leave Boa behind," the computer replied, much to Idrella's delight.

She had played a hunch, threw out a piece of bait and discovered that Oku was definitely biting. Private meetings with him were rare and his insistence on secrecy emphasized the uniqueness and importance of the occasion. As she left her quarters by way of the private exit, confidence punctuated each stride and if she could have seen herself, Idrella might have recognized a sparkle in her eyes not unlike a certain flame-haired pilot.

****

As the *Götterdammerung* retraced the *Hyperion*'s path back through the system, a thousand eyes were upon it, or at least, they tried to be upon it. Defense stations attempted to keep a constant watch on the ship's progress, but the anomalous scanner readings the ship produced often had them tracking nothing more than space flotsam. That fact created even more panic, as every particle of debris now came under suspicion. Oku's single ghost ship seemed to multiply a thousand-fold across the length and breadth of the system, as well as in the deepest recesses of the minds of his enemies.

The Union fleet was dispersed to find the *Götterdammerung* and after several days, one Union squadron finally stumbled upon the bizarre ship, making visual contact with the huge vessel their scanners insisted was not there. Keeping a discreet distance, the squadron fanned out around the *Götterdammerung* under the pretext of an official escort. A large contingent of Oku's conventional fleet then positioned themselves around the Union ships, forming an offensive sphere, ready to descend upon the Union ships if they imprudently made a move on the *Götterdammerung*. So, in the configuration of mutual distrust, they rolled through the system like a giant snowball, gathering more ships and more tension with every passing kilometer.

****

"Anything new today?" Mardo asked between a stretch and a yawn as he emerged from his bedroom into the central living area.

"Everyone's still breathing down everyone else's neck," Granny replied from his seat at the information terminal, his words slightly garbled because of something in his mouth.

"What is that you're stuffing into your face?"

"Cherries!" Granny declared, tossing his friend a handful that even a juggler wouldn't have been able to catch. "The sweetest, juiciest cherries I've ever had."

"Where did they come from?" Mardo asked, his teeth sinking into the moist, pitless flesh of the one to which he had managed to hold on.

"That wonderful woman, Kiya," Granny growled through gritted teeth as he squeezed the guts out of an innocent cherry. "Sweets from the sweet!"

"I bet she took the transport pod of fruit from the *Hyperion*," Mardo said as he gathered the precious orbs from the floor. "Is this her lame attempt at a peace offering, or a last supper for the condemned?"

They knew Kiya had taken command of the *Götterdammerung* when it reached the *Hyperion*, but she hadn't dared to show her face to those she had betrayed. The carton of fruit delivered with the simple note, "Compliments of the Captain", was the first acknowledgment of her presence. Any information they had received had been from junior officers and members of the medical staff who checked them every other day. It was always a point of bitter irony, the age-old custom of making sure prisoners were in perfect health before they were shot.

"How's life on the chain gang this morning?" Walter asked from the doorway of his room.

"A present from the warden," Mardo said, winging a cherry across the room. "I guess it was the least she could do for ruining our lives."

"Damn decent gesture," Walter laughed, tossing the piece of fruit in the air and deftly catching it in his mouth. "Very civilized of her."

"What are you in such a good mood about?" Granny asked, seeing Danan smile for the first time since their capture.

"I don't know, Gran, but something feels different. Maybe I just had a good night's sleep, or maybe the pressure is finally getting to me," he laughed again, messing his hair up into a mad scientist coiffure.

"Well, whatever it is, how about spreading it around?" Mardo said, leaping over the back of the couch and settling down for another of Danan's lessons.

Walter had been teaching Mardo and Granny some of the basics of his theories and they had already shown some positive results. It was like the tranquil feeling that pervaded the *Hyperion*, only now the two officers were able to generate traces of that feeling themselves. Their progress had certainly been a boost to Walter, but he knew the real lift came from Kiya. Even after all she had done, Walter knew without a doubt that she was still practicing all the techniques he had taught her. He was tempted to try to walk through a couple of walls to see her, but decided that the initiative must be hers.

Jesse's condition was also encouraging. The cries of anguish had been replaced by a growing confidence and strength that made Walter suspect that Jesse was not facing his ordeal alone. He imagined that his brother-in-law had taken a shine to one of the medical staff, or perhaps a petite security guard who displayed her weapons at an alluring angle. After all, it had to be someone on staff, Walter reasoned, because the only other people with the clearance to visit such a prisoner without special permission were the Monitors themselves. He toyed with that thought for a moment and then laughed it away, proving even living legends weren't infallible.

****

Much to Rial's horror, Council warrant prisoner Jesse Dimont and Monitor Idrella Croix were officially a hot item in the upper circle gossip parties. Despite a lifetime of despicable behavior, she felt that it was her daughter who had brought shame to the family name. Complaining bitterly to her husband Justinian, Rial claimed that she would rather leave the Croixs and retake her maiden name than suffer the humiliation of Idrella's disgraceful behavior.

Instead of sympathy, Justinian produced a lawyer on the spot and concluded the divorce before a dumbfounded Rial had time to think twice. Quickly convincing herself that her foolish husband would be begging to get her back the next day, she packed a few things and went to her ancestral home. The next day, a transport full of crates arrived to deliver the remainder of her belongings. After a stunned gasp, Rial fainted. In the Croix household, for the first time in decades, Justinian felt like he could breathe again.

Expecting that Silas' shoulder would be available to cry upon, as well as having plans for the rest of his body, Rial called the Monitor late that evening. Sobbing and wailing as she detailed her plight, Silas listened patiently until she got to the part about the divorce.

"You signed? You mean you're no longer a Croix?" he demanded more than asked.

"Well, of course not, dear, that's what I've been trying to tell you," she said with trepidation, shocked by the violent response. "But all that means is that I'm now free for us to be together."

"All that means, you repulsive leech, is that you are no longer any use to me. All that means, is that you've gone from belonging to one of the most powerful, influential families to being nothing but a...Forget it, Rial, you're not worth a slander suit."

Stabbing at the transmission disconnect button with a triumphant finger, Silas mused that it was the most satisfying movement of their brief relationship. Without the Croix name to wield, Rial's ability to gather information from intimidated underlings would vanish. And now that Idrella's traditional filial obligations to her mother had been legally dissolved, there would be no chance of obtaining anymore inside information on his adversary.

For the first time in her life, Rial felt as if *she* had been used, but was able to console herself with the thought that she still had enough money and talent to continue her lifestyle, albeit somewhat diminished in stature. And in time, she would probably convince herself that Justinian and Silas were stricken with remorse and would regret losing her with their dying breaths.

****

Idrella and Jesse were once again together in the decidedly unromantic setting of his maximum-security cell. They at least had the ability to speak in privacy thanks to the field generated by the disks perched on their shoulders, but the circumstances were definitely not conducive to much more than talking.

"When will Walter arrive?" Jesse asked the instant the blue haze of the field snapped on.

"They are scheduled to dock in forty-six hours," she replied nervously, paused, and then added, "Are you sure you don't want to know anymore?"

"Absolutely not," he emphasized by waving his hands back and forth in front of his chest. "If you or anyone else has a plan, I'm the last person to tell."

"Jesse, please don't think that you-"

"It's true, and you know it. They've tricked me once, and I don't intend to have anything to tell them if they trick me again. Idrella, we're all safer this way. What if they send in a surgically altered double of you and I can't tell the difference?"

Leaning forward, she gave him a long, passionate kiss. He was sure the privacy field was going to short circuit.

"If anyone else can do *that*, tell her anything she wants to know," Idrella whispered sensuously in Jesse's ear, half-sorry she ignited a fire that she was not in a position to quench.

"This is the cruelest torture of all, Monitor Croix," Jesse accused with a sigh. "I suppose security would figure it out if they saw a blue blob of light rolling around on the bed?"

"It wouldn't take a rocket scientist," she laughed, trying to cool her own jets. "Look, Jesse, I'm certainly no prude, but-"

"I know, I know. Showing a bunch of surveillance technicians a good time is not exactly my idea of a romantic interlude, either. I just wish..."

"Hold that thought, Jesse. I'll see you as soon as the trial is over. Wish us luck!" she said, rising to leave while she still could.

"Wait! Please tell Walter...tell him...I'm sorry."

There were a dozen things she wanted to tell Jesse to ease the anguish in his words and eyes. But she simply nodded her head and left, praying that the next time they met, everything would be different. Everything.

Chapter 22

Faces throughout the Council Hall were pressed against every available viewing portal as the *Götterdammerung* made its final approach. Distant beamcutters, like a string of lighthouses, cut a huge path for the mighty vessel. Everyone had already seen images of it a hundred times on the news, but this was something that had to be observed in person to be truly appreciated, and believed. There was a terrifying, gothic beauty about it; a long, pointed-arch hull embellished with intricate tracery and mysterious raised features of lace-like delicacy. It was almost a hypnotic vision, a transcendental work of art, until one realized that every curve outlined the deadly lips of a megacannon. There was no innocence to be found in a single wisp of its architecture.

Its sheer size was also frightening. This ship had returned in roughly the same time it would have taken a stripped, four-man fighter, and there were no assurances that the *Götterdammerung* had even approached its top speed. But here was a vessel with a crew of hundreds, with cargo bays capable of carrying enormous payloads. It had been assumed that the bays were empty for the flight, but as the most important members of the Union looked on in horror, the bay doors slid open and dozens of one-man fighters spewed out, like tiny insects bursting from their mother's belly.

Warning sirens screeched throughout the Hall and Union forces scrambled to defense positions. The nimble fighters swarmed like gnats around the huge, orbiting complex, darted through formations of government ships with dizzying speed, looped back to the *Götterdammerung* and disappeared back into the bays. The entire display seemed to take less than the blink of an eye, and surely less time than a single breath, but that was only because so many had their breaths frozen in their throats.

The sirens stopped and were replaced by Oku's voice ringing throughout the Hall. Assuring everyone that it had merely been a demonstration, he stressed that there was absolutely nothing to worry about.

"After all, for two weeks I have been besieged by requests for information about the ship," Oku continued with an unmistakable tone of amusement, "So, I thought, what better way to present my new fighter carrier than by displaying the fighters?"

"Fighter carrier?" M'bai gasped, digging her triangular-cut nails into the fabric of her sofa, from where she had had a bird's-eye view of the spectacle. "My god, if that thing is just a transport, what is the rest of the fleet like?"

The dozen members of the Monitor's staff watching with her, suddenly all thought that it might be a good time to request a vacation or seek other employment. It was already accepted that if there was one such vessel, Oku would no doubt have an entire fleet hidden somewhere. But the revelation that the *Götterdammerung* was merely a beast-of-burden and not the flagship was almost too terrifying to fathom.

"I want an analysis of those fighters immediately," she shouted. "Are they of the same material, what is their firepower, what kind of drive do they have?"

The composition of the fighter's hulls was apparently similar enough to the mother ship so that the Hall's scanners were unable to gather any coherent data. As far as the security network was concerned, nothing more than a shower of wood chips had exited the *Götterdammerung*.

"What do you mean there's nothing to report?" Lindquist bellowed at his new computer. "A swarm of fighters just passed so close that I could see the pilot's tonsils and you tell me you didn't get any readings?"

"I believe that is what I just said," the computer replied icily, not realizing how close it was to suffering the fate of its predecessor.

"Damn him!" Silas shouted as blood rushed to his cheeks and temples. "Damn that conniving bastard Oku! He had better deliver Danan for the interrogation or I swear I'll turn the beamcutters on his precious ship."

The idea soothed his anger and cooled the molten fury he needed to keep in check for the trial. It had been decided to begin the proceedings as soon as the vessel docked in order to minimize any possible escape plans. Silas assumed the sentence for the three prisoners was a foregone conclusion and a smile actually returned to his face when he realized that by this time tomorrow, Walter Danan could be streaking out of the system in an isolation pod. The image so delighted him that after a moment he broke into a fit of joyous laughter.

"Let Oku play his games!" he declared boldly. "Once Danan is gone, I can concentrate on the other little ants beneath my feet."

Grinding his heel into the carpet, lost in a rapturous vision of power and glory, the threat of the *Götterdammerung* dwindled into insignificance. The universe itself had singled him out for a higher purpose, and nothing could change that no matter how many killer rabbits Oku pulled out of his hat.

****

"Interrogation proceedings will begin in exactly one hour," a voice announced throughout the Hall. "All proceedings will be confidential. Security will be upgraded to level one, repeat, level one. No one will be permitted to leave residential sections. You have one hour to conclude your business and leave the Council meeting area."

Security personnel were urging outsiders to get to their transports and leave immediately. Only staff members and full-time station support crews were allowed to remain and those not on duty were prohibited from leaving their quarters. Guards and Peacemakers were posted every few yards and nonessential areas were sealed off. Paranoia was the order of the day, and no one could decide who was the greatest threat on the menu, Danan, Lindquist or Oku.

When Monitor Lindquist entered the meeting room, he felt a keener sense of anticipation, a stronger rush of adrenaline, than the day of his inauguration. Pride swelled within him as he realized he was the culmination of generations of Lindquist hopes and dreams. He imagined his great-grandfather Harod was with him, inside of him savoring the sweet taste of revenge his mighty descendant had made possible for all the members of the family forced to endure the disgrace the Danan's had inflicted.

Silas had not actually seen Walter for almost two decades. Despite the recent images available in Danan's general file, Silas still pictured him as the awkward outcast with the "dirty genes". Lindquist scoffed at the reports of remarkable powers and refused to believe a word that portrayed his enemy as anything but a treacherous charlatan. Meeting him face to face after so many years would be a great pleasure in itself; the inferior freak of nature forced to confront the magnificence of genetic perfection.

Idrella shook her head in disgust as she watched Silas strut into the room and take his seat, with the now trademark flip of the cloak over one shoulder. There was blood in his eyes and a snarling smile twisting across his lips, as if he was about to dine on the carcass of his prey. The other Monitors were too preoccupied with Oku and the *Götterdammerung* to notice Lindquist. For that matter, the emergence of the fighters had struck such terror in them that they really didn't give a damn about Danan at the moment.

"May I remind my distinguished colleagues of the historic importance of this day?" Lindquist said with enough force to draw their scattered attentions. "We are about to conduct the interrogation of Walter Danan and his conspirators, not to discuss Oku's new toy."

"A few more toys like that and we can all kiss the Council good-bye," Rizzic declared to the agreement of the majority. "You had better reassess your priorities. Danan is harmless by comparison to this."

Monitor Rizzic pointed a trembling finger at the ghastly apparition filling the length of their expansive window. All the *Götterdammerung* lacked, in her eyes, was a bony hand wielding a scythe, although she half-expected one to emerge from the hull at any moment.

"Harmless!" Lindquist shouted, but quickly harnessed both his words and temper when he saw Oku entering the meeting room.

The entire Council sat stiffly as if the teacher had just walked in on an unruly class. Lindquist boiled inside, however, furious that on his day of victory Oku had stolen the limelight. He was sure the sole purpose of the fighter display was to spoil his moment of triumph. As Oku took his place, he signaled for the prisoners to be brought in. Idrella and Silas tensed, but the other Monitors were still so clearly distracted that some weren't even looking when the three men entered.

First in, flanked on either side by guards, was Granny, a towering sculpture of a man with defiance chiseled into every rock-hard feature. Next came Mardo, still dignified in his Captain's dress uniform despite the glowing restraining bands that encircled him. After half a dozen more guards entered, Walter Danan stepped through the doorway, accompanied by a strange surge of energy that struck everyone's solar plexus like a solid object. While the others felt lightheaded and energized by the jolt, Lindquist experienced it solely as a flood of disgust.

Walter was still dressed in his plain, blue *Hyperion* coveralls, bearing a patch with the name Recone and a pair of green stripes on the collar to denote the level his alias possessed in the botany department. There was a look of supreme tranquility on his face, in stark contrast to most of the Council members. Walter's gaze fixed on Lindquist and didn't waver as he moved across the room and took his place beside Mardo and Granny. Silas felt his skin crawl, and the unpleasant tingling didn't stop even after he forced himself to look away from the prisoner. He still steadfastly refused to believe the reports, but there was something about Danan, something obviously dangerous. Lindquist hated to admit it, but this was not the same helpless boy he persecuted with such delight in his youth.

Idrella was overwhelmed by Walter's presence. The sparks of light she had sensed from Jesse were like blinding beacons radiating from Danan. She was filled with shame and remorse that this was the same man she had so callously condemned only a year ago. As if reading her mind, Walter turned to her and smiled warmly. Idrella felt a wave of strength that dispelled any doubts about her future course of action.

"I conducted a brief, preliminary interrogation of the prisoners a short time ago aboard the *Götterdammerung*, as was my right," Oku added quickly, daring Lindquist to object when he had conducted his own investigation of Jesse. "There will be no need for a lengthy trial. Walter Danan will freely submit to isolation on two simple conditions."

"Conditions! Danan is in no position to do anything but accept our sentence," Lindquist shouted, pounding the table with his fist, a murderous crimson flushing his cheeks.

"You underestimate your old friend, Monitor Lindquist," Oku said as he pointed to the prisoners.

Once again, Walter stepped out of the restraining rings as if they were a mirage. Walking directly toward Lindquist, he stopped only a few meters away when the momentarily surprised guards threatened to shoot.

"How does he keep *doing* that?" one of the nervous and frustrated guards complained to his equally spooked comrades.

"You can do what you want with me, Silas, but I refuse to let you continue to make others suffer because of your hatred for me," Walter said with restrained, but still potent, power. Lindquist could do nothing but stare dumbly and blink. "I did not kill my wife Valery. I wish the official record to be cleared of that charge. These two men who helped me are guilty of nothing more than loyalty and friendship. If they are shown leniency and my first condition is met, I will walk into that isolation pod immediately. If not, well, if not, I'll make things *very* interesting."

After looking each Monitor directly in the eye, Walter returned to his spot and stepped back into the restraining rings. The sight was too much for the frazzled nerves of the majority of the Council and the last thing they wanted was any more surprises. Deferring to Oku, they asked his opinion on the request.

"It seems quite reasonable, in lieu of our clever prisoner's unique abilities. His admission of treasonous activities and previous escape are sufficient to condemn him to isolation. The murder charge is inconsequential. As to the Captain and Commander of my ship the *Hyperion*, I naturally feel a personal responsibility for their actions. If they were to be released into my custody, I would be willing to save the Union the expense and personally see to their rehabilitation."

"They're just as guilty of treason!" Silas protested vehemently. "We must stamp out all of Danan's supporters, once and for all."

"Don't you have anything else to worry about?" Rizzic said impatiently.

"I agree with Oku, too," M'bai chimed in, not deeming it a wise course of action to openly oppose the man currently carrying the biggest stick.

"And what about you, Monitor Croix?" Silas asked with a sneer, realizing she was unnaturally quiet. "Surely, you aren't just going to sit there and not even lift a finger to help your precious miracle worker."

"The law is the law," she stated with no emotion. "Danan admits his guilt. Let's just get it over with, strike him from the records and get on with our lives."

Idrella was referring to what was commonly called the "Moses Law". The moment a prisoner was blasted into deep space in an isolation pod, he officially was never born. Except for the central file and a record of Council proceedings, the name of the prisoner was eliminated from every school, company, charge account, health club; anything that he ever owned or accomplished. It was that little extra touch, the insult added to injury to make sure the memory of the prisoner did not live on. Walter Danan's name would be stricken from the records and legally he would cease to exist.

"We all seem to be in agreement," Oku said, looking at Lindquist and waving his hand in a circle. "Will you delay the sentence by quibbling about two insignificant individuals and a meaningless charge?"

Silas didn't really care about Mardo and Granny. He would have preferred to see them isolated, but he imagined Oku would make things sufficiently unpleasant for them. The murder of Valery Danan was another story. If Walter were officially cleared of the charge, that meant the case would be reopened. Even though Dr. Frye had been silenced, Silas didn't want any fingers pointing at him. Yet, if he protested too much that would also attract suspicion. It was not the one hundred percent satisfaction for which he had hoped, but the annihilation of Walter Danan would still provide an exhilarating ninety-nine.

"No. I do not wish to give this dangerous criminal another minute of hope. I agree," Lindquist said with a tone and expression of pure hatred.

Danan's expression didn't alter as the official vote to eliminate him was cast. Mardo and Granny stood silently by, unable to protest beneath the mouth restraints. A look of deep sadness filled their eyes and an anger that Lindquist could almost taste as he viewed the two helpless conspirators.

"By a unanimous vote," the Council computer announced coldly, "the Captain and Commander of the *Hyperion* will be placed into Monitor Oku's custody. Walter Danan, in accordance with section three of the criminal code, will be placed in isolation at the earliest possible date. The case is now closed."

Normally, it would take at least several days to carry out the ultimate sentence, but Lindquist just happened to have an isolation pod already prepared. Union experts would examine it thoroughly, however, checking to make sure the food generation and life support systems were fully operational. There was sufficient reason to suspect Lindquist might have tampered with the pod, but they couldn't know that he wanted Danan to live a long, long time, the pain and misery of isolation slowly driving him insane. It was a thought Lindquist wanted to savor the rest of his life.

"While we are sweeping out the trash," Lindquist began with a gloating smile, "may I request we conclude the Dimont case also? I think my little ruse proved his competence, such as it is."

Granny strained beneath the energy rings, but the best he could manage was a muffled growl. Mardo surely would have spit at Lindquist if he wasn't restrained.

"But Monitor Lindquist, we couldn't possibly do that. Further interrogation of Jesse Dimont would violate Council Amendment thirty-seven, section E," Idrella reported casually, leaning back in her chair with an expression of satisfaction that proved she was not beneath gloating herself.

"What the hell?" Silas snarled, summoning the obscure code from the computer while glaring at Croix.

"Council Amendment thirty-seven, section E states," the computer began, "that whereas Council members are exempt from prosecution of any offense, except for that of murder in the first degree, so too is the spouse or declared intended spouse of a Council member currently in office. In the case of-"

"Silence!" Lindquist shouted as his breaking point seemed a mere hair's breadth away. "Spouse, Idrella? Are you actually expecting us to believe that you and that-"

"I hereby state for the official record my Declaration of Intent to marry Jesse Dimont," Idrella stated, rising to her feet and pronouncing every word with defiance and emphasis.

A gasp rose from the circle and no one seemed to know quite how to react. Finally, Oku chuckled and applauded several times.

"Well, if my rude colleagues can't speak, may I extend you my congratulations at this happy announcement. It appears, Monitor Lindquist, that Monitor Croix has found the one loophole in your plan. But cheer up, you should consider yourself fortunate that she's not marrying Walter Danan!"

Oku's joke did not pacify the enraged Lindquist. Leaping from his chair, his blind fury carried him around the table toward Idrella. The guards' attention was focused on the prisoners, but the security sensors detected threatening intent and instantly produced a holding screen around Silas, stopping him only a meter away from her. Lights flashed, sirens sounded and guards and Monitors collided, as all hell broke loose. Not even Oku's voice of reason could be heard over the confusion. Fortunately, the computer took the necessary steps.

Screens were energized around everyone and the computer ordered silence in a booming voice. Never in the history of the Council Hall had such measures had to be taken and no one was quite sure what would happen next.

"The holding screens will be deactivated in thirty seconds. Anyone persisting in what could be interpreted as an aggressive action will be further restrained and incapacitated, if necessary," the computer stated with complete authority.

The seconds ticked by on the grandfather clock with tense anticipation. Then one by one, the screens faded. No one dared move at first, but then M'bai cautiously took the first step and returned to her seat with as much dignity as she could muster. Walking slowly back to their places, all eyes still remained on Lindquist who had yet to move.

"My apologies, Monitor Croix," he finally said with a gracious bow, his rage bottled up within his fragile, diplomatic veneer. "My actions are inexcusable. You can understand the shock, given the nature of our past relationship, of course."

"Of course," she replied with identical, icy cordiality. "It was callous of me to make such an announcement in that manner."

"My apologies also to my fellow Council members," Silas continued humbly. "A Monitor should never allow personal affairs to interfere with one's duty. Since our business is now concluded, I beg you to excuse me."

Bowing again, and then heading for the door, he paused in front of Danan and gave him a vicious look.

"As for you," Silas said in a whisper, "I will be there to personally push the button to send you to hell!"

Chapter 23

Idrella spoke briefly to Walter in his holding cell before leaving the Council Hall for Mars. After Lindquist had left the meeting, she had requested the visit to relay a final message from Jesse to his doomed brother-in-law. Messages and personal meetings were often allowed the condemned, a gracious act of compassion before the authorities sent the prisoner to a horrible end.

Boa thought he had seen his mistress in every conceivable mood, under a full range of conditions. But when she exited Walter's cell, there were so many emotions fighting for control of her features that he barely recognized her. By the time they made it back to her quarters, however, the professional face had taken control and she was once again the determined Monitor.

The faithful bodyguard waited reluctantly by the hatch to Red's ship while Idrella went to her study. Opening the case to the transmitter, she deftly entered a series of codes that she had painstakingly committed to memory. Holding her breath, she entered the final command and sighed with joy and relief when the unit responded. It indicated that all systems were functional and the program would commence as soon as the desired coordinates were entered. Triple checking the calculations on her handscreen, she punched in the data and like a skilled programmer, crossed her fingers and prayed. Leaving the unit to its work on her desk, she raced to join Boa and an ever-anxious Red.

"Get in there, you big baby," Idrella laughed as she slapped Boa playfully on the rear end, trying to urge her reluctant bodyguard into the ship. "Oops, I better cut that out, I'm almost a married woman."

"Excuse me, Monitor Croix?" Boa said as if his mistress had just lost her senses.

"Don't worry, I'll explain everything during the flight. That is, if Red gives me the time."

Red couldn't resist a quick pass around the *Götterdammerung* before heading for the hospital. He was practically drooling over the controls as his eye traced what to him were the seductive features of power and speed. Since its initial disclosure two weeks earlier, he had spent every free minute poring over all the technical reports available. For the first time since becoming a Council runner, he had found something he would rather do.

"I would work for free if I could pilot a ship like that!" Red dreamed out loud as he completed his pass around the *Götterdammerung*.

"I'll put in a good word for you with Oku," Idrella said before launching into her lengthy explanation to Boa.

Red was so excited by her offer that he went even faster and strayed even further out of the beamcutters' cleared path. Both passengers tried not to notice and Idrella sorely regretted her remark.

The second night shift was on duty at the hospital when they arrived and Idrella requested to see the now-familiar assistant supervisor. She was informed that the poor man was on medical leave due to a nervous condition and she was given the acting supervisor's name and location. Letting Boa enter first, Idrella followed to find a young, dark-haired woman barely out of her teens cowering behind her desk.

"Are you the acting supervisor," Idrella asked, peering over the edge of the desk at the frightened woman.

"Monitor Croix! Yes, yes, that's me. I, I was just looking for something I dropped. What can I do for you? Anything I can do, just ask!" she declared rapidly in semi-hysteria.

"I'm here to obtain the release of Jesse Dimont," she replied, motioning for Boa to wait outside so the woman wouldn't lose consciousness. "Sorry about the scare tactics, its just that we've encountered resistance here before."

The Monitor placed a round, fist-sized box on the desk, bearing the Council emblem on the lid. Inside was a data crystal containing the authorization for the release, which Idrella placed on the desk with great satisfaction. After inserting the crystal into her handscreen with trembling fingers, the acting assistant supervisor reviewed the order.

"Looks fine to me," she concluded after two or three seconds. "I'll inform the guards. Take him away as soon as you would like."

"Thank you, I will," Idrella said and then added before leaving, "And you can tell your boss I won't be back."

A guard was waiting in front of Jesse's cell. When he saw Boa coming, he unlocked the door and hurried away. Idrella's pulse quickened and she fought to keep the tears from building in the corners of her eyes. Opening the door, Jesse rushed to greet her with only one thought on his mind.

"Walter! What's happened to Walter and the others!"

"I'm sorry, Jesse, there was nothing I could do for Walter," she replied, watching the impact of her words bring him to his knees. "But Mardo and Granny have been spared, isolation at least. Oku will be taking care of them."

"When?" he asked blankly, referring to Walter's sentence.

"I'm afraid any minute now," she whispered, lowering herself to the floor and placing the privacy disk on his shoulder and activating the field. "But Walter told me to tell you he will personally kick your butt if you give up hope!"

"You spoke with him? He has a plan?" Jesse asked, rocketed out of the depths of despair.

"Yes, and I hope so. But let's get out of here and then I'll explain everything."

"Very funny," he replied, clearly not amused at what he thought was supposed to be a joke.

"Jesse, I wouldn't joke about something like that. I found a way to get you out, but there's a catch," she said with a wink.

"Out? You're serious? What do I have to do?"

"The spouse of a Monitor is granted amnesty for past offenses and is exempt from prosecution," she stated triumphantly, but was puzzled by the lack of reaction. "I know that wasn't the most romantic proposal in history, but I meant it."

"So, in order to gain my freedom from this type of imprisonment, you're asking me to give it up again for another kind?" he declared in complete seriousness and then burst into laughter when he saw Idrella's horrified expression. "Of course I accept your proposal, my love. It's just that, well, I was kind of hoping I would get a ring."

"I ought to leave you here to rot, Jesse Dimont!" she yelled, while laughing and crying simultaneously.

"Come on, let's get out of here," he shouted, picking her up and sweeping her across the threshold of his cell. "We have the rest of our lives for you to make me pay for that one."

****

The isolation pod was certified to be in complete working order. A full squad of guards came to escort Walter to the launch area. Hallways were cleared, although viewing areas were unusually crowded for such a late hour. People whispered about a last second rescue being planned by Danan's supporters, while others said the man they had captured wasn't really Danan. Across the Union, stories were already circulating about his escape and dozens of witnesses millions of kilometers apart swore they had seen Danan on his way to freedom. It was clear that the "Moses Law" would not strike the memory of Walter Danan from the hearts and minds of the populace.

The launch area was at a site out beyond the rocky band of debris and a heavily armed transport carried the prisoner to the temporary station. As Walter was led out of the ship, he could see the hatch of the pod opening before him, and Silas Lindquist waiting by the control panel, an expression of supreme exaltation melting his usual look of hatred. The restraining bands were removed and Walter was summarily shoved into the small compartment that was to be his eternal home, and eventual tomb.

"Does the condemned man have any last requests?" Lindquist asked, filling the hatch opening with his huge frame. "Care to make my day and beg and plead for your life?"

Walter made no reply and sat calmly in the one chair provided in the pod.

"Nothing to say? Too bad. Well, I have just one thing I'd like to tell you," Lindquist said with a monstrous grin. "For years I've dreamt of this moment and the thousand different things I would want to say. But before I seal this door forever, I would like to leave you with just this one thought. I am responsible for your dear wife's death."

The door slammed shut an instant before Danan flung himself against it. The last thing Lindquist saw was the glorious anger in Danan's features as he hopelessly lunged toward him. It was a sight Silas Lindquist would always cherish.

"Revenge is the sweet nectar of the gods!" Lindquist declared triumphantly, as he activated the drive units that sent the pod hurtling toward oblivion.

At that very instant, the central network began erasing everything from Walter Danan's birth certificate to the latest item on the news announcing the completion of his sentence. By the time the thrusters disengaged from the pod, leaving it to the mercy of its inertia, it would be as if the man had never existed. Lindquist experienced an ecstasy beyond description.

While one pod raced helplessly toward the black depths of the unknown, another pod, roughly the same size, passed by following a steady course toward Earth. It carried no weapons, gave no unusual readings and was therefore unanimously ignored by scanning technicians. One tech did casually notice that the two craft almost collided, but almost is just wide enough in space.

CHAPTER 24

It was a small party, a family affair with just two hundred of Silas Lindquist's closest relatives. It was an occasion of unrestrained joy, a symbolic dance on Walter Danan's grave. Brothers, aunts, cousins and most of all, Silas' parents, hailed him as the redeemer of ancestral honor, the champion who fulfilled the dreams of generations.

The adulation softened the disappointment of his less than picture perfect victory and enough derogatory remarks were circulated about Idrella to pacify his anger. His family members also assured him that the impending marriage would be portrayed on the networks as a degrading spectacle, a Monitor lowering herself so far as to marry someone who not only was an ex-con, but wasn't even a member of the upper circle. The Croix family had been revered since the time of Jupiter and Silas thought it was high time that their sterling image should be tarnished as much as possible.

The centerpiece of the gathering was a full-color, holographic display above the buffet tables, charting the initial course and possible current positions of the isolation pod. Just in case anyone ever had any ideas about following a pod to attempt a rescue, deviators were always placed around the hull. Programmed to fire in random bursts at random times, the units would render the pod's course impossible to track. But just for fun, the Lindquist's computer speculated as to what barren region of deep space the tumbling pod might be headed.

Oku and the *Götterdammerung* were also hotly discussed issues. Various Lindquists spoke openly about assassination, armed confrontation and possible topics for blackmail in their discussions as to how to deal with the menace. Sabotage experts were already trying to infiltrate all areas of O.I.T. and the city-stations. Operatives were both gathering information and trying to instill negative images of Oku in the minds of those who would be most helpful during a war. Progress was slow, but Silas felt confident that time was on his side.

****

A collective sigh of relief arose from the Council Hall when Kiya ordered the *Götterdammerung* out of port. The vessel that also carried Mardo and Granny set a course for Oku's estate on Earth. Onlookers pitied the former high-ranking officers of Oku's fleet and everyone was sure that whatever the Monitor had in store for the traitors had to be worse than isolation.

When the delicate feet of the giant *Götterdammerung* touched gently down on the landing base in the desert southwest of North America, the crew was dismissed for shore leave. But Captain Kiya Oku left strict orders for them to remain on the planet and be prepared to leave on a two-hour notice. The rigorously trained crew knew that their talents and expertise had not been sought merely for the purpose of prisoner transport. And no one was ever summoned on a two-hour notice just for maneuvers.

The Council had a forty-eight hour recess before the final week of the session and no one was surprised to see Oku disembarking from the ship and getting into the same landjet that was carrying the prisoners to his estate. Kiya remained behind for a few minutes in order to greet the blazing red Laserswift that streaked through the atmosphere like a meteor and came to rest on the landing platform as softly as a feather floating to the ground. Three passengers staggered out and the vessel darted away again. Kiya stepped up to formally greet the guests.

Monitor Croix, Mr. Dimont, we are honored to have you at our home," she said bowing and then nodded a brief acknowledgment to Boa, who stood dutifully in the background, swaying unsteadily.

"Wait a minute!" Jesse said with angry confusion. "What are we doing here? Isn't she the one who turned in Walter?"

"I see the Monitor has yet to fill you in on all the details," Kiya said, automatically taking a step back as she remembered Granny's violent reaction. "Your recent experiences should have taught you that when the stakes are very high, you can never be sure who is an ally and who is an enemy."

"So which are you?" he asked clenching his fists, suddenly suspicious of everyone.

"I'm sorry, Kiya, but Jesse didn't want me to explain anything. After what he's been through, he has to see something to believe it, and maybe not even then," Idrella said, putting a soothing arm around Jesse. "So, what do you have to show him?"

"Not everyone has arrived yet, of course," she replied cryptically, yet as if Idrella would know exactly what she meant. "But, hopefully, there will soon be enough proof to ease Mr. Dimont's mind."

Kiya led them to her landjet and the red rock terrain became a rusty blur as they raced through the vast compound toward the main house. Her perplexed passengers thought she had made a mistake when they finally landed, because there were no towering structures of glass and marble. In fact, there didn't appear to be any structures at all, just russet-colored hills and cliffs rising out of the desert floor. Then a figure seemed to emerge from a crevice in the cliff face nearest them and they realized the surface was dotted with window holes and natural terraces.

"Father didn't wish to interfere with the natural landscape so he carved our home into this hill," Kiya explained when she saw the startled look on her guest's faces.

Idrella and Jesse had expected that the man responsible for the Florid Keys would have built himself a glittering palace, the most extravagant dwelling in the Union, a high-tech miracle of art and engineering. Instead, it appeared as if they were entering a glorified cave.

The rooms were spacious and beautifully furnished, but still retained the natural rock walls. The floors were thickly carpeted which added to the considerable silence of the place. At least two windows and a balcony were in each room and airshafts in the ceilings and walls allowed a constant, fresh breeze. The complex, though on a much grander scale, reminded Jesse of Walter's island, and at the thought of Walter's current predicament, Jesse found it difficult to restrain himself from lunging at the betrayer and current host, Kiya Oku.

Jesse's anger was about to erupt when they stepped into a room carved into the corner of the hill with a sweeping one hundred and eighty-degree terrace and a panoramic view of the desert stretching to the horizon. Shirtless and lounging in the sun, were Mardo and Granny, and Monitor Shiro Oku was in the process of pouring them a cool drink. Jesse thought he was having another hallucination until Granny jumped out of his chair and squeezed Jesse's breath away in an elevated bear hug.

"Let him go, Gran," Mardo laughed as he joined them, "We didn't bring Jesse here to kill him!"

After the enthusiastic greetings, introductions were made. Jesse hoped no one noticed his hand trembling as Oku shook it warmly.

"Welcome, young man. If you are half as wonderful as Idrella tells me, we will get along splendidly. Can I get you a refreshing beverage?" Oku said cheerily, the tough, Monitor persona nowhere in evidence.

"What you can get me is an explanation. When I see mortal enemies having a tea party I think it's time I heard the whole story," Jesse replied, shaking his head in disbelief.

For the next few hours, the unlikely assemblage explained their individual parts in the drama that had unfolded over the last few months. Jesse listened in amazement as seemingly random events revealed themselves as carefully, premeditated acts and the full range of Oku's genius and cunning was uncovered.

The first step of Oku's plan began when he made Mardo captain of the *Hyperion* and selected the ship for the construction of the new city-station. Mardo didn't know that he was not selected for the mission because of his skill, but because of his loyalty to Walter Danan. Oku knew that if Danan needed to escape out of the system, his clever and devoted friend would find a way to get him on board the *Hyperion*.

The same informers that initially tipped off Lindquist about Jesse had also sold the information to Oku's people. Knowing that Lindquist would tear planets apart looking for Danan, and that the fugitive would be forced to flee his hideout, Oku directed Kiya to join the crew of the *Hyperion*. Kiya's mission was to identify Danan and discover if the reports of his incredible abilities had any validity. From the time of Walter's first interrogation, Oku had recognized the man's potential, though he masked his curiosity and reverence by voting for isolation; a single vote for innocence would not have changed the verdict and would only have just brought suspicion on himself.

On the night of Lindquist's inauguration, Oku had consulted with the Astromancer, just moments before his death, and discovered that a new age was indeed beginning that night. But what the Astromancer did not reveal in public was that Walter Danan had to be the philosophical and spiritual leader during the critical transition period, or it would be an age of great suffering. That knowledge, plus Kiya's startling reports, convinced Oku that he must do whatever he could to protect the fugitive Danan from Lindquist's vengeance.

Monitor Oku would have been content to leave Walter and Kiya on the *Hyperion* for the next eight years, with Lindquist thinking he had vanquished his enemy. But when Jesse revealed during the fake escape that Walter was alive, it was clear that it would only be a matter of time before Silas' death squads tracked him down. As painful as it was, Kiya was forced to turn Walter and the others in for their own safety, hoping they could then devise a plan for their eventual salvation.

As for the *Götterdammerung*, the ship that terrified the entire system, it was the biggest hoax ever perpetrated. While it did possess blinding speed and awesome firepower, the miraculous new composite of which it was made was just slightly more stable than a house of cards. O.I.T. scientists had yet to determine why after several months, the material simply crumbled.

"If we are to use the *Götterdammerung* as an intimidation factor to help overthrow the present government, we had better do it in the next couple of weeks before the hull turns to dust beneath our feet," Oku said with a mixture of humor and concern.

"If that has been your goal all along, why didn't you do it years ago?" Jesse asked, his mind reeling beneath the onslaught of mind-blowing facts. "Didn't you have the support and the resources?"

"Yes, but I didn't want a bloody conflict. The *Götterdammerung* might be just frightening enough to make the Union forces give up without anyone getting hurt. And just as importantly, while I knew the present regime was corrupt and destructive, I honestly didn't know what to put in its place if I was victorious. Walter Danan has shown me that an entirely new way of life is possible. It's his theories and practices that must form the basis of a new government. I will simply be the muscle behind his brain," Oku smiled at his own joke, flexing biceps that barely registered a change.

"This is all marvelous, but aren't you all overlooking the little fact that Walter has been blasted into oblivion?" Jesse managed to say before emotion choked in his throat.

"That's where the Croixs come in," Idrella said crossing her fingers.

The plan Idrella went on to describe was even more fantastic than the incredible explanations that had preceded. It was a flimsy plan suspended by a slender thread dangling over thin ice. The odds of success were so outrageous that Jesse began to think that it wasn't his own sanity he should be questioning.

****

The Union's fears that Oku had an entire fleet made of the same material as the *Götterdammerung*, began to be realized. Throughout the system, reports were filtering in about a wide range of vessels giving bizarre scanner readings. From small fighters to enormous cargo carriers, glimpses of the new ships were recorded in strategic areas everywhere. These elusive and terrifying ships were always accompanied by numerous squadrons of conventional vessels. The tenuous readings on the new ship would somehow get confused with the others and then disappear from their screens altogether.

This brought frenzied rumors about the ships having the ability to vanish, either by jumping between dimensions or simply becoming invisible. What the Union scanning techs couldn't have known, and what Oku was not about to tell them, was that sheets of the composite were being temporarily fitted over conventional vessels. After parading around long enough for someone to make visual contact, the squadrons would go into a tight formation around the sheep in wolf's clothing. In the midst of the tangled knot of readings, the skin of material was quickly stripped off. Ships would come and go in groups to avoid getting a proper count and when the squadrons dispersed, the new ship would seem to have vanished.

Oku operatives within the fleet were diligently fanning the flames of fear. It was a fire that spread swiftly through Union forces and many were easily convinced that the present government was not worth dying for. Even captains and commanders were discussing that it would be better to be a well-paid officer of Oku's empire than a dead Union hero. Within twenty-four hours, the domino effect of fear had tumbled through every level of the government fleet. Even Lindquist supporters aboard the Union vessels tasted the terror Oku's ghost ships were instilling and began to wonder if they were backing the right Monitor.

CHAPTER 25

The innocuous pod held faithfully to its course, but traveled substantially slower than its modern counterparts. Speed was not, however, one of the designer's concerns when he created the unique vessel. If it had been, he surely would have made it the fastest ship for its time.

The anxious inhabitants of a desert estate on Earth tracked the pod's every move. More than once they were tempted to send a larger vessel to intercept it, but restrained themselves so as not to attract any attention. Oku and his organization were under tight surveillance and they didn't want any suspicion to fall on the tiny craft. Nothing would be unusual about a pod making a delivery to his estate, so they would all just have to be patient and wait.

It was early the following morning after everyone's arrival that the craft finally began its entry into the Earth's atmosphere. In the delicate dawn light, Oku and his daughter, the ex-*Hyperion* officers, Idrella, her fiancé and bodyguard all gathered at the landing site like a group of marooned people anxiously awaiting rescue. An emergency medical team was also standing by, with orders to be prepared for anything. No one was quite sure what to expect, or who, for that matter.

Granny paced like an expectant father and Idrella didn't believe it was humanly possible to be so nervous without losing consciousness. Even Oku, master of stoicism, chewed an occasional fingernail. When the antique craft finally appeared, emerging from the eastern glow of the horizon, it was like a ray of light shining at the end of a very long, dark tunnel. The craft made a slow, plodding, but flawless approach, and the landing gear softly kissed the earth. A cheer went up from the small gathering, an instant before they all ran to the vessel's hatch.

The release mechanism could only be activated from the inside and seconds seemed like an eternity as their ears strained to hear sounds from within, any sound. The awful silence was broken by a series of muffled beeps, followed by a whooshing noise, as the seal to the door was broken for the first time in generations. The hatch parted in the middle and slid back to reveal Walter Danan, and standing next to him on shaky, but determined legs, was none other than Jupiter Croix himself.

"For heaven's sakes," Jupiter finally said with a deep, resonant voice that still boomed with authority, "you all look like you've never seen an old man before!"

Idrella rushed into the arms of the great-grandfather she had never met, while Jesse almost knocked over Walter in a Granny-style hug. An instant later, both travelers were besieged by the medical teams and a barrage of questions. Walter was quickly pronounced fit and Jupiter was found to be in remarkably good condition, considering both his age and the fact that he had just come out of stasis.

"I have my buddy Walt to thank for that," Jupiter declared, slapping his new friend affectionately on the back. "I was in damn sad shape when I first woke up."

During the initial, frenzied greetings and activity, Kiya had stayed quietly in the background, eyes downcast. Though she had acted in Walter's best interest, she could not dispel the feeling generated from his heart-piercing look at the moment of her apparent betrayal. As she was about to leave the happy group, Walter caught her hand and pulled her into a powerful embrace.

"Forgive me for not trusting you," he whispered, infusing her with a fierce heat that melted away all her anguish and doubt.

"No…it, it was my fault for not confiding in you," she said as they parted, a deep flush filling her cheeks.

"Enough of that, Walt," Jupiter chuckled. "Let's get out of this damn blazing sun and get something to eat. I can't remember when I had my last meal!"

While the others walked back to the house, a medical transport carried the old man and his still-breathless great-granddaughter on ahead to commence a more thorough examination. Protesting good-naturedly every inch of the way and asking probing questions about every piece of equipment, he was the model of the feisty genius Idrella had always imagined.

****

"I can't stand it anymore!" Jesse exclaimed when they entered Oku's house. "Tell me everything that happened. How did you get on Jupiter's pod?"

Walter's glowing features suddenly darkened and he told his brother-in-law to sit down.

"I almost wasn't able to pull it off," Walter began solemnly, "after what Lindquist told me as he sealed the door."

"What did that bastard say to you?" Mardo asked with concern, as he placed some food on the table between them and took a seat next to Jesse.

"Just before the hatch closed, he looked me right in the eyes, and with great satisfaction, told me that he was the one who had Valery murdered. I guess the news was his going-away present to me," Walter stated, his jaw still tense with emotion.

"I'll kill him," Jesse shouted. "I'll kill him myself!"

"Jesse, I know you're upset," Idrella said, entering the room in time to hear Walter confirm what she had already suspected, "but you have to leave Silas to Oku and I. You have to let us complete our plan. Then we will deal with that son of a bitch."

Idrella was right, of course, but Jesse had suffered so much at the hands of the cruel Monitor that patience became an almost impossible virtue. Oku calmly assured him that justice would come, very soon.

Walter continued with the story, restating the details about Idrella obtaining the control unit for Jupiter's stasis pod from her father and then revealing it to Oku. She knew that having Jupiter's awesome presence behind a coup attempt would have been like resurrecting Napoleon during World War II to lead the French resistance. He was revered as a Thomas Edison, George

Washington and Plato all wrapped into one brilliant, lovably unpredictable man. Idrella felt confident her great-grandfather would want to help their cause, because Walter Danan represented everything Jupiter had hoped for mankind.

When Oku met with Walter on the *Hyperion* before the trial, they decided to recall Jupiter's stasis pod and direct it to pass close to Walter's isolation pod as it streaked out of the launch area. Idrella's calculations couldn't take into account any unforeseen delays in Walter's scheduled departure, and she prayed that the deviators wouldn't kick in until after the transfer had been completed.

The "transfer" as Walter termed it, was the basis of the entire plan. Relying on the principle similar to that used to walk through walls, Walter believed that if he could establish a mental link with Jupiter's stasis pod, he would be able to "dissolve" himself, and then "reintegrate" on Jupiter's craft. If it worked, in theory he would be able to send himself over any distance, but since he was going to try it for the first time, they all decided it wouldn't hurt to have the two vessels pass very close.

As with the other special abilities Danan had displayed, a serene state of concentration was necessary to accomplish them. When Lindquist confessed to Valery's murder right before the launch, Walter was so agitated that he couldn't even sit still. He knew he only had minutes to settle down, sense the location of the approaching craft and pull off one of the most remarkable feats of human history.

"I guess I did it," Walter said with some uncertainty, squeezing his arm and legs to make sure he was really there. "You know, sometimes this stuff even gets too weird for me."

When everyone stopped laughing, Walter went on to describe how he activated the resuscitation units and revived the ancient legend. After aiding the old man's recovery with a few of the tricks he had up his sleeve, Walter explained the situation and asked if Jupiter wanted to join them or go back into stasis. With a story such as Walter presented, he really didn't need to ask.

"So now it's all very simple," Oku declared. "Walter and Jupiter will accompany Idrella and I to the Council meeting tomorrow where I will announce that we have decided to disband the present government and begin a new order."

"It's that simple, huh?" Jesse said, more than slightly skeptical.

"I never said something couldn't go wrong," Oku admitted, but was quick to add, "but I think we're holding a winning hand."

"He's got a point there, Jesse," Granny agreed. "Two of the most powerful Monitors and their families, a resurrected legend, a miracle worker and a fleet of invisible ships sounds pretty tough to beat!"

"I suppose, but what's to stop the others from arresting Walter again, and the rest of you for that matter?" Jesse continued as the devil's advocate.

"Walter, who?" Danan asked facetiously. "By law, I no longer exist. I'm as free as a newborn baby. That's why I wanted to wait to escape until after the sentence was carried out, so I wouldn't still be a fugitive if the planned coup failed."

"And as for Oku and I," Idrella said thoughtfully, "we can't actually be arrested because of our immunity. We can, of course, be kicked off the Council, but I think we have enough surprises to sway the others to our point of view. Except for Silas, who will no doubt have to be restrained the instant he sets eyes on Walter."

"Damn!" Jupiter cried, hobbling into the room with one hand on Boa for support and the other holding a handscreen that he was studying intently. "I'm a regular historic figure! When I get back into circulation I'm going to have more women than I can handle."

"At the moment, that figure stands at one," Idrella quipped. "Now sit down and take it easy."

"That girl definitely has Croix blood in her veins," Jupiter laughed as Idrella swelled with pride at the complement. "Now I told those damn doctors to stop poking at me because I had something important to say. I was just looking at the way the system's communications networks are configured, must've been designed by an idiot. With half a brain and a screwdriver anyone could disrupt the whole thing. When the Council or this

Lindquist character tries to contact the fleet or make a broadcast, we could block it and put in our own messages. Must've been an idiot!"

Kiya rushed over to see Jupiter's calculations and shook her head in approval and amazement at every step of his plan.

"We can effectively cut off all conventional lines of communication!" she stated, awed in the presence of such remarkable genius.

"That will certainly make our life easier," Oku smiled and then said to Jupiter, "What took you so long to figure it out?"

"It's all these blasted interruptions," Jupiter replied and then realized it was a joke. Turning to Kiya, he continued with a wink, "Come on, honey, let's you and me go someplace quiet and do some serious calculating."

"Shouldn't you be resting?" Kiya asked, eager to work with one of the greatest minds the world had known, but hesitant to put any strain on his aged physiology.

"I've been resting for almost forty years! I'd say it was time I got off my butt and did something constructive!"

Boa again served as support as Jupiter followed Kiya to her private lab. As Oku served another round of cool beverages, the others continued to discuss the details of the plan that would either ruin them all, or change the course of mankind.

****

Lindquist slept on the short hop back to the Council Hall, the first time in almost two days he got any rest. The party was still going strong when he left, the number of participants doubling each day, and he wouldn't be surprised if it still was in full swing when he returned after the final week of the session. For the most part, the celebration had degenerated into a wild orgy, which had been fine with Silas because the thrill of his victory had fueled an overwhelming, insatiable sexual drive.

However, now due to exhaustion, his eyes currently had difficulty focusing and he had some trouble just walking in a straight line, but he had earned a bit of fun. He could only hope there wasn't anything on the day's agenda that would require his full attention. Cleaning up and putting on a new cloak, he asked the computer to calculate how far into space Walter Danan might be at that moment. The computer informed him that it had no record of such a person and Lindquist howled with delight.

"Computer, if you check the central file record, oh, never mind, it doesn't matter. No record of such a person! I like the sound of that."

Gulping down half a dozen energy drinks and stuffing some nutrition tablets in his pocket, Silas took one last look at himself in the mirror and headed for the meeting. He knew he was going to be late, but felt certain they would never start without him. When he entered the room and saw the horrified looks on the other Monitor's faces, he couldn't believe they would get so upset about him being a few minutes late. Out of the corner of his eye, he saw three additional figures standing by the clock and realized that was the direction the stunned Council members' jaws were swinging.

"What the hell is going-" Silas' words caught in the pit of his stomach as he rubbed his eyes and then forced them to re-focus on the unannounced visitors.

Boa was easily recognizable, and the first he spotted. Silas then saw the ancient man leaning on his arm, the untamed white hair and beard, and piercing, sparkling eyes making him appear very much like he imagined Jupiter Croix would look in person. With effort, he removed his gaze from the fascinating old man and stared right into the eyes of Walter Danan.

What followed next was one of those indescribable moments when time and belief seem to be indefinitely suspended. There was the man he personally sent into isolation, standing next to someone who was supposed to be orbiting the planet Jupiter in a stasis pod. Obviously, it could not be a reality. As his intellect remained bogged down in a quagmire of incredulity, his animal instincts decided to take command. Charging like an enraged bull elephant, Silas didn't get three steps before a security shield froze him in his tracks.

"Damn Lindquists," Jupiter cried. "Always was a hotheaded bunch."

"This can't be! I sealed the door myself! This can't be," Silas cried in muffled shouts, struggling against the shield that registered no notice of his efforts.

"It can be, Monitor Lindquist," Oku said, rising. "It is, or more correctly, was Walter Danan, but by law he is a new man. And this is *the* Jupiter Croix, returned to help us bring a more enlightened way of life to the Union. I suggest you outgrow your hatred and join our cause."

"What's the matter with all of you! Arrest them!" Silas growled in ever-increasing fury.

"For God's sake give it up, Lindquist!" M'bai shouted, pounding the table with open palms. "They've got a fleet of ghost ships we can't track, they've cut off our communications, what are we supposed to do?"

"And can you imagine how the people will feel when they see Jupiter and Danan practically risen from the dead?" Rizzic added, almost glad it had finally come to a head.

"And if that isn't bad enough, they've threatened to release the reports on our d-chip tax revenues!" M'bai added frantically. "The people would tear us apart with their bare hands!"

"It's all over, Silas," Idrella said solemnly. "Half of the Union forces have already pledged support for a new government. If you resist, it only means a lot of innocent people will get hurt."

Danan had yet to speak, and in the brief silence that followed Idrella's words, he walked over to the seething figure trapped within the shield. With a wave of his arm, the energy field vanished. Silas was too stunned to react.

"For once in your life think of others," Danan said without malice. "Despite your crimes, I've recommended that you be allowed to live at your estate under house arrest. None of your family will be persecuted. We don't want to begin this new world with bloodshed."

Silas' expression took on a strange transformation. The crimson faded from his cheeks and the murderous glint in his eyes dulled to placidity.

"I, I must have time to think about this," Silas said backing away toward the door. "Yes, I must think this over."

"Should we have someone follow him?" Idrella asked with concern.

"The *Götterdammerung* will make sure no ships leave the area, he has no way of contacting the outside world and the security system will keep him from hurting anyone," Oku said thoughtfully. "Let's just give him time to chew on it."

While Kiya broadcast Oku's message from Earth, using Jupiter's jamming-transmitting system, the Union watched in amazement. She gave amazing accounts of Walter's mid-space "transfer" to Jupiter's pod, the old legend's return to usher in a better world, Lindquist's confession of Valery Danan's murder, and Oku and Idrella joining forces to end the admitted corruption of the Council. The Union fleet, badly shaken by scores of ghost ship sightings, didn't have to be told twice not to fight.

Danan supporters began pouring out of the woodwork and dancing in the streets. Many who had been staunch Lindquist supporters suddenly encountered acute memory problems and were unable to recall that they had ever endorsed such an evil man. Even the members of Lindquist's vast espionage ring sensed the ship sinking and immediately scurried to dry ground.

After Lindquist had fled the meeting, Oku convinced the seven overthrown Monitors to prepare brief statements explaining their willingness to cooperate with the new government. While the Council would be disbanded, Oku graciously offered them places on the reorganization committee, once their d-chips were removed and they completed a class in Danan's Theories 101, of course. And as Danan eloquently explained the plans for the new enlightened democracy, the Monitors actually began to feel enthusiastic about the change. There was a palpable energy in the air, something that managed to convince them that their apparent loss was in actuality a wonderful gain.

Then there was a deafening crash that shook the entire Council Hall and set off screeching decompression sirens throughout the complex.

"Silas!" Idrella yelled, ordering a schematic to see where the damage occurred.

"Hull rupture in residence quarter five," the computer stated calmly. "Section sealed off. Estimate twenty-three casualties. Recommend immediate evacuation of all personnel."

The computer had barely finished when a second and third explosion rocked the room.

"How could he get explosives through the security system!" M'bai shouted with more anger than fear.

"Not explosives," Jupiter said calmly. "He's shut off the beamcutters."

Running to the panoramic viewing port, to their horror, they all saw that Jupiter was correct. They also saw a field of debris toward which they were headed on a collision course. A tiny fragment struck harmlessly right above the window, but it was enough to send the terrified Monitors racing to their ships. The Council Hall was a scene of panic as they pushed their way to overcrowded transports. The complex continued to shudder beneath the constant hail of particles and section after section needed to be sealed off.

"He's really pissed me off now!" Jupiter hooted while Boa helped him to a computer terminal as his precious creation was being pulverized. "I can activate some reverse thrusters to try to keep us floating with the debris and not into it, but that won't work for long."

"You all have to get out of here!" Danan ordered.

"We will all leave together," Oku said, taking Idrella by the arm. "The *Götterdammerung* will take us safely away."

"Access to docking area seventeen has been sealed off," the computer stated casually.

"Seventeen! Then there's no way to get back to the ship," Idrella said, thinking not of herself, but of Jupiter. She didn't have him revived only to die like this.

"Damn! Lindquist deactivated the beamcutters and imposed his own code on the override," Jupiter growled. "It could take fifty years to break this code. What fool changed my security system? He should never have been allowed to get near the beamcutter controls!"

"Monitor's privilege," Oku replied wryly, thinking that the excess of privileges might be the end of them.

"If I could find Lindquist, I could convince him to give me the code," Walter said with grim determination.

"What would you do, twist my arm?" Silas said, emerging from the private entrance with a crazed expression contorting his features. "What's the big deal, anyway? If there's to be no Council, who needs a Council Hall?"

Another blast struck with such violence that everyone was thrown to the floor and half of the ceiling collapsed. This impact was not from an asteroid, but the wreck of an unlucky transport ship, pushed helplessly through the huge windows of the reception hall. As everyone struggled to his feet, Lindquist tried to run toward Danan, but was stopped by the massive hand of Boa darting out to grab his throat. Lifting him off the floor, Boa slammed Silas onto the smooth, black Council table and pinned him down like a purple-winged bug.

"Care to give us the code?" Idrella asked the prone Monitor.

"Care to go to hell?"

"There's nothing I can do without the code," Jupiter sighed.

"Why doesn't your messiah go inside my brain and find it?" Lindquist laughed like a madman.

"Not a bad idea," Walter replied with a smile that instantly sobered his adversary. As Danan approached, Lindquist fought to escape, but Boa gladly tightened the grip on his throat to keep him down.

"I believe it's too late for that," Oku said, pointing to an enormous chunk of rock tumbling straight toward the viewing port.

It was narrow, but half the length of the Council Hall and it spun ominously, end over end. It would only be a matter of minutes.

"Anyone in there need a ride?" a familiar voice cracked over the failing intercom.

"Red? Red is that you?" Idrella shouted.

"Yes, Ma'am. And if you don't mind my saying, I think you had better get your pretty little butt out of there!"

"Where are you?" she cried, never so happy to hear anyone's voice before.

"I'll be outside your quarters in about fifteen seconds."

"Boa, let him go and help Jupiter," Idrella commanded, more concerned with saving her great-grandfather's life than with ending Lindquist's.

"I'm not leaving here without my baby!" Jupiter stated stubbornly, pointing to the grandfather clock against the wall. "It was our ancestor's you know."

Boa looked to an exasperated Idrella who shrugged her assent. The faithful bodyguard hefted the clock under one arm and Jupiter under the other and hurried down the corridor. Oku was pulling Idrella along and shouting to Walter to hurry, when Silas arose from the table, gasping for breath through his half-crushed throat. Grabbing a splintered section of a fallen ceiling beam made of beautifully carved wood, Lindquist raised it in preparation to crush Danan's skull. Darting nimbly to his left, Walter dodged the makeshift club that crashed down on the spot where he had stood.

"You still don't get it!" Walter said as if talking to an unruly child. "Can't you bury your hatred long enough to save yourself?"

In answer to Danan's question, Lindquist took another swipe with the beam. Another explosion shook the floor sufficiently to ruin his aim, but he raised the deadly piece of wood for another attempt. Walter dodged that one too, by leaping onto the table. He shouted for Oku to get Idrella to the ship and turned back to Lindquist with an expression that said he had had enough. Closing his eyes for a second, he took a deep breath and extended his hand. A reddish spot of light glowed in his upturned palm and suddenly the beam disappeared from Lindquist's hands and materialized in Walter's grip.

"Your tricks don't impress me!" Lindquist shouted, his mind too warped to see the truth. "And I don't need a club to kill you."

Lunging for Danan's feet, Lindquist grabbed nothing but air as his ribcage impacted with the hard, stone table, knocking the wind out of him. Incredibly, Danan was now standing in the doorway to the private corridor, at least fifteen meters away.

"My patience is wearing thin, Lindquist. Are you coming?" Walter shouted above the sirens and constant pounding on the hull.

As Lindquist fought for breath, the self-preservation instinct finally overwhelmed his rage and he staggered toward the door. But he hadn't gone two steps when a jagged piece of rock three meters wide smashed into the lower corner of the window, compromising the structure sufficiently to trigger the decompression alarms and shut the emergency hatches. The last thing Danan saw as the door slid shut, was the terror and desperation in Lindquist's eyes as he tried to claw his way through the wreckage. It would be a sight that would haunt him forever.

Realizing there was nothing more he could do, Walter raced to Idrella's quarters where the others were already on board the Laserswift.

"For heaven's sake hurry, Walt!" Jupiter yelled as Danan squeezed in between the old man and the even older clock.

"What about Monitor Lindquist?" Red asked and immediately understood the look on Danan's face. "Then we're out of here!"

The shortest way out of the asteroid belt was to head back in front of the meeting room, which would put them right in the path of the oncoming, colossal asteroid. Red figured they would have plenty of room, and he always preferred the shortest distance between two points. Activating the drive units, the vessel lurched forward and prepared to thread the rapidly shrinking eye of the needle formed by the spiraling hunk of rock and the Council Hall.

"If we live through this," Oku said, fingers crossed, "you can have the pick of my fleet!"

That was all Red needed to hear as he headed straight for the twisting rock pillar. To his frightened passengers, it appeared as if they were all about to add another crater to the craggy wall of stone. With split-second timing, Red pitched sharply, just in time to miss the leading edge of the asteroid by just a few meters. Rolling into a nauseating series of maneuvers, he dodged dozens of smaller, but no less deadly, fragments. Climbing steeply through a cloud of micro fine dust, the Laserswift shot out of the field of debris without a scratch.

No one cared to look back to see the trailing arm of the mighty asteroid rise up and slam down on the Council Hall like a fist crushing a walnut. A series of massive explosions completed the job of destruction and Jupiter shook his head sadly when he saw the sickening crimson flashes of light reflecting off the windows. But after a moment of deep concentration, that gleam returned to his eyes.

"I just got an idea for a better structure," he reported happily and then sank into silent calculations.

"What happened to Silas?" Idrella asked Walter with a far-off voice and expression.

"He thought it was more important to kill me than to live. The hull was rupturing, there was no time..." his voice faded away, overcome by a dozen different emotions.

"Did the *Götterdammerung* make it?" Oku asked his new pilot, Captain Red.

"It was the damnedest thing," Red replied in amazement. "I thought it was a goner when I saw this huge boulder bearing down on it. But it just bounced off like a rubber ball!"

"Thank god," Oku said with relief. "Too bad that material doesn't last."

"Oh, that stuff. I'll have that stabilized by next week," Jupiter said distractedly and then plunged back into his new structure's design specifications.

"I don't doubt it," Idrella laughed. "And I hope the rest of the Union's problems will be so easy to fix. It looks like we all have our work cut out for us."

"Not work, Idrella," Walter said, managing a smile. "No, not work. This will be pure pleasure."

As the vessel altered its course for the shortest distance to Earth, its occupants began planning nothing less than to alter the course of human history. That path would not be so fast or direct, but this time it would be pointed in the right direction.